Pride Publishing books by K. Evan Coles

Boston Seasons
Third Time's the Charm

with Brigham Vaughn

Single Books
Wake
Calm

The Speakeasy
With a Twist
Extra Dirty

Boston Seasons

THIRD TIME'S
THE CHARM

K. EVAN COLES

Third Time's the Charm
ISBN # 978-1-913186-09-8
©Copyright K. Evan Coles 2019
Cover Art by Erin Dameron-Hill ©Copyright May 2019
Interior text design by Claire Siemaszkiewicz
Pride Publishing

THIRD TIME'S
THE CHARM

Dedication

For my son, who makes me laugh every single day and supplies me with terrible jokes.

For the people in and around my life who inspire me and make me feel brave.

For anyone who tells me to know my limits. You're making me push myself harder.

My sincere thanks to Shelli Pates, Beth Greenberg, Shell Taylor and Sally Hopkinson. You all make my words better.

Chapter One

"Hey, Luke, I'm going to Starbucks to buy coffee for everyone. You want?"

Luke Ryan stared at the code on his computer monitors and nodded absently. "Sure."

"Okay. Grab your stuff and come with me."

Luke blinked. "What do you need me for?" He turned away from the monitors and faced his best friend and business partner, Simon Martin.

Simon stood and eyed Luke across their shared office. "To help me schlep back the orders."

"Ugh." It was nearly two p.m. and Luke's concentration was flagging. As much as he wanted to keep working, fresh coffee sounded wonderful. The idea of going to fetch it, however, not so much. He stood and picked up his wallet and phone from his desk. "We wouldn't be having this conversation if you'd let me buy a new coffeemaker."

"I said I'd buy it, didn't I?"

"Yes, you said that two weeks ago. And here we are, making the trek to Starbucks once again."

Simon sighed at Luke's grumbling. "Oh, goodness. I'll buy one this weekend, I promise. In the meantime, you could stand to go outside for a few minutes. Your ass has been bolted to that chair all day. You didn't even break for lunch."

"Yes, I did."

"You ate a plastic squeeze tube filled with something green."

"It was yogurt," Luke said. "I bought a box of mixed flavor tubes but Ella doesn't like lime, so they're all mine."

Simon grimaced. "That sounds appalling. Serves you right for feeding that girl junk."

Luke chuckled as they started for the door. His niece, Ella, was ten years old and particular about what she ate. Luke had been stuck eating food she'd rejected before, but he didn't mind—weird foods came with the territory of raising children. Or helping to raise them, anyway, as Luke had been helping his brother, Peter, do for the past several years, ever since Peter's wife had walked out on her family and Peter had moved Ella from the Marine base in Virginia back to Boston and into Luke's Back Bay apartment.

Once outside, Luke and Simon walked a block and a half to Winter Street, navigating around shoppers and tourists. The line at Starbucks stretched nearly out of the door, and they stepped up to its end while Luke read over the orders his coworkers had scribbled on a scrap of paper.

"I don't know what this says." He pointed at one messy line. "This looks like Klingon."

Simon squinted. "You would know, I suppose. I'm fairly sure everyone ordered cold brew, by the way. That's all those hipster punks drink anyway."

Luke laughed. "Good point. Gillian wants an almond milk Macchiato, though." Gillian Vasquez was the third partner in their software development business. Petite, red-haired and whip-smart, her easygoing personality provided an excellent foil for Simon's brashness and Luke's hyperfocus. Gillian kept Simon and Luke in line and they knew it.

"Is she still doing the dairy-free thing?" Simon asked.

"I'm not sure. I think she just likes almond milk, to be honest. Ella's the same."

"That doesn't make those bowls of sugar cereal you feed her any healthier, you know."

Luke rolled his eyes. He'd never understood why kids' cereals got such a bad rap. Beyond the high sugar content and their dubious nutritional value, that was.

"I found a recipe for Cap'n Crunch cookies," he said. "I was thinking Ella and I could make them over the weekend." He snorted with laughter at Simon's obvious disgust.

"Where on earth would you find such a thing?"

"Pinterest. It's loaded with all kinds of questionable recipes."

"Oh, Pickle." Simon made a sympathetic noise. "This only underscores what I've been telling you for months—you need to get out more."

Luke winced. "Please don't call me Pickle in public." He glanced around, hoping no one had overheard the ridiculous nickname, and met the gaze of a dark-haired guy standing behind them.

Well, hello there.

Luke flashed a grin and the guy blinked, clearly surprised. He offered Luke a shy half-smile of his own just before the line shifted.

Luke faced forward. "You know I don't have time to go out," he said to Simon. "Even if I did, the men I'd meet would take one look at Ella and run for the hills."

"Surely not every man you meet is averse to the idea of family." Simon frowned. "I like children. Or Ella, at least."

"Yes, but you and I are not dating."

"Not since I kicked you to the curb a decade ago, true." He smiled at Luke's laughter. "Still, I can't imagine anyone you meet not being charmed by Ella. She's loveable even when she's being difficult."

They stepped forward as the line moved again. Luke hazarded another glance back and felt a pang of disappointment to find the cute guy talking on his phone. He met Luke's eyes again, however, and Luke smothered a curse when Simon nudged him with his elbow.

"Ella likes you, so of course you think she's fun," Luke said. "Not everyone thinks the way you do or wants to stick around while I fill in for her dad, though."

"Are you so sure?" Simon asked.

"I'm still single, am I not?"

"Yes, though I confess I don't know why. It's not because you're lacking in looks and your personality is certainly adequate."

"Nice." Luke shrugged off both the compliment and the tease. He knew he was easy to look at. He was tall and fit with a heart-shaped face and gray-green eyes, and his friends joked he couldn't take a bad photo. Luke didn't suffer for lack of attention from men.

Keeping a man's interest presented the real challenge these days, and that had a lot to do with the fact that he was taking care of a young child.

"I'm thirty-two years old," he said. "The men I meet who want children are either already parents or in committed relationships and headed in that direction."

"This is why you need to meet *new* men," Simon replied. "Ella isn't your daughter, Luke. Pete'll be back from deployment in a couple of months and that'll take some of the pressure off you. There's no reason for you to be celibate until then, either."

"I'm hardly celibate," Luke muttered, his cheeks hot. "And please keep your voice *down*."

He paused as they approached the counter. Simon placed the order and Luke glanced at the guy behind them again. Thankfully, he was still on his phone instead of being forced to eavesdrop on the saga of Luke's sad single life.

"I know I haven't had a boyfriend since Ella moved in with me," Luke continued while Simon paid for the order. "Taking care of her complicates my life, but it's nothing compared to Pete's wife taking off on them. *And* I do go out on occasion, Simon. I date."

Simon cocked a well-groomed eyebrow at him. "Okay, and when exactly? Because we both know you don't have time to yourself anymore."

Despite Simon's gentle tone, Luke winced. Even with help from his parents and his babysitter, Melissa, he rarely had a minute to himself outside his own bathroom. Even then, odds were Ella would knock on the door and blithely ask questions while Luke showered or shaved.

"In all seriousness, when did you last go out with a man?" Simon asked. They moved aside so the baristas could mix up their magic, and he patted Luke's arm. "Hell, when did you last pick someone up?"

"I met someone while I was grocery shopping last week, believe it or not," Luke replied. "We emailed a couple of times, but he dropped off the map. I picked someone up a couple of months ago, the last time Pete came home on leave." He grinned at Simon. "You and I went out for dinner and drinks, then over to that bar in Back Bay named after Oscar Wilde. Remember?"

"That's the bar with the boozy milkshakes?"

"Yes! I met Jeremy that night."

Realization flashed in Simon's eyes. "I'd forgotten that's where you met. Where was I?"

"Sucking face with some bartender, I think." Luke smirked at Simon's raucous laughter.

"Oh, God, that's right. Those milkshakes are lethal!"

"Believe me, I remember." Luke reached up and ruffled Simon's hair. "Anyway, I didn't take Jeremy home that night, but we exchanged numbers and spent time together for a couple of weeks."

"What happened between you two, anyway? I don't think you ever said."

"There was nothing to tell. Pete's leave ended and I canceled a couple of dates because Melissa was busy and I couldn't find a sitter. Jeremy just faded out." Despite his careless tone, Luke's heart twinged a little. He'd enjoyed spending time with Jeremy and watching him withdraw had stung.

Simon clasped Luke's shoulder with one strong hand. "I'm sorry. It doesn't have to be that way all the time, you know. I can watch Ella for you if Melissa is busy — I just need some notice. Gillian will, too. Hell, ask around the office if you need someone for a couple of hours. I'm sure at least one of the kids on staff is the babysitting type."

"I know, and thanks. It doesn't matter, though. The reality is I'm with Ella a lot because I want to be and guys usually bolt after they figure that out."

Simon's gentle scowl warmed Luke's heart. He loved that his friend cared enough to listen. Then Luke saw the cute guy with the dark hair pay for his single coffee and leave. *Damn.* Once upon a time, Luke would have struck up a conversation with him instead of watching the opportunity slip away. Maybe Simon had a point.

"It's fine," he said. "And you're right. I should make an effort to get out there and meet new men. Especially since things will go back to normal after Pete gets home. For a while, anyway."

"That 'for a while' is kind of a problem." Simon's expression sobered. "Your brother will still be at Quantico more rather than less. I don't even mean that in a bad way because I know you love having her here."

Luke nodded. He'd never thought twice about welcoming his niece into his home. "I do. All the more reason to find someone who's okay with Ella being in my life."

Is that such a bad thing to want? Luke didn't think so.

The barista called their order and Luke handed Simon the bags he'd been holding. "At any rate, it'll be great having Pete back, even if he's not in Boston. Ella hasn't been the same since her dad was deployed." Carefully, he collected the trays of cups.

Simon led the way out, talking over his shoulder as he held the door for Luke. "You think so?"

"Oh, yeah." Luke sighed. "She really misses him, and it's not like we can visit. She worries about his safety, just like my parents worry, and I do, too. Life will be a hundred times easier for all of us with Pete on US soil, whether he's at the Marine base or not."

"I understand," Simon replied. "I'm just sorry I can't do more than listen."

Luke smiled. "Don't be. I'd have gone bananas a long time ago without you and Gillian around to listen and keep me sane."

"Girl, you've always been bananas," Simon said, his tone airy. "But we're used to it and don't love you any less." He shot Luke a wink and they headed for the office.

Chapter Two

"The answer is no, Finn. You are not staying in again, especially when we both know the food will be excellent."

Finn Thomason eyed his friend, Paul Gallagher, and tried not to scowl. Finn was dog-tired and in no mood for a lecture while sitting at Paul's kitchen table with a bottle of beer. He'd worked a ten-hour shift at Massachusetts General Hospital before doing errands and now, as four o'clock came and went, he wanted a hot shower, another beer and a big steak, preferably in that order.

He'd be lucky if he got any of those things, however, because while Paul had also worked a long shift, he was attending a fundraiser at an oyster bar in the South End tonight and was determined that Finn would tag along.

Finn cast a pleading glance across the table at Paul's husband, Mick, but he simply shrugged. "How are you so perky right now?" Finn asked Paul.

Paul's blue eyes twinkled. "Mick made me take a nap after I got home. I'm not sure how much sleep we got, of course."

Finn wrinkled his nose. "Way more than I needed to know about your afternoon, man."

"You should have napped yourself," Paul replied. "Or at least bought a coffee while you were out doing whatever you did after work."

"I went clothes shopping," Finn muttered. "I had a coffee, too, thank you very much. It didn't do anything for me, that's all." The guy standing in front of Finn in the line for coffee had done something for him, however, that was for sure.

Finn smiled to himself. Yeah, Mr. Starbucks had definitely caught Finn's attention with his striking features and head of dark hair, not to mention his beautiful suit. Or the way his broad shoulders filled out the suit's jacket.

"What's that dreamy face about?" Finn could practically see the wheels turning in Paul's head. "Anything you want to share with the class, Finn?"

"Nope." Finn shook his head. "I've got nothing to share, Nosy McGee."

Unfortunately, that was an all-too-true statement. Finn hadn't even spoken with Mr. Starbucks. He'd been in the company of someone blond and elegant who'd been dressed in his own fine suit, and they'd appeared to know each other well. Finn had felt at a disadvantage in his jeans and blue shirt and had gone tongue-tied when the guy had flashed him a grin. Just as Finn had decided to say something the next time the guy turned around, the hospital had called with a patient update. Before he'd really thought about it, Finn had walked out of the coffee shop with his phone and cup, and left Mr. Starbucks and his handsome friend behind.

Lame.

Paul looked unimpressed by Finn's non-answer. "Why don't you grab a shower before we go?"

"Because I still think it'd be nicer to go lie down and sleep for ten hours," Finn replied.

"Yeah, no," Paul said. "You're coming out with us and that's final. It's going to be fun, dammit."

"Ooh, I can't wait." Finn smiled as Mick smothered a laugh behind his hand. "It's not that I don't want to come out with you, by the way," he added. "Any other night and I'd be happy to join, but I'm beat. Not sure I'm up for dinner and drinks with a bunch of strangers."

Paul's expression turned coy. "Not everyone there will be a stranger to you."

Finn's mood tanked further. He dropped his gaze to the floor where Daisy, his calico cat, lay stretched out, ignoring them all. Paul no doubt meant his friend Chad would be at the party. Chad Lawry was interested in Finn, and Paul kept trying to set them up, despite Finn's insistence that he didn't need a matchmaker. Never mind that Finn and Chad had nothing in common. Or that Chad seemed more interested in Finn's title and medical degree than his personality. Finn hadn't told Paul any of that, of course—he couldn't help his friend being a problematic prick.

Finn cleared his throat. "Knowing people there doesn't change the fact I'd much rather take a nap than shuck an oyster."

This time, Mick set down his beer bottle. "Maybe Finn's got a point, Paul. We both know he's been working like a dog all week. If he's tired, why shouldn't he stay here tonight and chill?"

"Because being tired comes with the job, love." Paul laid his hand over Mick's where it rested on the table. "Now, I know what you're going to say — working hard can make any job tiring. You clock a ton of hours when you're on a big project. Finn and I don't have a set work structure, however. We don't know when or how long we'll be on until the shift schedules post.

"All that said, we need to get out of the house and see people, no matter how tired we are. Luckily, I have you to remind me of that." Paul grinned at his husband. "I wouldn't go out even half as much if you weren't around, and Finn's much worse. He has a tendency to go full-on hermit if he's not forced to socialize."

Finn nodded. "That's true," he told Mick. "Paul's been dragging me out since we were in med school, so I shouldn't be surprised he's trying to force me now." He glanced back at Paul, whose expression softened.

"Honey, I won't *make* you come with us, but I think you should. You've been holed up in this place since you got off the plane from Chicago."

"That's a stretch," Finn scoffed. "I go to work. I've been out with you and Mick most weekends looking at apartments, not to mention our excursions for fried seafood."

Paul hummed in agreement. Finn had made it his mission to try fried seafood all over the city, a project Paul supported with great enthusiasm. "Granted. Sullivan's on Castle Island is next on the list, by the way." He eyed Mick, who was chuckling. "What?"

"Nothing. I love that you're a shameless slut for fried clams." He ruffled Paul's golden-brown curls. "Why don't you hit the shower while Finn and I finish up here?"

"Okay." Paul looked askance at Mick. "You're not planning on talking him out of going to dinner tonight, are you? Because I can tell by his face that he's already given in."

Finn lifted his bottle with a snort. "You keep talking like that and I swear to God, I will fall asleep at this table just to spite you."

Paul cheerfully flipped him off before he stalked out of the kitchen, and Mick splutter-laughed around a mouthful of his beer.

"This may sound weird, but sometimes, I wish I'd known you both when you were dating," Mick said.

Finn let out a laugh of his own. "We weren't much different back then. I mean, besides being more, you know, handsy."

Mick wrinkled his nose. "Okay, that I don't need to see. You're a good-looking guy, but I'm not one to imagine Paul with anyone that way, if you know what I mean."

"Yeah, same. No offense to you, of course," he said with a laugh.

"None taken." Mick studied Finn with his pale green eyes. "You okay? I know you're tired, but you seem kind of down tonight."

"Oh, I'm fine." Finn rubbed a hand over his hair. "Despite my bitching, Paul's got a point. I need to work on expanding my social circle."

"You'll get there," Mick replied, his deep voice soothing. "Making friends in this town can be tough. Everyone's rushing and busy, earbuds in, staring at their phones." He grinned. "I've lived here long enough to be used to the chronic lack of eye contact."

"It doesn't bother me, either," Finn said. "I feel more at home here than I ever thought I would."

Having grown up in Chicago, Finn was used to an open brand of Midwestern friendliness in the people he met every day. While he sometimes missed it, he'd acclimated to Boston's more standoffish vibe with ease. Well, maybe that wasn't entirely true. He'd dropped the ball with the guy at Starbucks a couple of hours earlier. And that guy had even *smiled*, for crying out loud.

"There's that look again."

Mick's voice drew Finn him back to the present. "What are you talking about?"

"The look you're wearing right now," Mick said. "Kind of dreamy and maybe the tiniest bit drunk. You've hardly had any beer, though, so I've got a hunch there's more to it. You gonna tell me what's going on?"

"There's nothing to tell," Finn replied. He wished he had a story about meeting Mr. Starbucks. Yet another reminder Paul was right about Finn's need for human interaction.

"And you're sure you're up for going out?" Mick asked. "Paul's all talk, you know — he'd be the first one to tell you to stay home if you're feeling ill."

"Oh, I know. I'm good, Mick. A little melancholy maybe, but some good food and company will cure that." Finn reached out and patted his friend's arm. "I wish I'd come back for a nap too, though. You guys need to make sure I don't pass out face-first into my plate tonight."

"So, go lie down." Mick picked up the empty bottles. "I'll make sure you're up in an hour."

Finn cast a doubtful look at him. "Don't cocktails start at six?"

"They do, and dinner is at seven-thirty." Mick sipped his beer. "Paul and I can go ahead and you can meet us there. He won't care that you're late, as long as you show up. I'll even run interference with Chad for you if you want."

Finn sighed happily. "You are a good friend."

"I know." Mick gave him a knowing smile. "It'll cost you, though."

"I already told you I'd hire you to decorate my apartment — what more do you want?"

"Paella, like you and your mom made the last time Paul and I went to see you in Chicago."

"Done!" Finn pushed himself to his feet with a laugh and Mick rubbed his hands, his satisfaction evident.

Daisy followed Finn to the guest room and jumped onto the foot of the bed while he stripped down to his boxers. He was still dog-tired but felt lighter as he crawled under the bedding. It was Friday night, he lived in a new city and he had plans to eat good food with his friends. A quick nap and he'd be ready even for Problematic Chad.

Chapter Three

Fueled by food and caffeine, Luke spent the afternoon pushing through the code that had been dogging him and by five o'clock, he was smiling.

"You look very pleased with yourself," Simon observed. "Everything back on track?"

Luke gave him a thumbs-up. "I just turned everything over to the design team."

"Well done. Are you about ready? We need to leave soon to meet Miss Ella."

Every Friday, Luke treated his niece to dinner at the restaurant of her choice. For almost a year, Ella's favorite eatery had been Two Men and a Grille, a retro diner not far from their neighborhood. Simon tagged along, as did Ella's babysitter, Melissa, when she was free.

"I have one more thing to wrap up," Luke told Simon, "but I'll text Melissa and let her know we're running behind."

Simon held up a hand. "Don't worry about it. I'll go ahead and meet them."

"You don't mind?"

"Of course not. This is my chance to convince Ella to eat something other than macaroni and cheese." Simon closed his laptop.

"Thank you. And what have you got against mac and cheese?" Luke asked.

"Nothing. I have no idea how Ella can order it *every* time she goes out, that's all."

"You never complain when you're cleaning up whatever she didn't eat," Luke replied.

Simon opened his mouth to respond, but stayed silent when Gillian appeared in the doorway.

"I'm calling in sick Monday unless there's a new coffee machine," she told them, a hand on her hip.

"No, you won't." Simon smirked at her. "You have a meeting at nine with a subcontractor and we both know you can't have that meeting from home."

Gillian met his gaze over the top of her glasses. "I hate you."

"Liar." Simon stood and slung his bag over his shoulder. "You *love* me, Gilly."

"Only when your mouth is so full you can't speak." Gillian turned to Luke. "You boys headed out?"

"Soon, yep," Luke replied. "You out, too?"

Gillian nodded. "Charlie says Shelli wants macaroni and cheese, and I need to start cooking."

Simon made his way to Gillian's side and draped his arm over her shoulders. "What is it with you people and the mac and cheese?"

"It's easy, reasonably nutritious and children like it. Duh." Gillian poked Simon's ribs with her elbow and made him grunt. "Besides, it's not like you don't eat it if it's in front of you."

Luke grinned and waved his friends out. Once upon a time, he, Simon and Gillian had spent every Friday night together downing snacks and drinks at a tavern in Charlestown. They'd made many decisions — both good and bad — during those beer-and-nacho-fueled nights, including starting their own company. Now, twelve years later, the Friday beer nights were a thing of the past. None of them could tolerate that much booze, for one, and Gillian was usually with her husband and daughter while Luke spent time with Ella, often in Simon's company. Luke wouldn't have changed any of it, but he sometimes missed those carefree, beery nights.

Maybe I miss being carefree, he thought. He pulled up a worksheet and began making notations. It had been a while since Luke had truly felt such a thing.

Thirty minutes later, he gathered his things and locked up the empty office. Thunder rumbled over the downtown area as Luke stepped outside, and he eyed the dark, threatening clouds overhead.

"I can make it," he muttered and set off.

He put some speed into his step in an effort to beat the impending showers and made it two blocks before the skies opened up. The fat, fast-moving drops sent pedestrians scrambling and umbrellas popped open while those without them dashed for shelter in shops and anything providing cover.

Luke skidded to a stop under a gray and white awning at the entrance of a high-rise condo tower across the street from Boston Common. He glanced down at his damp jacket and shirt and sighed. The downpour was too heavy to go on if he didn't want to get soaked, and lightning streaked through the clouds over the park, followed by a low rumble of thunder.

Luke pulled out his phone. *Rain delay*, he wrote to Simon. *Stuck on Tremont without an umbrella.*

Simon replied at once. *Bad show. El and Missy just got here — we'll grab a table.*

The double doors behind Luke swished open, but he was too busy staring gloomily at the flow of rain-streaked traffic to pay much attention. He pocketed his phone with a sigh.

"That bad, huh?"

Luke blinked. He turned to the figure beside him and blinked again as he recognized the cute guy from Starbucks, whose expression of surprise Luke knew mirrored his own.

"You were ahead of me in line for coffee today, right?" the guy asked.

"That's right," Luke said and laughed. "I'd try to hold back a corny remark about small worlds, but wow." Delight zinged through him when the guy grinned.

"I won't hold it against you."

Luke caught himself staring but didn't stop. This guy was actually gorgeous. He stood about as tall as Luke's six-foot-one height but looked lean where Luke was broad. His dark hair and warm olive skin set off his clear gray eyes, which shone when he smiled. His stylish black jacket and trousers also made Luke excruciatingly aware of his own soggy state.

Ugh.

"I'm sure this won't last much longer," the cute coffee guy said. He gestured at the rain falling beyond the awning, unaware of Luke's struggle. "Another ten minutes and you should be fine."

"You're right." Luke licked his lips. "I'm just annoyed because I'm late meeting my niece and some friends for dinner. It's my own fault for not bringing an umbrella, of course, and the subway's not much help where I'm going."

"Where are you headed?"

"Stanhope Street in Back Bay." Luke raised his eyebrows when the guy held up a black umbrella.

"I'm headed that direction, too," he said. "This thing's plenty big enough for both of us, if you don't mind sharing, and I can get you close to where you need to be." His expression fell slightly in the face of Luke's stare.

Luke gave himself a mental shake. "Really?"

"Sure." The cute coffee guy smiled. "You know it's impossible to find a cab or Lyft in this kind of weather, and I don't mind the walk if you don't."

"I absolutely don't." Luke grinned as his rescuer unfurled the umbrella and popped it open. "Thank you. You've saved me a lot of aggravation."

"No trouble at all." The guy dropped his gaze then and chuckled. "Um…yeah."

Luke swallowed. Good Lord, but he was adorable. "What is it?"

"I've never made someone's acquaintance under an awning in the rain before." The cute coffee guy's cheeks flushed. "Especially *after* almost meeting them in line for coffee. I'm Finn," he said.

Luke stuck out his hand, and warmth spread through him as Finn shook it. "Luke. I've never met anyone in the rain, either."

"Well, it's nice to meet you, Luke." Finn caught his bottom lip between his teeth for a moment before he let go of Luke's hand. "Shall we?"

They fell into step together, and Luke glanced up at the black nylon shield above them, marveling at how well it covered them both. They had plenty of room to walk side by side while staying dry, even with Luke's bag over his shoulder.

"Okay, this has got to be the biggest umbrella I've ever seen," he blurted. He was too charmed by what was happening to be embarrassed by his own silliness.

"It's not even mine," Finn said with a smile. "It belongs to my friend. He and his husband live in that building, and they're putting me up while I find a place of my own."

"Are you new in town?"

"I've visited Boston many times, but essentially, yes. I relocated here in April from Chicago."

"That explains it," Luke mused. "Midwesterners are super friendly compared to New Englanders."

"I didn't say anything to you in the coffee shop." Finn grimaced. "I fell down on the job there, even after you smiled at me."

"True, but I didn't say anything to you either."

"Fair point. Can I assume this congeniality you're showing now means you're from out of town, too?" Finn asked.

"Nope. I was raised here and I'm as crabby as anyone else in the city when I want to be."

They paused at an intersection and waited for the light to change while traffic sped by.

"Oh, I don't know—you seem pretty friendly for a local guy," Finn said with a teasing grin.

"Well, you broke the ice." Luke shrugged at Finn's disbelieving expression. "If you hadn't, I'd still be standing there, staring at the traffic and sulking until the rain stopped."

Finn laughed. "Oh, no! You did look pretty dejected."

"I'm sure the wet head doesn't help." Luke ran a hand through his hair. "I'm probably the only gay man in the city who doesn't carry an umbrella on his person." Finn's chuckle made his stomach flip pleasantly.

"Well, I'm glad you don't," Finn said. "Otherwise, I'd have missed another opportunity to be a big Midwestern nerd."

Luke smiled. "You're about the furthest thing from a nerd I've ever seen, Finn. I'm a software developer, so I know what I'm talking about."

"No way." Finn scanned Luke out head to toe as they crossed the street. "But you're built like a brick shithouse!" he blurted and his cheeks flushed again at Luke's laugh. "Wow, sorry."

"You should see your face right now!"

"I think my filter broke," Finn said. "But come on, you know you don't quite radiate stereotypical tech guy, right?"

"That doesn't change the fact that I *am* a tech guy, though. I just happen to work out, too." Luke softened his teasing with a grin. "Besides, it's 2018 — surely you've met nerds like me before."

"I went to medical school so, yes, I've met plenty of nerds," Finn replied. "I don't think I've ever met a nerd who looked like you, though."

Luke hummed. "I'm not sure if that's good or bad."

"Definitely good," Finn said, his expression so warm Luke's stomach gave another giddy flip.

They walked through Chinatown and continued chatting, and it was *easy*, Luke thought. The flirty banter came as if they knew each other well instead of having met only a few minutes before. By the time they turned onto Berkeley Street, he'd learned Finn worked as a trauma surgeon at Mass General, often alongside the friend he'd been staying with, Paul. Like Luke, Paul was a Boston native, and it had been through him that Finn had learned about the position at MGH.

"You mentioned house hunting earlier, so where are you looking to live?" Luke asked. They turned right onto Stanhope Street and, man, did he want to keep talking to this handsome doctor with the big umbrella and the pretty eyes.

"Beacon Hill's my first choice," Finn replied. "It's close to the hospital, and I'll appreciate that after a long shift. I really like Back Bay and the South End too, though, so I'm torn."

"You're not buying, right?"

"Right—I'm renting for now. I don't even know if I'll be here five years from now, never mind what neighborhood I'll want to live in."

Luke slowed his steps as they arrived at the diner, and he waited until Finn stopped and faced him. It felt risky pushing for more than this playful interlude—Luke didn't even know if Finn was single. Hell, he wasn't even sure Finn was into *men*. No chance in hell would Luke let the opportunity slip through his fingers twice in one day, though, not with Finn smiling at him.

"This is me," Luke said. "Would you like to grab coffee with me sometime, Finn? You got me out of a jam tonight, and I'd love to repay the favor."

Finn's face lit up. "I'd like that." He pulled a wallet from his pocket and Luke took control of the umbrella. Finn produced a business card embossed with the MGH logo.

"My cell's at the bottom." He handed Luke the card. "I'm working a lot of nights lately, but that'll change next week. Some days I work six hours, some days eight, then I'll work a string of twelve-hour shifts, so we could be having coffee at ten in the morning or three in the afternoon."

"I have no set rules for coffee drinking," Luke declared. He paused a moment and glanced over the card. "Griffin Thomason."

"My mother spent time in Wales as a child and developed a thing for Welsh names. Which is pretty random considering she's Turkish. My sister is Seren, my brother Aeron and Griffin for me." Finn took back the umbrella so Luke could grab his own wallet. "The traditional spelling reads something like 'Gruffydd,' but luckily, my dad convinced Mom to spare me a lifetime of explaining myself. My brother started calling me Finn after I was born and it stuck."

Luke smiled and tucked Finn's card away, then handed over one of his own. "My parents went with Biblical names, so my brother and I are Peter and Luke."

"Luke suits you." Finn grinned. "And if I haven't said it already, it's been a pleasure meeting you. Properly this time."

Luke extended his hand again. "Same here. Thanks for the shelter, Dr. Thomason."

"I'll look forward to hearing from you, Mr. Ryan." Finn's touch lingered an extra few seconds as they shook hands, then they each went their separate ways.

Luke jogged toward the diner's door but spotted a trio of familiar faces in the front window and stopped in his tracks. Simon, Melissa and Ella were seated at one of the front tables, each eyeing Luke with varying levels of curiosity. Luke gave them a smile and his insides fluttered at the way Ella studied him. *Oh, boy, am I going to have to answer a lot of questions.* At least he'd have good food and beer while he suffered through the interrogation.

"Who was that?" Ella asked before he'd sat down. She'd pulled her braids back off her face and wore a Black Widow T-shirt and jeans, and Luke thought she seemed far too grown up as she stared him down. He patted her hand where it rested on the table, his fair skin cool against her own golden bronze.

"That was a man I met named Finn."

"How come you were holding his hand?"

"I was shaking his hand, not holding it." Luke picked up a menu and wanted terribly to kick a snickering Simon under the table.

"That's not what it looked like to me," Ella said. "What kind of name is Finn?"

"It's short for Griffin, which is Welsh."

"Huh. That's cool, I guess." Her expression turned thoughtful.

"I met him on my way here. Simon told you I got caught in the rain, right?"

Ella's amber eyes gleamed. "Yep. He said 'that silly idiot's stuck without an umbrella.'"

"Charming." Luke shot a glare at Simon. "Well, I stopped to wait out the rain and ran into Finn. He offered to share his umbrella because he was coming this way, too."

"Oh, man. That sounds like something out of a movie," Melissa sighed. Her dreamy smile made Ella and Simon roll their eyes in tandem.

"It sounds like something out of a shitty soap opera," Simon muttered.

Luke bit back a laugh. "Finn's new to Boston, and I told him I'd buy him coffee as a thank you for sharing his umbrella."

A small grin crossed Ella's face. "That was nice of you. When are you doing that?"

"I don't know — we said we'd try next week after his work schedule changes. Finn's a surgeon," he added and felt very smug at Simon's arch expression. "He works in the Trauma Division at MGH."

"Of course he does." Simon almost sneered when Melissa went moony again. "Good to hear he's got a job at least. Other than rescuing stranded pedestrians with his mammoth umbrella, I mean." He winked at Ella's giggling.

"Anyway, we can talk about that another time," Luke said. "After I tell Ella my terrible joke."

This time, Ella smiled widely. "Okay, go," she urged.

"What did the cow say to the milk jug?" Luke kept a straight face and waited for Ella's answer. After a moment, she shook her head.

"Tell me," she said.

Luke made his voice deep and Darth Vader-y. "I am your father!" he boomed, and grinned as Ella burst out laughing.

Chapter Four

Finn stepped up to the door of the oyster bar and closed the oversized umbrella. The earlier downpour had weakened to a light shower, and he went still under the raindrops for a moment, a grin growing on his face.

He pulled Luke's business card out of his pocket and stared at the piece of cardstock. "I used an umbrella to pick up a man," he murmured to himself. Not just any man but big, broad-shouldered Luke with the cheeky smile — the very same guy Finn had thought about all afternoon after their run-in at Starbucks.

Finn's phone vibrated in his pocket and snapped him out of his daze. Quickly, he slipped the card away and reached for the restaurant's door, ignoring the persistent buzz. Once inside, he left the umbrella at the coat check and scanned the room until he spotted his friends at a table near the bar.

Paul nailed Finn with a glare as he approached their table. "What, you can't pick up the phone when I call?"

"Sorry, Mom." Finn sat down but flinched when Paul smacked his shoulder. "Hey!"

Paul scowled. "So rude."

"I was literally just outside," Finn replied. "It seemed ridiculous to answer when I could almost see you from the door."

Paul's glower softened. "Sorry. I thought you'd decided to blow us off." He reached for the bottle in the marble chiller at the end of the table, and Mick slid an empty wine glass toward him. "You can't blame me after all the bitching you did earlier today."

"I said I'd be here." Finn gestured at the room around them. "Mick doesn't seem surprised to see me, so why should you?"

"Well, unlike me, Mick is a kind and trusting soul." Paul glanced fondly at his husband and filled the glass with wine. "He was adamant you'd make it."

Mick nodded at Finn. "I told him not to call, but you can see how well that went."

"It's okay." Finn accepted the glass with a nod. "There are worse things in the world than to have someone overly interested in your well-being. My mother appreciates it. And she did ask you guys to keep an eye on me when I moved out here."

"That's because Ayla knows you need mothering from time to time." Finn's mother and Paul had always been fond of each other. "Take now for example," he said, then reached over and gently fingered the lapel of Finn's black blazer. "Why are you wet? Didn't you bring an umbrella?"

"Of course I did—I checked it at the door and got splashed a little when I closed it, that's all. It's one of yours and the thing is the size of a circus tent."

"Every umbrella we have is huge," Paul replied. "There's one with rainbow stripes that is one of the most glorious things you've ever seen."

"That means it *looks* like a circus tent, too. Thankfully, the one I picked up was plain black."

Finn was arrested by a sudden yen to open a giant rainbow umbrella over Luke's head, just to see his expression. Paul and Mick went quiet then, and Finn glanced up to find them watching him closely.

"O-o-kay — what's going on with you?" Paul drew his eyebrows together until the skin of his forehead puckered. "You've been acting goofy ever since you got home this afternoon."

"Don't say it's nothing because neither of us is buying it," Mick chimed in. "At least, not right now because, holy shit, I think you are actually *blushing*."

Finn laughed. His cheeks were on fire and he kind of wanted to kick himself, but another part of him was excited that he had a story for his friends. Especially a story about Luke.

"I may have met someone," he hedged and laughed again at Paul's grimace.

"What the hell does that mean, 'may have met someone'?" Paul asked. "I mean, either you did or you didn't, Finn, unless this someone is an inter-dimensional being. Did you meet a ghost?"

"No, I met a man." Finn grinned at his friends' eager faces. "I met a man outside your building, and we shared your umbrella on the walk over here."

"Hey, that's great!" Paul exclaimed before his smile wavered. "Wait, 'sharing an umbrella' isn't a euphemism for something sexual, right?"

"What? No! Or, not that I know of?" Finn clapped a hand over a laugh while Mick and Paul cackled across the table. "I literally shared an umbrella with a guy so he wouldn't get rained on," he said. "And get this — I saw the same guy earlier today in line at Starbucks."

"Really?" Paul asked. "You met him buying coffee?"

"Well, we didn't quite meet — he was ahead of me in line and we smiled at each other, but I chickened out and never said anything to him."

Paul frowned. "That doesn't sound like you. He must be smoking hot for you to go all shy."

"He's so that," Finn agreed. "Big and built with a killer smile. Very much my type."

Understanding flashed across Mick's face. "Aha! That's why you were moody earlier today."

"Yeah, I was pissed at myself for blowing it. But whatever, I ran into him again and didn't lose my shit."

"This happened outside our building?" Mick asked.

"Yep. It was raining when I came down and the guy had stopped under your awning to stay dry. We recognized each other and somehow got talking. I realized we were headed in the same direction and offered to share the umbrella."

Paul's jaw dropped open. "Seriously?"

"Seriously."

Mick reached over and tapped his glass against Finn's. "Very nice, Finn. That is some next level chick-flick kind of chivalry, my friend."

"Thank you. I didn't even think about it at the time — I was just happy I got another chance to talk to him." Delight shot through Finn as he recalled the way Luke's smile had lit up his big eyes, and he grinned.

Paul hummed. "Oh, my God. You are smitten."

Finn didn't bother denying it — he'd seen enough of Luke during their short time together to become infatuated. If only he knew where Luke's blond friend fit in the picture.

"Are you going to tell us more about the umbrella man or keep us in suspense?" Mick asked.

Before Finn could respond, a familiar voice cut through the buzz of the crowd around them and popped his happy flirt bubble.

"Finn! What on earth are you doing hiding out over here with the old married guys?"

Problematic Chad squeezed behind Finn and plopped down at the table's remaining empty chair. He was impeccably put together in a sleek black suit and clearly didn't care that he'd interrupted their conversation. He aimed a smile at Paul and Mick and leaned over to kiss Finn's cheek.

"Hey, Chad," Finn replied. "I just got here a minute ago. I'm here at Paul and Mick's invitation."

"Pfft, I'd have invited you if I'd known you had the night off," Chad replied. He set his glass beside Finn's and reached for the wine bottle. "How have you been since the last time I saw you? No, let me guess — you've been working crazy hours and continuing to abuse your friends' hospitality. I'm sure they can't wait to have their place back to themselves."

Finn raised his eyebrows. He'd extended his stay in Paul and Mick's apartment several times since his move, but they'd assured him repeatedly he should treat their home as his own. Finn glanced across the table and felt relieved when he saw them staring at Chad with shock on their faces. Mick almost radiated offense.

"You're out of line." An edge lurked in his deep voice, and Chad's demeanor sobered.

"Oh, come on—you know I didn't mean anything by it. I was teasing!" Chad met Mick's stare over the rims of his stylish glasses. "Of course you've welcomed Finn into your home. You wouldn't be the men I know and love if you hadn't. I'm sure he's a very considerate housemate, too, but that doesn't mean you and Paul *aren't* looking forward to getting your privacy back."

"That day's not far off," Finn said. "I decided on an apartment this afternoon."

Paul's face lost some of its glower. "You did? Which one?"

"The place on Primus Avenue," Finn replied. "The one with the garden courtyard."

"I loved that place!" Paul beamed. "Are you sure it's still available?"

"I called the realtor on my way out of the hospital today," Finn said. "I hadn't quite decided at the time and asked her to hold Primus and the apartment on Spruce."

Mick snapped his fingers. "Did the apartment on Spruce have a lofted bedroom?"

"That's the one," Finn replied.

Chad waved a hand at them all. "Wait, wait, wait." His expression had turned peevish, probably at being left out of the conversation. "Primus and Spruce? Where are these streets? Neither rings a bell, and I pride myself on knowing this city quite well. Are you moving to Cambridge, Finn?"

"No, I'm staying in Boston. Primus Avenue and Spruce Street are on Beacon Hill."

Chad's haughty attitude deflated. "Ah. That's disappointing. Are you sure you've made up your mind? That part of town is so stuffy." He made a face.

"Lawyers and politicians and all those cobblestone streets that eat up your shoes."

"I'm sure I'll manage. I need to be near the hospital, what with all my crazy hours." Finn offered Chad a smile so fake his face ached, but Chad continued heedlessly.

"The South End is much more vibrant, Finn, not to mention more fun. Even Back Bay isn't half-bad in comparison. I've been trying to talk our friends here into moving away from that dumpy place on the Common for years, but they won't hear of it."

Paul pressed his lips together in what Finn recognized as a valiant attempt to keep his temper in check, but he lost the battle in seconds. He'd inherited his condo from his grandmother, and Finn knew Paul loved it and the neighborhood unreservedly. Finn felt sorry for Chad as Paul scolded him but not enough to insinuate himself into their argument. Mick simply sat back and a grin played about his lips as he watched his husband lay into their friend.

Finn sipped his wine and let the quarreling voices fade into the background. Despite Paul's and Mick's assurances he could stay with them as long as he needed, he wanted to get the ball rolling on his own apartment. Finn needed a place to call his own again, especially if he planned to get to know someone like Luke better.

Chapter Five

"So this guy doesn't know about Ella?" Gillian asked as Luke closed his laptop.

"I mentioned having a niece the other night when we met," Luke replied. He looked up as she leaned against the side of his desk. "But not that she's ten, lives with me and I'm effectively her single dad while Pete's away."

Four days had passed since Luke had met Finn under the awning on Tremont Street. They'd exchanged messages over the weekend and settled on Tuesday to meet for coffee, but now, with Gillian asking questions while Simon looked on from his own chair, Luke felt nervous.

"We didn't have time to get deep into family stuff," he said. "We talked about what we do for a living, where he's thinking he'll live — that sort of thing. I don't even know if Finn's seeing anyone."

"You were obviously stupefied by the man's good looks," Simon said. He cast a glance at Gillian. "He's gorgeous, Gilly. I did a double-take when I realized he was talking to Luke, of all people."

"Gee, thanks," Luke muttered. His insides tightened a little more with nerves.

"That came out wrong," Simon replied quickly. He frowned at the way Luke rubbed his palms against his trousers. "What's the matter?"

Luke grimaced. "Nothing. You're right, though. Finn's not the kind of guy I'd buy coffee. I mean, I couldn't bring myself to talk to him the first time I laid eyes on him and we were *in* a fucking coffee shop."

"Whoa, Pickle, slow down." Simon scooted his chair close and rested his hands over Luke's to stop his restless motions. "I never said you shouldn't buy the man coffee. And what do you mean, the first time you laid eyes on him? Wasn't the thing with the umbrella the first time?"

"No." Luke told his friends about spotting Finn in line at Starbucks and couldn't hold back a smile at the pride that crossed Simon's face.

"You and that hot man were eye-fucking right under my nose and I never even noticed," Simon said. "What is wrong with me?

"So many things," Gillian replied. Simon gave her the finger.

Luke scoffed. "Dude, we were barely flirting. You've also missed the point of the story."

"No, I haven't," Simon said. "You didn't do anything the first time you ran into Finn, and neither did he. But you got a chance for a do-over, so I don't understand why you're complaining."

"I'm not complaining. I'm coming to grips with the knowledge that Finn is both really good-looking and has his shit together while I am a big mess in comparison."

Simon frowned. "You are not a mess. I mean, maybe a little, but it's part of your charm."

Luke pulled his hands free and fought the urge to put his head down on his desk. "You're not helping."

"I'm joking," Simon protested gently. "You own a business and provide love and a home to a juvenile human, and you're one hundred times more organized than I am before you even eat breakfast every day. You're the *opposite* of a big mess. Besides, Finn said yes when you asked him, right?"

"Yeah, but that's because he had no idea I know more about Ariana Grande than the city's social scene."

"What is an Ariana Grande?" Simon asked before his eyes widened. "Oh! She's a singer, right? Like a sort of baby Christina Aguilera?"

"I love that you both know this," Gillian said with a laugh. "Welcome to my world!"

"And that's my point." Luke shrugged helplessly. "Finn is a trauma surgeon, and all his friends are probably doctors, too. I imagine he meets people who attend symphony galas, not bake Cap'n Crunch cookies. I eat yogurt from tubes, for crying out loud, and even my friends give me crap for that."

"That's because the yogurt in those tubes is revolting," Simon countered, his tone stern. "You're being a wee bit hard on yourself, don't you think? Who says your doctor will even care that your social calendar slants toward kid things, anyway? No doubt he has trouble finding time to eat, never mind hobnob with society types."

Gillian nodded. "Simon's right. The doctors I've met work way more than they socialize."

Luke licked his lips. He appreciated his friends trying to talk him down, but their words couldn't dispel the knots in his belly.

Simon searched his face for a long moment. "You really like the guy, huh?"

"I don't even know him." Luke uttered a feeble laugh. "I'd like to, though. Finn offered me his umbrella in a rainstorm, for God's sake. I can't remember the last time I saw someone do something so chivalrous in real life, and he hooked me good."

Gillian laughed. "I can't fault you for that. The whole story is ridiculously swoony and a thing I can see a man doing for you, too." She leaned in and smoothed Luke's hair back from his face. "You don't see yourself clearly, Luke, and never have. Not only are you gorgeous, you're a grown-up. For the most part, anyway. That's not always an easy combination to find in this city."

Simon reached up and ran his hands over Luke's shoulders, his touch gentle. "Relax, Pickle. From what you've said, the doc gave off all the right signals the other night. He's interested in you."

Luke drew in a breath. "You're right," he said on the exhale. "We're just having coffee and even I can handle that."

Simon smiled. "Good boy. Now get your ass in gear or you'll be late." He and Gillian laughed as Luke shot upright in his chair.

"Where are you meeting him?" Gillian asked. "At the Starbucks around the corner?"

"Uh, no—I asked him to meet me somewhere else." Luke grabbed his wallet and bag from his desk. "I don't think you guys would crash my coffee thing on purpose, but I didn't want to tempt fate. Especially as we still don't have a working coffeemaker," he added with a laugh.

* * * *

Luke and Finn met outside the Roasted Bean, which was conveniently located one block from the building where Finn was staying. They shared a smile, and Luke fought not to stare as he got a gander at the doctor.

Finn's dark blue scrubs flattered his golden complexion and highlighted the lines of his shoulders and narrow waist. They also made his legs appear miles long. Luke nearly reached up to touch the name embroidered in white thread on Finn's left breast pocket before he caught himself.

"Nice scrubs, Doc."

"I just threw these on," Finn joked, but he checked Luke out with an appreciative gaze. "I feel underdressed next to you."

"You shouldn't." Luke smoothed his tie against his chest with one hand. "I had to change before I left the house this morning. Almond milk may have fewer calories than cow's but it makes just as big a mess when it spills."

"Yikes." Finn grinned. "Hey, are you still in the mood for coffee? I was up working all night and now I'm awake again, my body needs some fuel."

"I'm always in the mood for coffee," Luke said. He led the way to the shop's door and Finn rubbed his hands together, his expression eager.

They chatted while they waited in line, and it struck Luke again how easily their conversation flowed. There were none of the little snags or pauses he'd expect between two almost strangers, and his stomach sank to think that might change the moment Finn knew about Ella.

Luke racked his brain as they placed their orders, trying to decide how to broach the topic. He continued dithering after he'd paid and they'd carried their cups to an empty table and sat. Then a face Luke knew emerged from the patrons around them and forced the issue without even trying.

"Hiya, Luke!"

Luke smiled at the girl who stood beside his chair while his insides twisted. "Hi, Sofia—fancy running into you here!"

"We're going to the Frog Pond," Sofia said as her mom, Bev, emerged from the crowd too. Sofia and Bev wore pink sundresses that set off their deep brown skin, and Bev carried a beach bag Luke recognized from past afternoons they'd spent at the wading pool in Boston Common.

"Looks like you guys are geared up for the whole afternoon," Luke said.

Sofia nodded. "Yeah, my dad went to find some spots in the shade."

Bev stepped up behind her daughter. "Hey, Luke. Where's your sidekick today?"

"Ella's at swimming class," Luke replied. "After that, she and Melissa are going to the Museum of Science and we'll meet up for dinner in a couple hours."

"You guys should come here," Sofia told him. "I had a brown sugar lemonade that was *so* good."

"I'll remember that," Luke replied with a chuckle. He forced himself to focus on Finn, whose expression had gone blank. "Finn, these are my friends, Sofia and Bev. Sofia goes to school with my niece, Ella."

Finn gave them a small wave. "Hello there."

"Finn is from Chicago," Luke told Sofia. "He just moved to town and he's been living out of boxes." Hiding behind the kid was a shitty move, but it gave him some time to delay having to explain himself. Luke badly wanted that reprieve, however brief.

Sofia turned her big brown eyes on Finn. "You don't have a place to live?" Her solemn manner cracked his and he smiled.

"Not of my own, nope," Finn replied. "I've been staying with friends, but I found an apartment a couple of days ago."

Sofia fingered the blue beads decorating the ends of her braids. "My dad says moving sucks," she said, then grinned at the adults' laughter.

"It really does," Finn replied. "But it'll be nice to have space to put my stuff again."

Bev put a hand on the top of her daughter's head. "Speaking of your dad, he's saving our spots and we should get going before he thinks we forgot about him. Maybe we can set up a playdate with Ella this weekend if Luke says it's okay?" She aimed a questioning look Luke's way.

"Definitely okay," Luke replied. "How about I call you tomorrow?"

"Sounds good. Enjoy your coffee, guys." Bev flashed a smile at Finn, who nodded goodbye.

A heavy silence followed, and Luke's heart fell a little further with every second that passed. He'd expected Finn to be annoyed with him for not saying anything about Ella. Maybe Finn was staying quiet because he didn't care. Or maybe he'd already checked out and was just finishing his breakfast before he shook Luke's hand and walked away, never to be heard from again.

Ugh.
So much for not fucking up a simple thing like coffee.

Chapter Six

"Ella's ten."

Finn looked up at Luke's abrupt statement and immediately noticed his somber demeanor. It didn't sit right on his expressive face.

"She's my brother's daughter," he said. "Pete's a helicopter pilot in the Marine Corps. He's been stationed at Quantico in Virginia for a while now. He moved Ella up here to live with me when she turned six. He stays with us whenever he can, but he was deployed overseas in the spring. He's been on base in Norway since then."

Finn nodded. The last several minutes had thrown his entire state of mind for a loop. "And Ella's mom?"

"She left them." Luke ran his fingers over his lips, clearly considering his words before he spoke again. "My family liked Carly. We were happy when she and Pete got married. But something happened to her after she had Ella. *With* Carly, I mean. She pulled away from all of us. She told Pete being a mother wasn't what she expected. That she got tired of his shipping out and leaving her behind and she didn't want to do it anymore. They were in couples' therapy but one day she dropped Ella at school and didn't come back. Only Pete has seen her since, and not very often."

Luke paused for a beat. "Pete was on his own in Virginia after Carly," he said at last, "but here he's got me and our mom and dad to help."

The barista called Luke's name then, and both of them glanced toward the counter. Finn pushed back his chair.

"I'll get it," he said quietly. He went to the counter, still processing the information that had been thrown at him.

Finn had been more than surprised to learn Luke had a child in his life—he'd felt deceived. He'd sat silent while Luke smiled at his friends and talked about swimming lessons and play dates, and a numbness crept over him at the possibility Luke was married— maybe to the blond from the coffee shop—and had a child. That maybe he planned to cheat on his family with *Finn*, for fuck's sake, because Finn had been so starry-eyed he'd somehow missed the fact that he'd been flirting with a married man. He hadn't seen a ring on Luke's finger, but he hadn't even checked, had he?

Of course, it turned out Luke didn't have a husband or wife—he didn't even have a daughter called Ella, but a niece instead. *Thank God*, Finn thought as he picked up the tray of food. He didn't need that kind of guilt on his conscience. He knew how much it hurt to be cheated on. His last boyfriend, Adam, had taught him that lesson repeatedly.

Finn set the tray down and handed Luke a plate of macaroons. Just because Luke wasn't married didn't mean Finn liked the way this had all gone down. From the sounds of it, Luke was practically a parent, and that was no small detail. When had he planned to mention it?

Finn tucked into his sandwich and mulled over what to say. He'd assumed Luke would defend his decision to stay quiet about his niece or perhaps talk more about her, but Luke sat silent. Maybe he wasn't saying anything because he didn't care what Finn thought.

No, Finn thought. *That doesn't add up either.* If Luke's tight expression and body language were anything to go by, he wasn't happy about how this get-together had turned out, either. He appeared dejected as he and pushed the untouched plate of cookies away.

Finn had finished his sandwich before Luke met his gaze again. "Something wrong with your food?" he asked.

Luke gave him a weak smile. "Not as hungry as I thought, I guess."

Finn picked up his coffee and held Luke's stare as he sipped. The unhappiness in Luke's eyes troubled Finn almost as much as the idea that he'd lied by omission. And that didn't sit well with him.

"Luke, can I ask you something?" Finn set the cup back in the saucer.

Luke seemed to steel himself before he answered. "Sure."

"Is there a reason you were keeping Ella a secret?"

"I wasn't." Luke shook his head. "I never got a chance to tell you the other night and today I just couldn't figure out how. I was trying to get there before Sofia walked up to say hi."

Finn cocked his head. "What stopped you in the first place?"

"I wanted to avoid an awkward conversation like this." Luke sighed. "Historically, the topic of Ella and my ad hoc parenting doesn't get a lot of traction with new people I meet."

"I see." Finn thought about that for a moment. "And you assumed I wouldn't be interested in someone with a child? Or maybe that I don't like children?"

"No, not at all."

"For the record, neither is true."

"Honestly, I didn't know what to think or even that you were interested in me." Luke worried his bottom lip between his teeth. "I mean, I hoped so, especially after you agreed to have coffee with me, but I wasn't counting on it."

The tight feeling in Finn's chest loosened. Luke had no idea how attractive he was, that much was plain.

"Here I thought I'd been so obvious," Finn murmured. "I'm definitely interested, Luke. Heck, I've been trying to figure out if the guy you were with at Starbucks last week is your boyfriend."

"Oh." Luke blinked twice before a grin transformed his whole face.

"Why do you think I offered to share my umbrella with you in the first place?" Finn asked. "I was so relieved when you said you were gay I nearly walked into a parking meter."

Luke laughed. "God, what a mess. First, the guy from Starbucks isn't my boyfriend—he's my business partner. Second, I'm sorry I didn't get a chance to tell you about Ella myself. That's not at all what I wanted to happen."

"It's okay," Finn said. And it was. He wanted to fist-pump now that he knew Luke's blond friend was just that—a friend. The fact Luke took care of his niece didn't alter Finn's interest in him either. If anything, Luke's obvious love for his family impressed Finn and made him want to know even more about the man in front of him. Sure, he would have liked to have known about Ella before they'd sat down for coffee, but he believed Luke's explanation that the timing had just been wrong.

"Look, can we start over?" Luke asked. "This time, I won't hesitate when it comes to awkward stuff. Like the fact I'm super excited for the third movie in the *How To Train Your Dragon* series."

A burst of warmth filled Finn's chest. "I'd like that." A sudden burst of inspiration swept through him. He stood and grabbed his bag, then held a hand out to Luke. "C'mon, I have an idea."

Luke stared at Finn's hand for a second before he smiled and grasped Finn's fingers. Finn pulled him to his feet and Luke flailed slightly, but he reached for his bag as Finn pulled him toward the door. Once outside, Finn marched them both up the block toward the gray and white awning where they'd first spoken.

Luke was chuckling by the time Finn came to a stop. "What's going on?"

"We're starting over." Finn dropped Luke's hand and turned so they faced each other again. "Now I say, 'I've never made someone's acquaintance under an awning in the middle of a sunny afternoon before. Especially *after* checking them out over coffee and a BLT with avocado. I'm Finn. I'm new to Boston, I have a calico cat named Daisy and I think kale is vastly overrated.'"

Luke's laughter filled the air. His eyes sparkled as he stuck out his hand.

"I'm Luke," he said. Finn took the hand and didn't let go. "I checked you out, too, even though I didn't eat my cookies. I run marathons, watch way too much *Star Trek* and take care of a ten-year-old niece who likes bad jokes and runs my life. Would you like to have lunch with me sometime?"

"I would love it." Finn bit his lip. "But you just bought me lunch, so how about I make the plans for next time?" He waited for Luke's nod and smiled, then reluctantly dropped his hand. "Listen, I need to get going—my shift starts in a half-hour. Feel like walking with me a bit?"

Luke met Finn's smile with a big one of his own. "I'd like that."

They crossed Tremont Street and headed onto Boston Common, chatting as they walked through the old park. Finn swore the skin on his hand tingled everywhere it had touched Luke's.

He bit back another grin. Luke made him think all kinds of goofy thoughts. They'd only spent about an hour together total, but Finn already wanted to know more about him. A lot more, and as soon as possible.

"Do you really run marathons?" he asked. With a start, he thought he should have asked about Ella, the newly discovered niece, but Luke didn't miss a beat.

"Yep," he said. "Not professionally or anything, but just for me. I try to run at least two every year and shorter races in between. I ran Boston in the spring and I'm planning for New York in November."

Finn nodded. He was no stranger to working out but anything over five miles sounded like an invitation to have his ass kicked. "How much mileage do you put in during a week?"

"Depends on how hard I'm training. Right now, around forty." Luke chuckled at Finn's low whistle.

"There's a treadmill in my basement and that baby gets a lot of use."

"I'll bet. Do you run solo?"

"Mostly, yes. But my brother runs too, and he'll come along when he's around. My friend Simon's good for shorter distances, but he starts whining at around the eight-mile mark. Simon's the business partner I told you about," he added.

"The guy from Starbucks?"

"Yes. We co-own GLS Solutions with our third partner, Gillian."

Finn raised an eyebrow. "GLS? As in—"

"Gillian, Luke and Simon, uh-huh. Officially, the acronym stands for Global Language Systems, but I think most people figure out the not-so-hidden meaning without trying very hard." Luke chuckled. "That's what happens when you dream up an idea for a company over appetizers and beer."

"For real?"

"Absolutely." Luke held a hand over his heart. "Simon and I met at MIT as undergrads, and we were recruited by a firm based in Charlestown after graduation. Gillian already worked there, and she's the one who decided we'd be friends."

Finn hummed. He thought Gillian might have some things in common with Paul. "I have a friend like that, too. Bossy and brilliant?"

"That sounds about right," Luke said. "Gilly's one of my favorite people in the world. Anyway, there we were—just starting out and broke, like every other recent graduate in the office. A group of us started pooling our money on Friday nights and we'd go to a pub near the office that ran a special on wings and nachos. It got so we could buy enough to qualify as dinner, though I use that term very loosely."

"Hey, you covered some major food groups, so I'm not going to judge."

Luke laughed. "Good point. Gillian, Simon and I got to talking one night about how great it would be if we could write our own stuff instead of getting stuck working on projects we didn't like." Luke stepped out of the way of a group of passing kids wearing towering balloon hats. "Obviously, that's not uncommon talk among people with boring jobs, but Gillian kept bringing it up, even weeks later. One day, I threw the idea back out to Simon over lunch. He surprised me by wanting to talk about it, like how we could get funding and where we could set up shop. We realized we didn't want to let the idea go either, so we didn't."

Finn cocked his head at Luke. "So that's it? You upped and created a business?"

"No. I *wish* it had been that simple." Luke smiled at him. "We knew we needed investment money, and the three of us built a business plan and took it to my dad. He's kind of a stock market wizard, and he and my mom are loaded," he added.

"Wow. Talk about lucky."

Luke nodded. "My parents invest most of their money and they live comfortably, but you wouldn't guess they're pretty well off. They paid for Pete and me to go to college on the condition that we were on our own after graduation and figured out how to support ourselves."

"Which you did," Finn prompted.

Luke made a 'so-so' gesture with one hand. "If living in a crappy studio apartment and pooling my spare money with friends for beer and cheap eats is supporting oneself, then yes, I did."

"I've been there," Finn replied with a laugh. "Pretty sure I ate enough ramen noodles during med school to feed my hometown."

"I ate more than my share of ramen trying to get GLS launched. I still love it."

"Hah, me too!"

Luke beamed. "Anyway, we worked out of my apartment for the first year. Simon and Gillian practically moved in with me—which sucked, by the way, because it was a very *small* crappy studio apartment."

Luke paused, and Finn could tell by the intensity of his gaze that he wanted to say something more.

"I told you I wouldn't hesitate with awkward stuff, so let me get this out in the open. Simon and I dated for a while, back when we were first getting the business off the ground. We were together about a year before it ended," Luke added when Finn's eyes widened. "Things were pretty tense for a while, but Gillian made sure we stayed friends."

Finn nodded, though his insides were a sudden jumble of surprise. The chemistry he'd seen between Luke and Simon in the coffee shop hadn't been his imagination after all. "She ran interference for you?" he guessed.

"Yep. Made sure we stayed on the straight and narrow and saved arguments for after work. And we did a lot of arguing." Luke smiled sheepishly. "It seems ridiculous now that so much time has gone by, but she helped us make our friendship stronger. With each other *and* her."

"I think I know where you're coming from," Finn replied. "Paul and I were together in med school," he said. "We broke it off after he got matched at MGH. Then he met Mick, his husband. We're still tight, though. I told you he's the reason I found out about the job here."

"You guys work together a lot?" Luke asked.

"Yes and no. Paul specializes in infectious diseases while I'm in emergency surgery, but we team up regularly. We had time to work things out after we split, though. I can't imagine running a business with someone during a breakup."

"I wouldn't recommend it." Luke smirked. "It wasn't easy, but we figured out ways to make it work. The three of us still met up for beer and snacks with our friends from the firm every Friday, too, and by the end of year one, we'd poached a couple of them and completed four major projects."

"How long ago was that?" Finn asked.

"Twelve years now." Luke spoke lightly but with obvious pride. "We were in an actual, teeny-tiny office space by the middle of year two and hired more staff in year three. We were tired and stressed and terrified a lot of the time and it was hard — really hard. Sometimes, it still is. But the beer and nachos idea became a reality."

"And you stayed friends," Finn mused. "That's quite something, Luke."

"I can't imagine going to work every day and not seeing Simon and Gillian," Luke told him. They exited the park and crossed Beacon Street. "I know a day could come when one or more of us decide to leave GLS, but I hope it's a long time before that happens. Sounds corny, right?"

"Frankly, no. I think it's kind of amazing. You have real roots here, Luke — family, friends, your business. And you're still so young. It's a little mind boggling."

Luke eyed him askance. "Like you're old. Not to mention you save people's lives for a living."

"Sure, and I was trained how to do that. I still don't have a permanent place for my stuff right now, and I've been changing jobs every couple of years."

"I see your point, but my life seems boring in comparison."

"Oh, I wouldn't say you're boring at all." Finn licked his lips. An odd longing had grown in his chest as Luke spoke, and Finn felt surprised to understand he was ready for something different in his life — stability.

"I've been so focused on my career for such a long time," he said. "Undergrad and med school, followed by my internship and residency. Training to be a doctor has been my whole life and anything outside of it is a blur. I dated and kept up friendships, but it's almost as if it happened to someone else. I was too busy to focus for very long on anything outside of hospitals and patients and it's like I floated through Chicago for years without ever touching down. That's a shame because it's such a great city."

Finn shook his head. The intensity of his own regret took him off guard.

"You can always go back, Finn," Luke said. "I'm sure you already have your choice of hospitals in any city that interests you."

"Sure, I suppose." Finn hitched his bag up on his shoulder and smiled as Luke reached over and helped him. "My family would love it if I ended up back in my hometown, but I'm not sure *I* want that. Besides, I'm here now, and I want to focus on Boston. I'll still be working a lot, of course, but I don't want to look around a year from now and realize I don't know anything about my new home city or the people in it."

"Sounds like you're on the right path," Luke replied. They paused on the corner of Charles Street. "Your friends got you out for dinner the other night, right?"

"More like guilted me into going out. But I ended up meeting you, and that made my night."

Luke shared a smile with Finn. "Mine too."

For a moment, the world around them seemed to slow. The noise of the crowds and traffic faded out, leaving just the two of them, standing on a busy street corner on a summer afternoon. Luke captured Finn's hand again, and the simple touch warmed Finn's whole body. His heart squeezed a bit when Luke finally stepped away and the world sped back up.

"I should go," Luke murmured. "I'll message you, okay, Doc?"

Finn wanted to roll his eyes at the nickname, but it made him grin. "Okay. I'll call you when I can, too. If you don't mind waiting a week for lunch, I'll be back on a human sleep schedule by then." He paused. "I'd like to know more about Ella, if you feel comfortable talking about her."

A big smile spread across Luke's face. "I'd like that. By the way, I can always bring you coffee and sandwiches in the event you need an emergency lunch."

Finn laughed and forced himself to let go of Luke's hand. "I like the way your mind works, Luke."

Chapter Seven

A week later, Luke met Finn for an early lunch on Tuesday and told him about Ella and Peter and how they made their family work. Finn asked Luke to lunch again on Wednesday, and they met for a third time on Thursday.

"Is eating lunch at eleven-thirty in the morning a doctor thing or a you thing?" Luke asked as he and Finn worked their way through a platter of fish tacos. "I'm digging the brunch vibe."

Finn laughed. "Maybe a combination of both. I'm at the mercy of my schedule and if I work all night, I wake up feeling dead hungry and wanting food as soon as possible."

"Good to know. Would it be weird to meet four days in a row, or is that pushing the laws of responsible lunch dating?" Luke ignored the heat in his cheeks and focused instead on the way Finn's eyes warmed.

"I'd love to break some laws with you tomorrow, but I can't. I'm working a double, seven to eleven."

Luke's disappointment mixed with genuine sympathy. "Ugh. I hope you don't mind me saying, but that sounds terrible."

Finn barked out a laugh. "It's not my favorite thing, but I'm used to it." He wiped his fingers on his napkin and studied Luke for a moment before he spoke again. "What about Saturday? Do you think you could get away for dinner? Or do you need more notice than two days?"

"Actually, your timing couldn't be better. Ella's having a sleepover with some friends and our babysitter is staying overnight to chaperone. I am, for all intents and purposes, a free man for the whole evening." He remembered how many hours Finn would be working and his smile faded. "You won't be too tired to hang out?"

Finn waved off Luke's concerns. "Meh, I've been tired for the last ten years—a double shift is no big deal if I get some sleep ahead of time. Why don't you come over to my place? I'll get some dinner together and show off my new furniture so you can ooh and ahh as appropriate."

"I like this idea." Luke wiped his mouth with his napkin to disguise his grin. "I'll bring some wine and sweets, if that works?"

Finn's eyes twinkled. "I'll take the wine, but I bought some ice cream yesterday. Just bring yourself, Luke, and that'll be sweet enough."

Back at the office, Luke didn't bother hiding his broad smile, even after Gillian and Simon pounced and demanded details. He was too busy riding a goofy, Finn-inspired high to mind being teased.

"So let me get this straight," Gillian said as the three of them exited Starbucks later that afternoon. "Finn wants to cook dinner for you at his new place, which he somehow managed to furnish while working nights at the hospital?" She exchanged a glance with Simon. "That can't be right."

Luke frowned. "What do you mean?"

"He's obviously hiding something, Luke. Like a house-elf."

Luke grinned at her over Simon's snort of laughter. Gillian's daughter had long been obsessed with *Harry Potter*, and this wasn't the first time Gillian had mentioned the magical creatures who acted as manservants to the wizarding world.

"I hate to disappoint you, but I'm almost certain Finn's not a wizard — he wouldn't be healing Muggles if he were," Luke said. "And I don't know if he's cooking. For all I know, we'll be eating Szechuan food out of cardboard cartons."

"He'll probably set up a picnic." Simon gave an enormous eye-roll. "There'll be a box of wine, cartons of noodles, and you'll throw out your back when you and Finn try to make out on the floor. I swear to God, Luke, this level of romantic dreck makes me want to vomit."

Luke leaned past Gillian and smacked Simon's arm. "I hate you so much."

Gillian tucked her hand into the crook of Luke's elbow. "It's nice to see you having fun, you know. You haven't been this smiley in far too long."

"It's preferable to all that moping around you've been doing," Simon threw in with a smile of his own. "What's Ella doing on Saturday?"

"Hosting a sleepover at my place," Luke replied. "Melissa's planning a popcorn candy thing, which means there'll be rainbow-colored stains all over the kitchen. Again."

"Girl, just paint the whole kitchen over in rainbow swirls and get it over with." Simon sipped his latte with undisguised relish. "Are you planning on introducing Ella to your beau anytime soon?"

Luke pursed his lips. He'd thought about introducing that very topic several times since his first coffee date with Finn. However, he and Finn were still getting to know each other, and Luke knew it wasn't the right time.

"Maybe a bit further down the road, sure," he replied. "In the meantime, Finn seems interested when I talk about Ella, and I think that's a good sign."

Gillian hummed. "Agreed. What about Ella? Does she know about Finn?"

"Please." Simon scoffed. "Ella saw Finn and his big-ass umbrella that first night. She stared hard enough I thought her eyeballs might fall out of her head. There's no way she's not curious about him, not if she knows how often Luke's seen him since."

"She knows we've been out a couple of times," Luke confirmed. "The odd thing is that I can't get a read on how she feels about it."

"What do you mean?" Gillian asked.

Luke stared down at his coffee cup and gathered his thoughts before he spoke. "She doesn't seem put off *or* enthused, really. It's not like my social life has anything to do with her day-to-day life in fourth grade, but I guess I expected something stronger than vague semi-interest?"

Simon and Gillian exchanged a glance and a bubble of apprehension formed in Luke's chest. "What?" he asked.

Gillian shrugged. "Ella may not want to admit she doesn't like you having a boyfriend."

"I don't have a boyfriend."

"Are you sure about that?"

Luke huffed out a laugh. "Pretty sure. We're still working up to an actual date, Gilly."

"You've seen Finn three times this week alone, Luke," Simon said. "That's atypical behavior for you, and we all know it. You're also having dinner with him in two days and Ella's not going to ignore that."

"Point taken. Still, she never showed interest in the other guys I dated. Maybe I shouldn't be surprised this isn't any different."

"This *is* different," Simon insisted. "Ella's never met any of the guys you dated. But she's seen you with Finn and that's different from hearing you talk about some faceless guy."

Luke ran a hand over his hair. "None of the other guys stuck around long enough for me to introduce them."

"Is that why you're hesitating about introducing her to Finn? You think he'll disappear too?" Gillian asked.

"I'm not hesitating at all," Luke said. "It just seems too soon. Finn and I have only been out a few times, and he hasn't seen me in uncle mode. He also doesn't know how much work it takes for me to keep up with Ella. Or that I'm embarrassingly obsessive about scheduling everything."

Gillian flapped a hand at him as they approached the entrance of their building. "It sounds like Finn knows Ella's a big part of your life. What's the worst that could happen if you introduce them?"

"Oh, I don't know." Luke slowed to a stop. "Maybe they'll hate each other on sight. Maybe every moment in each other's presence will be like lighting myself on fire, ending with me having to say 'Hey, Finn, you're gorgeous and lovely, and I still can't believe you want to talk to me, but this isn't going to work out because my niece hates you and doesn't give a damn about my sex life.'" Luke stared at his wide-eyed friends and drew in a deep breath. "That. That could happen."

"Or not," Simon said slowly. "They could get along great, Luke. And even if they don't, what does it matter?" Luke started to shake his head and Simon raised a finger. "Hear me out for a second. Let's say you're right and Ella and Finn can't stand each other. Does that mean you and Finn can't keep dating? You're a grown man, and I'd say you're allowed to go on dates without your niece's approval."

Luke groaned. "I know. But Ella's important to me. It would feel weird to *always* exclude her if I spent time with Finn and vice versa."

Simon's expression softened. "Man, you're such a big softie. It makes me want to kick you right in the ass."

"That's because you have the emotional range of a sock puppet," Gillian muttered.

Simon shot her a withering glare. "Anyway, you're a pretty good judge of character, Luke."

"Okay." Luke uttered a laugh. "What's your point?"

"You're freaking out right now that you'll lose Finn's interest after he sees how much kid stuff you have to do with Ella." Simon shrugged. "Introducing them is the best way to get a solid idea of what kind of guy he really is."

* * * *

That evening, Ella came to the dinner table wearing blue Starfleet Academy pajamas and pink and black paper flowers in her hair. Luke smiled at the crown she'd made herself. He and Ella had worked diligently on her braids, and he enjoyed the touch of whimsy.

"What's the occasion?" he asked.

"You made Sloppy Joes." Ella executed a smart little twirl and took her seat. "You know how much I like them."

"I like that you tell me that every time I make them." Luke glanced down at himself after he'd sat down. "But now I feel slightly underdressed."

Without missing a beat, Ella peeled a big pink blossom off the end of one braid. Luke leaned forward so she could thread the wire stem behind his left ear, and when he sat back, decorated and grinning, she laughed. They spent a minute taking photos of each other with Luke's phone, then tucked into their meal.

"I have a joke for you," Ella said after Luke bit into his sandwich. "How did the cow blend into his surroundings?"

Luke chewed and thought for a minute before he answered. "Cam-moo-flage?" Ella held up a hand for a high-five and Luke smirked.

"Your dad emailed me this morning," he said after they'd smacked palms. "He says he can do a video chat on Sunday."

"Awesome!" Ella pumped her fist. "I can show him how much progress we've made building the Millennium Falcon." She and her dad shared a passion for complicated LEGO models, and neither hesitated to drag Luke into their projects.

"Just don't tell him I dropped it last week and we had to rebuild half of the hull," he said. "Also, I ate lunch with Finn today."

Ella's eyes went wide. "Again?! Damn, son."

"Dude, language. C'mon."

She winced. "Sorry. I couldn't help it. You guys have been having lunch a *lot*."

"Does that bother you?" Luke bit off some more sandwich and chewed.

Ella worked on her food for a couple of beats while his insides twisted. "It's sorta weird. You've never had a boyfriend since I've lived with you."

Luke choked and reached for his glass of iced tea. Ella watched him, her eyebrows slowly creeping upward as he flailed.

"Finn's not my boyfriend," he rasped out. "I have dated a few guys since you moved in, though."

"Yeah, but I never met them." Ella hummed thoughtfully. "How come?"

"Things didn't get serious with any of them." Luke shrugged. That was truthful enough without dragging too many details into it. "I didn't see the point of letting someone get to know you or your dad unless I considered them a boyfriend and not just someone to hang out with."

"So you'd sort of be in love already?" Ella suggested.

Luke silently thanked the universe she hadn't caught him with food or drink in his mouth a second time. "Well, it's not that I'd be 'in love,' as much as 'really like,'" he hedged. "I've never been an insta-love kind of person."

"Okay. What about Finn? You want him to be your boyfriend?"

"Um. I can't answer that." Luke smiled at Ella's eye-roll. "Finn and I are still getting to know each other, honey. I want more of that. He's a nice guy and funny, and super smart, too. I like that. Makes him interesting and easy to talk to."

"Not to mention you told Simon he's 'cute as hell.'"

Luke put a hand over his eyes. "Yes, I did, but please don't repeat that."

"Okay, fine." Ella worked on her potato salad for a moment. "So what happens if Finn is your boyfriend?" she asked then. "Like, you'd go out on dates, right? And he'd come over?"

Luke nodded. "Sure. We'd spend more time together and get to know each other's friends and families. Finn asked me to have dinner at his place, actually."

Ella's face went deadly serious. "You mean for tomorrow?"

"No, on Saturday." Luke stared, mystified by the change in her demeanor before the penny dropped. *Oh.* "I'm having dinner with you tomorrow, El, like always. Finn already knows you and I have dinner plans every Friday."

Ella gave Luke a lopsided smile that didn't quite reach her eyes. Her posture relaxed, though. "Okay, cool."

They fell silent again and Luke debated asking what had just happened. Why would Ella assume he'd blow her off for a guy? He'd never canceled their plans before unless he'd been out of town.

Luke recalled Simon's earlier words and his heart sank. This was all new territory for Ella. She really had gotten used to having Luke all to herself. That was already changing with Finn in the picture, and for someone like Ella, it had to loom large. She'd experienced more than her fair share of change after her mother had taken off and her father had moved Ella over four hundred miles — should it surprise Luke that she might be leery of someone new in his life?

He wiped his fingers on his napkin. "Hey, El?"

"Yeah?"

"You know you can ask me anything, right?"

Ella eyed him warily. "Sure, I know."

"Good." Luke smiled at her. "Do you have any other questions for me about Finn?"

Ella cut her gaze to the side, her face tense. "Does he know about me?" she asked, her focus back on Luke.

"Of course. I told him all about you, and your dad too."

"Do you want me to meet him?"

"Sometime, yes. I think that's a while off, though, while Finn and I figure each other out. What do you think?"

Ella stared at her plate for what seemed to Luke to be a very long time. "Sure, I guess," she said at last. "But can I think about it some more?"

The apprehension in her face when she met Luke's eyes made his chest tighten. Gillian was right — Ella didn't want to tell Luke no.

"Of course you can, love," he said. "You take all the time you need."

The corners of Ella's lips pulled up. "Thanks. Have Simon and Gillian met him?"

"Not yet. But not for lack of trying." Luke forced a chuckle. "Simon tried to crash my lunch with Finn today. He doesn't know I know about it, though."

Ella grinned. "What did he do?"

"He asked me where Finn and I were having lunch and I gave him a name for the wrong restaurant. Simon walked right past the window where Finn and I were eating, but he was so focused on all his sneaking around, he didn't see us."

Ella tipped her head back and laughed and that clear, carefree sound did wonders to loosen the knot in Luke's chest.

I can do this, he told himself. *Dating and unclehood? No problem.*

Chapter Eight

The unlikely aroma combination of fresh paint and hot pizza teased Finn's sense of smell as he stared at his surroundings. It was nearing ten in the evening and he'd worked an eight-hour shift before coming back to Primus Avenue to paint and move furniture. Despite being sweaty and splattered with color, he hardly noticed his fatigue. He had a dinner date with a handsome man in just under forty-eight hours and he felt fucking great.

"Place looks good," Mick drawled. He joined Finn at the kitchen counter.

"It does." Finn shot a smile at his big, rusty-haired friend. "Thanks for this."

Mick shrugged. "Thanks for being an easy client. It's rare someone hires me, turns over half a dozen pieces of furniture, and tells me to make up the rest as I go along."

"We both know I had no choice." Finn laughed. "My schedule doesn't exactly make it easy to go furniture shopping. Besides, I'm hopeless when it comes to paint colors."

"That's why you hire guys like me," Mick replied. "Working on this place was a pleasure. I love these old buildings despite the fact it's hell getting trucks up here."

A sudden burst of cursing echoed along the hallway outside the kitchen, followed by a mix of laughter and jeers. Finn hid a smile. Paul had been in rare form all night.

"Is he still bitching about the paint in his hair?" Finn asked Mick.

"Oh, yes. He's beyond pissed no one mentioned it until after it dried."

"It's not like it won't comb out."

Mick chuckled. "I think he cares less about the paint and more about the fact we've been calling him Cruella De Vil for the last two hours."

Finn snorted with laughter. "Food and beer in the kitchen, guys!" he called out to the crew.

Within seconds, Jude, Franco and Alec were swarming the table and cracking jokes while they gossiped about celebrity news. Finn didn't know what favors Mick had promised these men for helping Finn set up house, but at this point, he didn't care—the apartment looked far too nice to worry about incidentals.

"Where's Paul?" he asked.

"He went out for a sulk," Franco replied, his eyes bright with mirth.

Mick grunted. "That's not good."

"He'll be back soon," Alec said around a mouthful of pizza. "His stomach was grumbling so loudly I could hear it over the bitching."

Finn smiled. He'd met Mick's coworkers Jude and Franco before, but Alec was a new face. He was a tattoo artist who knew the others through a local softball league and had ties to Mick's favorite South End bar.

Mick moved to set his beer bottle down, and Finn held up a hand. "I'll go," he offered, and Mick nodded.

"You'd better feed the beast while you're out there," he said.

He stacked several pieces of pizza on a plate and popped the caps on two beers. After loading Finn up with the food and drink, Mick gave him a sunny smile and ushered him outside.

Finn found Paul seated at one of the wrought-iron tables in the courtyard, one elbow on its surface and his chin in his hand. In the low light of the gas lamps, Paul's eyes were bleary, and Finn knew his friend probably wanted to be sleeping.

"I come in peace, bearing food and beer." He set the plate and bottles down and took the seat across from Paul.

"Thank God," Paul dropped the hand and sat up straighter in his chair. "I'm so hungry I think my stomach is eating itself."

"What are you doing out here all by your lonesome?" Finn watched Paul tear into a slice. "You've got twenty minutes to tell me whatever's got you in a snit, by the way."

"What, you have office hours?"

"No—the courtyard is off limits after ten." Finn squinted at his friend. "What's going on? And don't tell me this mood is about paint in your hair. Even you're not that vain."

"Actually, yes, I am." Paul chuckled. "But you're right—it's not the paint that's bugging me." He sighed and drank some beer. "It's Franco. I came out here so I could get some air and feel less like smacking his stupid, smug face."

"Wow." Finn sat back. "Did something happen?"

"Nothing out of the ordinary," Paul replied. "Franco always acts like an asshole. This thing between us goes back a ways. Back to before Mick and I got married, to be specific."

Finn frowned at the somber note in Paul's voice. "Were Mick and Franco a thing?"

Paul nodded. "They used to fool around. Then Mick met me and we started getting serious. The thing with Franco tapered off and they settled into being co-workers." Paul blew a breath through his nose. "Unfortunately, Franco doesn't think I'm good for Mick and he'd be the first person to throw a party if things between us didn't work out."

"What's his problem with you?" Finn helped himself to the food.

"The usual. My hours are shitty, I leave Mick alone too much, and my patients mean more to me than he does." Paul pursed his lips. "Nothing that isn't true to some degree."

"Excuse me, but that last part is bullshit." Finn met Paul's eyes across the table. "Yes, you put your patients first, but you don't value them more than Mick and he knows it."

"Yeah, well. It's not totally bullshit. When I'm working a shift, the patients *are* everything. The world may as well not exist outside of that ED."

Finn hummed around his food. He understood what Paul meant. In the thick of things, the trauma rooms became their world. Focusing on anything outside of patient care felt not only unnecessary but also negligent.

"Mick gets it," Paul said. "That doesn't mean he's not resentful sometimes. His life would be a lot easier if he had some office drone for a partner."

"He's obviously come to terms with it, though. He wouldn't still be here if he hadn't."

Paul swallowed a bite of pizza. "Doesn't make tolerating Franco easier. And he's *always* around when Mick's got a shindig and I'm up to my neck in bodily fluids that aren't mine."

"Ew."

"I wish I were joking. A couple of months ago, Mick's firm threw a party to celebrate its twenty-fifth year in business. While they were wining and dining, I was stitching up two drunk yahoos who'd been using each other as dartboards."

Sympathy flashed over Finn at the regret in his friend's voice. He put down his slice and rested his fingers on Paul's forearm. "What does Mick have to say about it?"

"About my job eating my life?"

"I meant about Franco, but sure, the job, too."

"Mick copes with the job stuff and tells me if he feels neglected so I can fix it. He thinks the thing with Franco is just me being me," he said, his voice growing quieter.

Finn frowned. "You haven't told him it's more than that?"

"I can't." Paul chewed in silence for a moment. "They've been friends for almost ten years, Finn, and seen each other through a lot of shit. I can't tell my husband to give up one of his oldest friends because the guy makes me uncomfortable."

"Well, you don't have to go that far." Finn picked up his pizza again. "Mick would want to know his friend annoys you to the point of fleeing the scene, though."

"Or I could be a big boy and deal." Paul shrugged. "Mick's never given me reason to believe there's more going on than appears. I'm just not sure Franco's on the same page."

Before Finn could respond, Paul waved his hand. "Oh, my God, I'm whining so hard. Fuck that. And fuck Franco, too. It's not my problem he's a dick."

Finn tipped back his head and laughed. "That's *much* better. Remind me never to get into a heart-to-heart with you when you're hungry."

"Noted. Talk to me about anything else," Paul said. "Like your date with the hot nerd."

"Oh, God."

"Your words, not mine." Paul pointed his pizza slice at Finn. "Fuck, I can feel you blushing from here."

"I never called him a nerd. Hot, yes, but not a nerd."

"You are made of lies, my friend. You *totally* did. Which makes me want to meet him even more."

Finn narrowed his eyes at Paul. "Don't make me regret telling you about him."

"As if you could stop yourself," Paul scoffed. "All we've heard for the past week and a half is Luke, Luke, Luke, and now you're having him over for dinner. What are you feeding the big lug, anyway? A side of beef?"

"I don't know. I'll pick something up from a place on Charles Street once I'm awake and functioning again."

"Make sure you buy eggs for breakfast. You know, just in case." Paul's leer made Finn laugh.

"I like where your perverted mind is going, but Luke won't be staying over," he said. "His niece is having a sleepover at their place, and he'll need to be there at some point that night."

"Hmm. So, the niece—are you thinking you want to meet her?" Paul asked.

Finn worried his bottom lip with his teeth. He'd wondered the same thing many times. *Did* he want to meet Ella?

"Sure. After Luke and I know each other a little better." He shrugged at Paul's dubious expression. "I know—the rules of romantic comedy dictate I be eager to meet the adorable rugrat whose shenanigans push Luke and me closer together."

"I didn't expect romcom levels of giddiness," Paul said. "Slightly warmer than tepid would be okay, though."

"I'm not tepid!" Finn replied. "But this is serious stuff. I've never been with a guy who had a kid."

"The kid isn't *Luke's* kid."

"She may as well be," Finn said. He thought about the way Luke lit up at any mention of his niece. "From what I've gathered, Luke's as much Ella's father as any man could be with the exception of her actual biological dad. It's all a little intimidating."

"How so?"

"Luke owns a business and takes care of a child. No offense, but he's more adult than you and me combined and he's younger than we are. Who am I in the middle of all that?" Finn asked. "A guy who's been sleeping in my friends' guest room for months."

"Because you moved here from another city." Paul scoffed. "C'mon, Finn. You're thirty-five years old and talk like you don't have a decent job saving people's lives, a hot ass and student loans in the triple digits."

Finn laughed and snorted beer up his nose.

"Okay, right *now* you don't look like much of a catch," Paul said, his voice dry. "But you know you are, right?"

"Sure." Finn wiped his mouth with his napkin. "I just don't want to rush into anything then fuck it all up, you know?"

"You like him, huh?"

"Yeah, I do." Finn smiled.

"Did you tell your mom about him?"

"Yep."

Paul smiled back. "And?"

"She was excited, of course, like she always is when I'm interested in someone." Finn sipped his beer. "Luke and I have only been out a handful of times, but he's really great."

"You're too fucking cute, Finn. Watching you float around in a good mood for the last couple of weeks has been a pleasure. For what it's worth, trust your gut," Paul said. "If you think this situation with the kid needs care, then give it care. Just don't forget to take care of yourself, too, okay?"

Finn ran a hand over his chin. "What does that mean?"

"You were always super-focused on me being happy while we were dating." Paul's expression turned droll. "Which was great for *me*. I'd never turn down extra pampering, especially from someone as delicious as yourself."

"Dude, come on."

Paul continued as if Finn hadn't spoken. "I think I got too comfortable with the paradigm, though, and that sabotaged the whole thing. You gave me what I wanted but didn't speak up for yourself when you were unhappy or wanted more from me. So I had no idea you weren't getting what you needed and you resented me for that. By the time we got around to talking about my move back to Boston, you were already halfway out of the door."

Finn nodded. "I never thought about it that way."

"You put your partners first, even when you shouldn't. We both know something similar happened with Adam's cheating ass."

"Ugh, don't remind me." Finn's ex had pushed for an open relationship, something that just didn't work for Finn. Adam had eventually promised to be monogamous, but Finn then discovered he'd been picking up men all over Chicago. Things had gone downhill from there despite both their efforts to make the relationship work.

"You need to pay attention to what you need, Finn," Paul said. "So don't let this guy and the kid eat up your whole life outside work. You deserve happiness for yourself, and it's on Luke to make sure he's giving that to you. Remember that, okay?"

Finn held Paul's gaze. For all his bitchery and teasing, Paul knew Finn better than almost anyone, and he was right. Finn needed to make himself a priority, too.

"I will," Finn said. He gestured at the table and the remains of their meal. "Now, c'mon and help me get this stuff inside. It's ten o'clock and those guys have been unsupervised in my apartment for long enough."

Chapter Nine

On Saturday evening, Luke met Finn at the tall iron gate that led to Primus Avenue, and Finn's bright smile sent a thrill through him.

"Hey, Doc. I expected another sidewalk awning," he joked as Finn gestured him in. "This is about a hundred times cooler, though."

"It's definitely more dramatic," Finn said. He surprised Luke with a hug after the gate clanged shut behind them. "It's good to see you again."

"I missed you at lunch." Luke pulled back and laughed as he noticed Finn's choice of clothing. His white T-shirt and well-worn jeans were so similar to Luke's that they might have been purchased from the same store. "Nice outfit."

Finn chuckled. "Whoa. I'm not sure if this is cool or weird, but I'm being sincere when I say you look great."

"So do you." On impulse, Luke leaned in to kiss him and, *mmm*, Finn's lips were deliciously soft.

Finn rested his hands on Luke's waist. He gripped tighter when Luke slid his arms around Finn's shoulders, and he nipped at Luke's upper lip, the coarse hairs of his stubble rasping Luke's skin. Warmth flooded Luke's body in a dizzying rush. He slipped the fingers of one hand beneath Finn's shirt collar and cupped the side of his neck.

"Damn," Finn said after they broke apart. He smiled. "You should warn a man before you scramble his brain with a kiss like that."

"Sorry. I've been thinking about doing that since the first time we had coffee." Luke stole another quick kiss and made Finn laugh.

"C'mon, let me show you around."

He led Luke along the avenue, which was really a long, terraced alley with no outlet. They climbed a series of short concrete staircases and moved deeper among the buildings, Finn's arm around Luke's waist. A pretty garden courtyard sat outside Finn's door, lined with ivy and shaded by tall trees.

"This is beautiful," Luke said, his eyes wide.

Finn smiled. "Hopefully, the interior gets a positive reaction, too."

Inside the ground floor unit, Finn put the wine Luke had brought on the kitchen counter, then gave him a tour of the two-bedroom space, which he'd decorated in blond wood and shades of gray and blue. The furnishings made excellent use of the apartment's limited square footage, and everything was streamlined and organized in a way that appealed to Luke's need for order.

"Okay, yes, great interior," Luke confirmed after they'd moved back to the kitchen. "I can't believe how much you got done in less than two weeks!"

Finn picked up the wine bottle. "I had a lot of help, believe me."

Luke remembered Gillian's talk of magical house elves and grinned. "What kind of help?" He squatted down to pet the calico cat who'd trailed in behind them. "This is Daisy, I take it?"

"The one and only." Finn smiled. He grabbed two glasses from a cabinet and set them down. "Paul's husband gave me the most help. Mick is an interior designer and he took stock of my stuff and added a few things to pull the rooms together. He and Paul brought some friends over the other night to paint, too, and without them, I'd still be living out of cardboard boxes."

"Well, thanks for having me." Luke accepted a glass from Finn. "I'm still boggled that you worked an overnight shift and yet you're somehow coherent."

Finn waved him off. "I slept in and ordered takeout. I remembered you saying you like sushi and picked some up at a place in the neighborhood."

"Fantastic. I don't get to eat it for dinner much."

"Why is that?" Finn put his glass on the counter and moved toward the refrigerator.

"Ella. She prefers fish in stick form." Luke stepped forward as Finn set several plastic containers on the counter. "Here, let me help you. Anyway, she's not super-fussy, but she tends to pick certain things and stick with them. Like macaroni and cheese or breakfast as dinner."

"I love breakfast as dinner, too." Finn pulled a cutting board from one of the cabinets. "You guys ate breakfast the night you and I met, right?"

"Yes! Well, I did — I had eggs and Cheddar grits that night, but Ella had the aforementioned mac 'n' cheese with a side of bacon."

"Mmm." Finn bit his lip. "That all sounds insanely good. I'd need a nap afterward, though."

Finn was animated as they chatted and arranged the sushi rolls and salads on the board. He brushed his fingers along Luke's forearm and pressed his hand against the small of Luke's back while they maneuvered around the small kitchen, and Luke looked forward to each touch. He craved them, really, and made sure he returned every one.

They carried the meal out to the courtyard and a mellow warmth settled over Luke as they sat on a sectional with their food and wine. He rarely had quiet moments like this, just him and a man he desired, and he savored the peaceful mood as much as the heat of Finn's body beside him.

After they'd finished eating, Finn set down his chopsticks and took Luke's hand, threading their fingers together. That simple touch made Luke's nerves sing, and his insides tightened at the shine in Finn's eyes.

"I'd like to kiss you again," Finn said, his voice quiet.

"I'd like it if you did," Luke replied, and anything else either of them might have said got lost when Finn leaned in and pressed their lips together.

Heat swept through Luke. Finn deepened the kiss slowly, and Luke tasted wine and soy and ginger. A hum rumbled through Finn and the slide of his tongue made Luke shiver. Finn pulled back and stared at Luke, his expression intense.

"I know you have to get back home at some point, but will you stay a while with me?" he asked.

Goosebumps rose along Luke's skin. "Yes. I'd like that."

They left their dishes in the sink and Finn led Luke to the bedroom where he lit the bedside lamp. He stepped into Luke's embrace and slid his hands over Luke's chest, pressing heat through Luke's shirt and into his skin.

They eyed one another in silence, and the tension between them made Luke's heart race and his cock harden. He gathered Finn up and kissed him some more, going deeper until Finn groaned. Luke's breath caught at that low sound.

The kisses continued as they undressed as though neither could bear to let go for more than a few seconds. Desire stormed through Luke as Finn's long, lean limbs emerged, and it made his gut clench. Something in his face must have conveyed his dazed state because Finn smiled and stepped toward the bed.

"Come here," he murmured and held out a hand.

Threading their fingers together, he pulled Luke closer and held him tight. Their mouths met again and they fell onto the bed in a tangle of limbs, and Luke thought he'd die at the feeling of all that hot skin against his.

"Jesus, Luke," Finn whispered against his lips. His rough voice set a fire in Luke's belly.

Finn pushed at Luke until he lay flat, then settled between Luke's legs. Luke rocked his hips up. The motion brushed their erections together, and the naked lust in Finn's face made Luke ache. He bit his lip when Finn grabbed his ass.

"Oh, my God, you feel good," Luke ground out.

They shared a breathless laugh, and Finn kissed him again, hot and dirty, his hands moving and his touch like a trail of fire along Luke's body.

"I want you," Finn said and bent to lick the skin on Luke's chest.

He worked his way lower, tonguing Luke's ribs and turning his bones liquid. Luke brought a hand up to Finn's head and slid his fingers into Finn's hair. He let out a hoarse grunt when Finn palmed Luke's cock with one hand and watched, mesmerized, as Finn took him in his mouth.

"Finn. Oh, fuck."

Finn sucked. A hum rolled through him, and he snaked a hand between the mattress and his own body. His eyelids fluttered as he touched himself, and he let out a low groan. The vibrations in his throat curled Luke's toes and made sweat break out over his skin. Luke pushed his head back against the pillows, losing himself in sensation.

He gasped when Finn pulled off, but Finn crawled up over Luke and met his lips in a blistering kiss that had Luke rutting helplessly to find friction.

"Uhh, oh, God."

Finn reached down and fondled Luke's balls. "What do you want?"

"You in me," Luke said through his panting breaths.

Finn smiled and pulled away. Luke rolled onto his belly, drawing a pillow under his chest, and his cock throbbed against the sheets. He heard the drawer scrape open, then a click, and he closed his eyes. His heart thudded in his ears as Finn tore open a condom package, and he spread Luke's thighs wide. A slick finger slid along the cleft of Luke's ass with a teasing touch.

Finn settled over him and moved his free arm under Luke's chest, holding him in a loose embrace. "So gorgeous," he said, his voice gruff against the back of Luke's neck.

He slid a finger inside Luke, and Luke grasped Finn's arm. The burn increased as Finn slowly stretched him open, forcing a needy gasp out of Luke. God, he needed this — he'd gone too long without being touched.

Finn took his time. He kissed Luke's face and murmured dirty things in his ear, working another finger in beside the first, and each motion drove Luke to distraction. Finn chuckled darkly when Luke bucked against the mattress and whined.

"Finn, please."

Finn slid his fingers away and shifted his weight, and the loss of sensation hit Luke hard. He buried his face in the pillow. He held on as Finn nudged his cock between Luke's ass cheeks and pushed his hips up and back to spread himself wide. Finn pressed forward, breaching Luke's body in a long, slow drive and Luke clenched his teeth through the stretch. He shivered when Finn bottomed out.

"God," Finn whispered, his breath ragged. He dropped a kiss on Luke's shoulder.

He rocked back and forward, and the pain in Luke's body became a sweet ache. Luke moaned. He pushed back to meet Finn, desperate to get closer, and shuddered at Finn's gasp. Blindly, he craned his head over his shoulder for a kiss.

Finn moaned against Luke's lips. "Fuck!"

He drove into Luke, the thrusts coming faster, and Luke sank into pleasure. All he knew was need and heat and the man wrapped around him. Finn thrust deep, the move scraping at Luke's prostate and jangling every nerve in his body. Luke tore his mouth free with a grunt. Finn thrust harder, punching that spot inside Luke until he thought he'd scream. His heart squeezed when Finn's voice broke.

Finn pinned Luke against the mattress when he came. His movements slowed and turned lazy as he rode out his high, and his breaths gusted over the damp skin of Luke's shoulders and neck. Luke reveled in the weight of the body on top of him. He ground against the bed, his face pressed into the pillow again, and the ache inside him sharpened unbearably after Finn pulled out. Luke's throat went tight.

Finn urged Luke onto his back, Luke's limbs trembling with the need to come. He shook more under the weight of Finn's gaze and the desire he saw there.

"Come on, Luke."

Finn slipped his fingers back inside Luke, and Luke arched into the touch. His body jolted again as Finn took him in hand, and he gasped, his head spinning at the dual sensations of being filled and pulled apart.

"It's too much," Luke whispered. His chest constricted to the point of pain.

"I've got you, baby."

Finn's husky voice was all it took for Luke to unravel with a long, shuddering moan. He clutched at Finn and broke apart, his world narrowing to his heart thundering in his ears and the bliss that pierced him clean through.

Luke lay spent and stupid when Finn pulled his fingers free. Finn swiped at the cum on Luke's torso with the sheet and pushed it aside, then gathered him close. They lay quiet, exchanging lazy touches and kisses as the sweat cooled on their skin, and Luke coasted on easy pleasure.

He'd started dozing when Finn roused. He peeled his eyelids open and watched unabashed as Finn moved toward the bathroom, his lean body toned and strong. The play of light over Finn's bare skin made Luke long to touch him.

Finn caught Luke's eye on his way back to the bed with a washcloth in hand, and he grinned. "What's that look for?"

"Just taking in the view."

"You like it?"

"You know I do."

Finn chuckled. He sat beside Luke on the bed and wiped him down, then laid a hand on Luke's chest. "It's getting late," he said. "Got time for another glass of wine?"

Luke smiled. "I do, and I'd love one."

"Great."

Finn stood and helped Luke to his feet. Pulling the quilt loose from the bed, he wrapped it around Luke's waist, then tickled Luke's belly with his fingertips and made him squawk. They talked about the next time they could see each other while Finn staggered back into his boxer briefs, then headed for the kitchen together.

"Ella asked me about you," Luke said as they stood at the narrow granite counter, sipping wine and sharing pints of mango and coconut ice cream.

Finn raised his eyebrows. "Yeah?"

"She's curious about the man who keeps buying me lunch."

"That's fair." Finn chuckled. "What's her take on tonight's dinner?"

Luke stared down at his glass. "I'm not sure. She says she's okay with my dating, but I can't tell if she's just humoring me."

Finn sipped his wine. "That's not bad, right? It's not like she threw a tantrum when you left the house."

"Oh, God, no." Luke grimaced. "She was a little moody but nothing too unusual. She advised me to be cool if at all possible, by the way."

"Seriously?"

"Very seriously," Luke replied, his voice dry. "Ella's tolerant of my geek quotient but it's clear she didn't trust me not to embarrass myself."

"It's sweet she's looking out for you."

"Mmm, I don't know. I think she's looking out for *you*, Finn."

"I doubt that." Finn swirled his wine. "I'm sure Ella wants to make sure the guys in your life treat you right, that's all."

Luke slid a hand along Finn's ribs. "Maybe. I don't date much, though, so it's hard to say."

Finn cast him a dubious glance. "How do you not date much?"

"Haven't met anyone who's okay with all of the baggage that comes along with taking care of a kid. Finding free time to go out is where the problems start and things go downhill from there."

Finn pursed his lips. "Okay. I get what you're saying, but it's difficult to believe that'd put someone off entirely. I mean, scheduling problems aside, there's *you*."

Delight spiked through Luke. "You're good for my ego. I don't blame guys for not wanting to deal with the whole caretaking thing. There's a ton involved. A lot of the time, I'm right in the middle of it, too. Ella's not difficult, but she needs time and attention like any child. Sometimes, she needs more from us because of the stuff she went through with her mom leaving.

Mother's Day, for instance? Not a welcome holiday for Ella. Father's Day wasn't exactly a picnic this year, either."

Luke set down the spoon. "I don't have much freedom to be spontaneous, and my schedule can be unforgiving. I can count on one hand the number of times I've been out past midnight in the last year. I *can't* tell you how often I've had to bail on plans because Ella needs help with her homework, or is sick, or needs to be picked up from taekwondo or swimming. Yes, we have a babysitter and my parents help out, but it's on me to be there for her when Pete's not around and I take that responsibility seriously."

"I get what you're saying, Luke, I do. But again, you're still you." Finn gestured at Luke with his glass. "There's more to you beyond taking care of Ella."

"Of course," Luke replied. "But I won't lie, Doc. Being there for Ella is a lot of work. Some days it feels like a full-time job."

Finn nodded. "I admire you for taking it all on. I'm not sure what I'd do in your place."

Luke shrugged. "It wasn't a hard decision. I was happy when Pete brought Ella to stay with me, even though some shitty things went down for that to happen."

He went back and forth in his head for a moment, weighing the idea of really showing Ella to Finn, and he let go of Finn's hand. "Back in a second."

Luke went to the bedroom for his phone, which he found in the pile of clothes they'd left on the floor. Finn was still at the counter when he walked back into the kitchen and met Luke's smile with one of his own.

"I think it's time I stopped talking about Ella in the abstract," Luke said. He stepped up alongside Finn and pulled up the last photo he'd taken. In it, Ella sat at the dinner table in her Starfleet PJs with the paper flowers in her hair and a grin on her face.

Finn smiled softly at the photo. "She's beautiful, Luke."

Luke flipped through more images on his phone until he found one of Peter and Ella together, taken a month before Peter had shipped out. They'd been shopping at the stalls in the Boston Public Market, and Luke thought his brother looked especially happy. Peter's face was bright with laughter, and the glow that lit his rich brown skin and dark eyes was echoed in Ella's smaller features.

Luke swallowed past a sudden tightness in his chest. "I can't remember if I told you that Pete and I are adopted," he said. "Pete was born in the Dominican Republic and our parents took him in when he was a baby. They found me not too long after in foster care, and Pete and I were born only a few months apart. People used to joke that we were twins because we're so close in age, but they didn't have to work to tell us apart."

"I can really see Ella's dad in her features," Finn said. He reached out and touched the screen with his finger, tracing the sprinkle of tiny freckles that highlighted the bridge of Ella's nose.

"Ella got the freckles from her mother," Luke said. "We thought she'd keep Carly's blue eyes, but they turned amber as she got older. She does take after Pete a lot, but she's still young and we know she'll change a lot as she grows up."

He locked the phone and a knot of nerves formed in his gut. "It may be too soon for this conversation, but you already know I'm crazy for planning. What do you think about meeting Ella sometime?" The knot tightened at the concern flitting over Finn's face. "What's wrong?"

"Nothing at all." Finn licked his lips. "But I don't want you to misunderstand when I say I don't want to rush into anything right now. I've never dated a man with a child before, and I'm not exactly sure how. I'd really love to get to know *you*, Luke, before we start pulling in family." He rubbed his chin with one hand. "Am I making sense?"

"Yeah, you are." Luke's nerves melted in the face of Finn's uncertainty. "Honestly, I haven't had a lot of luck balancing my family life with dating in the past, so it may be for the best we ease into things." He wrinkled his nose. "Too much, huh?"

Finn shook his head. "No, that's not it. This is new for me, sure, but I'm okay with new. I just want to be *ready* for it, too. I like you and I'd really like to keep seeing you."

Luke couldn't hide his grin. "I like you too. How about you tell me when you think we're ready to meet friends and family, and we'll go from there?"

"I can do that," Finn replied, and smiled. "Thanks for being open with me about all this, by the way."

"I meant it when I said I wouldn't hold back on the awkward things."

"I know you did." Finn nodded. "I haven't always had that kind of honesty with guys. My last boyfriend lied to me about all kinds of things, big and small. After we broke up, I promised myself I wouldn't let that happen to me again and it means a lot that you're being so honest with me."

Finn leaned in and kissed Luke, and a while passed before they came back up for air. Luke's knees wobbled as he forced himself to speak words he didn't want to say.

"I need to think about going home soon." He ran the tip of his nose along Finn's cheek. "Mind if I take a quick shower?"

"Only if I can join you," Finn replied. "I'm not ready to let you go yet."

Luke slid a hand down and rested it against Finn's ass. "Of course you can join me." He smiled at Finn's appreciative hum. "I have big plans to blow you under the shower heads in that shiny bathroom of yours."

Chapter Ten

"I feel like your mom right now," Paul said as he walked through Finn's front door. "This is the first time in a while you've introduced me to a man and it feels so formal!"

Finn laughed. "Dude, I'm making Cobb Salad — this is hardly formal."

"What we're eating isn't relevant." Paul followed Finn to the kitchen. "C'mon, you can't deny tonight's got a 'meet the parents' kind of vibe to it, right?"

"It does now that you've said that," Finn said. "It's not supposed to feel formal, though. Just friends getting to know friends. Incidentally, I suspect your feelings stem from the fact that you mother me more than my actual bio mom."

"Fair point."

"And does that make Mick the dad in this scenario?"

"Probably, but for God's sake, don't tell him that," Paul replied with a laugh.

A strange, buzzing energy invaded Finn's body as he and Paul prepared dinner. He'd worked a brutal shift overnight, and while he'd managed a little sleep after getting home, he'd woken feeling unrested and almost hungover. Finn didn't let it drag him down, though. Luke was coming over to meet Paul and Mick, and that put a smile on his face.

Paul set a glass of Pinot Noir down by the cutting board Finn was using to slice roasted chicken breasts and eyed the ingredients spread out on the counter. "When did you have time to get all this together?"

"I went shopping after my shift and roasted the chicken when I got home."

"That explains why you look like shit." Paul pulled a smaller cutting board from a cabinet. "Have you slept at all?"

"I grabbed a couple of hours and I'm off tomorrow, so I can sleep in if I feel like it."

"You want to talk about anything?"

"Nah, I'm good, thanks." Finn didn't want to think about his shift, let alone talk about it. Besides, if he and Paul started talking shop, they'd go all night, and that wasn't fair to Mick or Luke.

Paul set about deseeding a bowl of tomatoes. "Luke's introducing you to his besties, too, right?"

"We're having lunch with his partners and coworkers on Sunday. They do a monthly thing at one of the partners' apartments."

"What about the niece?"

"She's spending the day with her grandparents," Finn replied.

"And will you meet the rest of the Ryans?" Paul met Finn's raised eyebrow with a shrug. "You know that's next, Finn."

"Mmm, I don't know. I'm not sure we're quite at family intros yet," Finn hedged. "That's why we're starting with friends."

Paul scoffed. "Seeing as your family lives halfway across the country, you can consider me a stand-in." He reached over and pulled Finn's ear.

"Gah, you're getting tomato juice all over me."

"And you're deflecting," Paul replied. "Which tells me you and Luke are getting serious."

"I think we're getting *around* to getting serious," Finn said. "I know that sounds like a cop-out, but it's the truth. We're still taking some things slow."

"Because you want it that way, yes." Paul turned back to the tomatoes. "What changed your mind about friend intros?"

"We've been seeing each other for a month. It seemed right." Finn shrugged.

"Aha." Paul smiled. "You really like him."

"I really like him."

"And he really likes you?"

"Sure seems that way." Finn couldn't stop his grin. "So, we'll keep dating and see where it goes, and maybe things will get serious."

"Just like that, huh?"

"Just like that."

Paul nodded, but his smile was fond. Despite his teasing, he wanted Finn to be happy. And Finn *was* happy, more so than he had been in a while.

In spite of their many scheduling challenges, he and Luke had continued seeing each other several times a week. They sometimes managed dinner on the weekends during Finn's time off, but Luke spent most weekday evenings with Ella, so he made a point of meeting Finn for breakfast or lunch in various eateries around Boston. When the need to be physically close became too much — and it frequently did — they met at Finn's apartment where they ignored meals in favor of making each other gasp and moan in Finn's big, new bed.

Damn.

Finn bit his lip. It had been years since he'd formed such a strong connection to a lover. The more time they spent together, the more he craved Luke. He wanted Luke's hard muscles and hot skin under his hands. To watch Luke's eyes, pupils blown, grow hazy with lust and hear his deep, honeyed voice waver over Finn's name.

Finn enjoyed his time with Luke *out* of bed just as much, even when they were doing something mundane like grocery shopping or watching endless *Star Trek* re-runs. Finn wanted to know everything about the big man with the bright smile and quick wit, from what kind of books he read — cyberpunk — to his favorite flavor of ice cream — black raspberry or peppermint stick, but never together.

Finn was mixing a honey Dijon dressing when his phone chimed on the counter. "That's probably Mick," he said. He wiped his hands and declined the call, then punched in the code that unlocked the Primus Avenue gate. "Luke's dropping Ella off at a friend's first, so I don't expect him before six-thirty."

"Finn, it's six forty-five."

Finn went still. "What? How the hell did that happen?" he wondered as his buzzer went off. He headed for the door.

Paul tsked. "You should have slept more. You'll be dead to the world by dessert if not earlier!"

Sure enough, Finn found Mick and Luke chatting on his doorstep as if they'd become good pals between the gate and Finn's building. Then Luke looked at Finn, and the way his face lit up sent a dizzy rush through Finn's whole body.

He waved them in with a grin. "Hey, guys."

"Hey, Finn." Mick leaned in for a quick hug and inclined his head toward Luke. "I met this guy outside and glommed on to him."

"Mick was walking in front of me on Charles Street," Luke said. "He stopped at the gate and I figured he must be either a friend of yours or an unbelievably friendly mugger." He held up a white paper bag while the others laughed. "I brought dessert, as requested, in the form of Key Lime Pie Bars."

"Oh, God, those sound good," Mick crooned. He held his hands out for the bag. "I'll take those and go pour us some wine, shall I?"

"You should say hello to your husband while you're at it!" Paul shouted from the kitchen. Finn clamped his lips together over a laugh as Mick cringed.

"Yes, love, hello!" Mick called back. He managed an epic eye-roll before striding off with the bag and leaving Finn and Luke behind.

"I should warn you that they're like that all the time," Finn said. "It's ninety-nine percent play-acting, though, so don't take anything seriously."

"Thanks for the heads-up." Luke met Finn's gaze and smiled. "Hey, Doc."

"Hey." Finn's chest seemed to swell as he wrapped Luke up in a hug and closed the remaining distance between them with a kiss. He meant to steal just one, but one became several and soon he had Luke up against the front door and both of them were laughing.

Luke brought his hands up to Finn's face and kissed him so desire zigged up Finn's spine and turned his knees jelly.

He pressed his forehead to Luke's with a hum. "Thanks for coming over."

"Thanks for having me." Luke tilted his head back, and his forehead puckered when Finn opened his eyes again. "You okay?"

Finn opened his mouth to brush the question off but went silent when Luke gently brushed his thumb under Finn's eye, no doubt tracing the dark smudge of sleeplessness. His touch made Finn sigh.

"I slept for shit last night. I worked a tough shift and never settled. It happens," he said at Luke's frown. "You'd think I'd be used to awful shifts by now, right? It's okay, though. You're here and we'll have wine and dinner, not to mention one of my favorite desserts, and all those things will make me feel better."

"Okay." Luke dropped another kiss against Finn's lips. "You let me know how I can help. You can thank Gillian for the dessert recipe, by the way. She passed it on to me along with some secrets for juicing key limes." He grimaced. "Those little suckers are a bitch to wrangle when you've got big hands like mine."

Finn grinned so wide his face hurt. "I can't believe you baked for this. Wait 'til Paul hears."

"Paul already knows because he heard every word you said." The man himself appeared at the end of the hallway, his eyes sparkling with amusement. "This apartment's not very big, Finn, and the bricks and hardwood floors make for some truly fantastic acoustics. So how about you stop macking on your boy and introduce me? Mick's in here about to eat all your bacon, by the way, so the sooner you two get your asses moving, the better."

Though tired, Finn felt purely content as the evening progressed. Paul wasn't always tolerant of the men Finn dated, but Luke's abundant natural charm proved too much even for him, particularly after he mentioned the Ryan family's fondness for Sullivan's on Castle Island.

"We were just there two weekends ago," Paul said once they were seated in the courtyard with their dinner and several citronella candles. "Finn and Mick said the lobster roll was excellent."

"And what did you eat?" Luke asked.

"Fried clams," Mick answered in Paul's place. "Paul always orders fried clams and if a joint doesn't serve them, it's like the world is ending."

Luke laughed as Paul and Mick started another round of verbal sparring, but Finn caught his eye and his mirth softened into a smile. "What's that look for?"

"Nothing," Finn replied. He captured one of Luke's hands between his. "Just glad we could be here together. You okay to stay for a while after dinner?"

"Yes. Ella and her friends are watching a Marvel marathon tonight, and I'm not expected for pick up until ten-thirty."

"Is your niece Team Stark or Team Cap?" Mick asked. He wrinkled his nose at Paul, who pretended to gag. "Shut it, you."

"Ella's Team Cap," Luke replied. "Black Widow, Ant-Man and Black Panther are high on her list of favorites, too. Oh, and Drax the Destroyer. I'm lucky in that she likes many of the same nerdy things her dad and I do. I'm not sure how we'd handle overtly girly things on a full-time basis."

"That may all change after she hits puberty," Finn said.

"Ugh, I know. She's already showing shades of teenager, believe it or not, and we're in no way equipped to deal with any of it." Luke swirled his wine. "Pete and I hope she'll stay a little girl for a while longer, but that's probably wishful thinking."

Paul shook his head. "I don't know how you do it, man. Being responsible for someone else's care and happiness on a twenty-four-hour basis would do me in."

Mick turned to Finn, his expression disgruntled. "He says this like he's not even married."

"Having a kid is different," Paul threw back over Finn's laughter. "You're a grown man, Mick, or claim to be — you're responsible for taking care of yourself."

"For what it's worth, I agree," Luke said. "Ella's not fully independent yet, so I have to view my decisions through a particular lens. Everything I do has the potential to affect her in some way, even if the things I'm doing aren't directly about her."

Finn sipped his wine and mulled over Luke's words. "Do you feel that way when your brother is around?"

"To a certain extent, yes, because Ella lives with me full-time." Luke licked his lips. "But I worry a lot less when Pete is here. And it's nice not being the only person responsible for ensuring everything is okay in Ella's world."

"See, that kind of pressure would wreck me." Paul shot a significant look at Mick over the edge of his glass. "I can't imagine dealing with that, *particularly* on top of caring for patients all day."

Finn's eyes went wide. "Have you two been talking about having kids?"

"God, no," Mick replied. "We barely coped helping you take care of Daisy. Even opening cans of cat food without your reminders proved difficult."

"And that litterbox." Paul grimaced. "I deal with enough poop in the ED, thank you very much."

"Daisy survived just fine." Finn chuckled. "That's the reason I've got a cat and not a dog, you know — cats are much more low maintenance."

Paul waved his glass in Finn's direction. "Even a cat is too much for me. My goal is to be the one thing in my life that *isn't* low maintenance."

"Trust me, darlin' — you are," Mick said with a laugh.

After their plates were emptied, Finn stood and started stacking them. He shared a grin with Luke and tipped his head toward the door. "Come and help me make coffee, handsome."

Finn wasted no time pulling Luke in for a kiss once they were inside and they ended up shoving everything they'd been carrying onto the counter. As Luke's body heat soaked into Finn's, he wanted nothing more than to lie down and kiss Luke until they both lost their minds. Several minutes passed before he remembered they'd come inside to make coffee, and his knees wobbled again as he flipped the switch on the carafe.

"I wish we were alone right now," he grumbled. He ran a hand over Luke's hair and admired his flushed cheeks. Lust curled in his belly. "Would it be very rude if I asked my friends to leave?"

"I'm afraid so." Luke kissed the tip of Finn's nose. "Though I suspect you'd risk the offense if it meant you could hoard all the dessert." The laughter that bubbled up out of Finn made Luke smile until his eyes crinkled.

"Oh, baby, you don't know how right you are," Finn said. "Don't sell yourself short, though—you're as tempting as any Key Lime goodness. I *really* love the idea of eating them off your naked body, by the way."

Luke grabbed Finn's ass, his touch deliciously rough, and he pushed Finn against the counter with a pleased-sounding growl. "Damn. I'm all for making that happen—if not tonight, as soon as we can manage it."

A dizzy desire snaked its way through Finn and made his head swim and his cock harden. He didn't know any more if he wanted to fuck or cuddle, but he wanted all of it and more with Luke.

"I'm holding you to that," he whispered.

An hour later, most of the Key Lime bars were gone, Paul and Mick had headed home and Finn's exhaustion had begun to take its toll. He weaved as Luke steered him toward the bedroom, and they shared a laugh after he almost stumbled.

"Tired, huh?" Luke asked as they neared the bed.

"Utterly wiped," Finn said. He turned and looped his arms around Luke's neck. "Glad we did this, though. Paul and Mick were looking forward to meeting you."

Luke took Finn's waist in his hands. "I'm glad, too. I had a good time."

Finn closed his eyes and nodded. His breath caught when Luke pressed his lips against the hollow of Finn's throat. Slowly, Luke peeled Finn's clothes off, taking his time to touch and kiss as the garments fell away, and Finn's skin prickled under Luke's trailing fingers. Luke skimmed his palm over Finn's belly and dipped his hand lower, and Finn bit back a gasp.

"Okay, Doc?"

"Yes. Very okay." Finn moaned. Heat pulsed in his groin. "Need to touch you."

"You want me to grab the leftover dessert before we get started?"

Finn laughed at the smile he heard in Luke's voice but shook his head. "Want you too much."

He brought his hands to Luke's waist and opened his eyes as Luke guided him down onto the bed. Finn watched Luke shuck his own clothes, his gut tightening as the muscled planes of Luke's body were laid bare. Luke stretched out beside him, and they stayed largely silent as they kissed and caressed one another, communicating through sight and touch rather than speech. Finn lost himself in miles of fair skin and freckles, and his erection lay rigid against his abdomen when Luke finally pulled away.

Luke covered Finn's cock with one broad hand. He kissed along Finn's belly and pelvis, teasing the skin with his lips and tongue, and nuzzled Finn's shaft with his lips. Finn stared, arrested by the lust in Luke's eyes, which never left his.

"Jesus fuck, baby."

Luke smiled. "Lube," he murmured, his breath warm against Finn's cock.

Finn made a grab for the nightstand and gasped as Luke licked along the base of his dick. He sighed with relief when his fingers closed over the bottle, and he passed it down to Luke, his hands shaking.

Luke pushed himself up onto his knees, his face flushed and his mouth swollen from kissing. His cock stood stiff as he wet his fingers, but he ignored it and spread Finn's knees wide instead. He wrapped a hot, wet hand around Finn before he bent deep and swiped his tongue over Finn's balls.

Finn bit back a shout. "Oh, *God.*"

Luke closed his eyes. He licked and kissed the sensitive skin of Finn's balls with utmost care, each touch over Finn's shaft and cockhead tender-rough and perfect. Wonder filled Finn as he watched the man between his legs. Luke rested his cheek on Finn's groin and held his amazing ass high in the air. He rocked his hips gently as he sucked and each motion made the muscles of his back flex and jump. Several beats passed before it dawned on Finn that Luke was fucking his own hand, and he sucked in a sharp breath as the coil inside him drew taut.

"Mmm. Luke."

Luke opened eyes filled with fire. He shifted upright and pinned Finn with that stare as he took him down in a long, slow slide. Finn wound his fingers in Luke's dark hair and fought like hell not to buck, but he was gone the moment Luke swallowed around him. Finn swore and pumped into Luke's face, and everything in him pulled tight when Luke's lids slid closed and he moaned. The vibrations in his throat sent pleasure jolting through Finn's body and a familiar ache pooled in his groin.

"You—oh, fuck. Coming," Finn ground out.

Luke tightened his grip and swallowed again, and Finn came apart at the seams. His body went rigid as the orgasm stormed through him with crushing intensity. It left him wrung-out and boneless against the mattress, and he floated high while Luke licked him clean.

"Look at you," Luke murmured, his voice rough and reverent. He shifted back and Finn peeled his eyes open in time to see Luke lift his knee over Finn's lax form. He straddled Finn's waist, and Finn's brain came back online as Luke's erection jutted up hard and red against his groin.

Finn ran his hands over Luke's thighs and smiled at the goosebumps that pebbled Luke's skin.

"Show me, baby," he coaxed. "Make yourself feel good."

Luke took himself in hand with a hiss. His shuddered as Finn intertwined their fingers around Luke's shaft, and his head fell back as they pumped him in tandem. Finn licked his lips at Luke's moan. Quickly, he slid his other hand around Luke and fingered his rim, and Luke's body lit up like a firework.

"Oh, God!"

Finn groaned, his dick growing stiff. "Fuck, yeah, Luke. Show me how you come."

Luke curled forward with a choked cry, streaking Finn's torso with his cum. He shook as Finn pulled him down and held him close, both of them silent but for the sound of their racing breaths. Finn lay still until Luke stirred, and though he tried to rouse himself, it was as if his bones were filled with lead. Even his eyelids refused to cooperate.

"Where you goin'?" he asked and both of them chuckled at his sleepy slurring.

"Just getting something to clean us up," Luke whispered. He ran a hand over Finn's head with a soft touch.

Finn's awareness waned further as Luke moved around the bedroom. He was grateful for the warm, wet cloth that cleaned him up and the cool sheets drawn up over his body, and for Luke's solid weight spooned up behind him.

I could get used to this.

"You should stay," he murmured without thinking, then felt a pang of regret at Luke's sigh.

"Mmm, I can't."

Damn. Finn knew better than to guilt Luke over things he couldn't control. But before he could apologize, Luke rested his cheek on Finn's shoulder.

"I'll work on it, Doc."

Chapter Eleven

Luke surveyed the Boston skyline laid out before him and sipped his margarita. He'd always loved the view from the roof deck of Simon's South End condo, especially the way the Hancock tower's sharp blue angles jutted into the sky. The picturesque view paled in comparison to the man at Luke's side, though.

"This is nice," Finn said, his tone admiring. "Much nicer than the courtyard at my place."

Luke frowned. "Oh, I don't know. The courtyard at your place is very you."

"What, slightly overgrown and off limits after ten p.m.?"

"I *like* the courtyard," Luke replied. "It's green and shady and cool, and so peaceful, even with all the traffic and tourists beyond the gate. It's like an oasis hidden away in the middle of the city."

Luke cursed inwardly at the surprise that crossed Finn's face. He had an unfortunate tendency to wax poetic around men he liked, and he liked Finn a whole lot. Heat crawled up the back of his neck, but he relaxed when Finn took hold of his hand, the simple touch soothing Luke's rough edges.

"I never thought about it that way." The fondness in Finn's gray eyes nearly mashed Luke's heart flat. "The courtyard was a big draw to rent the place. I wanted someplace I could unwind after work and sit and do nothing."

"Seems as good a reason as any to settle on a space to live," Luke replied. "Though you'll have to find someplace else after the cold weather arrives. I didn't have anything specific in mind when I bought my place, other than to call a space home for the first time since I'd moved out of my parents' house." He smiled. "And by home I mean someplace decent where I didn't have to worry about someone spilling pizza sauce on the furniture, wrecking my laundry or stealing my beer."

Finn laughed. "Those were your criteria, huh?"

"Yep. It took a while to find a place that spoke to me. I must have seen every condo in Back Bay, and I swear my realtor wanted to strangle me with her bare hands. We finally found a place I liked and could mostly afford with the right loan, and I couldn't wait to move in and make it mine. Of course, *my* place became *our* place about a year later because Pete and Ella showed up to crash and Ella never left." He squeezed Finn's hand. "Too bad I didn't know ahead of time because I'd have looked for something bigger than a two-bedroom."

"Where does Pete sleep when he's in town anyway?" Finn asked. "Because I already know Ella got the second bedroom."

"She totally did. She's got it covered so thick in kid things I don't even recognize it anymore." Luke sipped his drink. "Pete sleeps in a converted closet. It has a window and enough room for a bed and a chest of drawers, by the way, before you start thinking I treat my brother like Harry Potter."

Finn barked out a laugh. "You've painted a very amusing picture in my head."

"It is pretty funny, now that I'm thinking about it." Luke chuckled. "My place isn't huge but it has a glut of closet space, including what used to be a walk-in closet off the main living area. It always seemed like wasted space to me, though, and I used it as an office for a while. We changed it into a bedroom after Pete moved Ella back."

He cleared his throat. "I'll show you some time so you can see for yourself," he said, and his heart gave a funny jump at the way Finn's eyes lit up.

"I'd like that."

"Good." Luke raised their joined hands to his lips and pressed a kiss against Finn's knuckles. He wanted to say more—to tell Finn how happy he made him every time they got together—but a deep, familiar voice stopped him.

"Please stop with the romantic bullshit before I go into a diabetic coma and die."

Luke stifled a laugh. "Something I can do for you, Simon, or are you just here to rain on my margarita?"

"Hah, clever." Simon stepped beside Luke. He looked very tan and blond in his white button-down shirt and old jeans, and his blue eyes shone with mischief. "I'm happy to rain on anything you want, but I just wanted to let you two know that lunch is ready." He gestured over his shoulder to the far side of the deck where Gillian and the others were gathering to feast on a cold fried chicken picnic.

"Well, thanks." Luke glanced at Finn. "You're ready to eat, right?"

Finn smiled. "Um, yes. How'd you guess?"

"I heard your stomach growl a minute ago."

"Ugh. That's not embarrassing at all."

Luke grinned.

This man.

Luke had yet to find anything about Finn he didn't like just fine. He'd been checking, too, because he wanted to get a handle on the way Finn made him feel. Luke had been infatuated before, but this...this was different. He hadn't experienced a connection like this in years, and everything about it seemed bigger and more intense. Luke's feelings for Finn scared him a little. And he wasn't doing a single thing to put the brakes on.

The sound of Simon clearing his throat sent heat flashing across Luke's face. Had he really gone all moony over Finn right in front of his best friend? *Yes. Yes, I have.* There was no chance Simon would let that slide, either.

Luke braced himself as he and Finn followed Simon across the deck, but Simon surprised him by holding his tongue. He watched Luke and Finn over the course of the afternoon instead, his gaze sharp. Luke read questions in his friend's eyes, but it was the concern Luke glimpsed there that finally pushed him to his feet.

He smiled down at Finn, who was comparing notes about noodle restaurants with Gillian and Charlie. "I'm going to get a refill. Can I bring you one, too?"

"Thanks, yeah." Finn handed up his glass. "Better make mine water this time, though. I'm on duty in a couple of hours."

"You got it. How about you two?" Luke glanced at Gillian and Charlie, who waved him off, then headed for the staircase that led down into Simon's loft.

Inside, Luke went to the kitchen sink with the glasses and washed them, and it wasn't long before he heard movement behind him.

"You don't have to do that," Simon said. "There's clean glassware in the cabinet."

"I know. It's easy enough to reuse these, though." Luke set the glasses on the counter and turned toward Simon, who'd gone to the refrigerator. "Besides, this way we can talk about whatever's been putting that look on your face."

Simon pulled a cake box from the refrigerator's depths and let the door swing shut. He cut his eyes at Luke as he carried the box to the counter. "You should be more concerned with the look on your face than mine. I know I am."

"What does that mean?"

Instead of answering, Simon pulled a wide blue platter from one of the cabinets and started arranging slices of cheesecake from the box.

"Does Finn know?" he asked.

Dread trickled along Luke's spine. "Does Finn know what?" The way Simon's expression softened made his guts churn.

"That you're falling for him."

"I'm—I'm not," Luke croaked out. Simon stepped up beside him, and all of the feelings Luke had been trying to manage reared up inside him at once. He swallowed hard.

"That's a lie," Simon said, his voice quiet. He took Luke's hand in his. "I know you better than most people, Luke. If anyone in this world knows what you look like when you're falling for someone, it's me."

"I didn't mean to," Luke rushed out with a jagged little laugh. "I don't even know how this happened and I have no idea what the fuck to do."

"Damn, I didn't know we'd be playing rounds of Luke Loses His Shit today." Simon looped his free arm around Luke's shoulders. "What's wrong?"

"I'm scared shitless." Luke dropped his head and let his shoulders slump.

"What about?"

"So many things. Mostly that I'll fuck up a good thing because that's how I roll. And…that Finn won't feel the same about me."

Simon gave him a squeeze. "Has he done or said anything to make you think he wouldn't?"

"No, but we haven't been dating very long." Luke inhaled. "He's the one who wanted to take things slow so we could get to know each other, too. I don't even know if he's dating anyone else."

"Okay, I get that." Simon tipped his head back and forth, his gaze thoughtful. "You could ask him, you know. And for what it's worth, the guy clearly likes you. I've only been around him for a couple of hours and it's obvious. I think he's good for you, too."

"Yeah?"

"You're lighter these days. Happier about life in general, and more optimistic, which is nice." Simon gave him a crooked grin. "So, what's got you spooked?"

"Nothing. Everything." Luke shrugged. "I'm not sure I'm even ready to feel this serious about someone, but I don't want to let Finn go. Shit, sometimes I feel like I could make a future with him, you know?"

"What kind of a future?" Simon appeared very grave. "Married with a house in the burbs and six kids kind of a future?"

"Ugh, no. I like my apartment too much." Luke smiled as Simon's stone face broke and he chuckled. "Honestly, I don't *know* what I mean. As long as Finn is a part of whatever comes next, that'd be enough for me."

Simon blew out a low whistle. "You've got it bad, baby."

"I know. I feel ridiculous."

"Don't. This is a good look for you."

Luke cocked an eyebrow. "What do you mean?"

Simon scoffed. "You've been walking around all summer making stupid hearty eyes at everyone. It's like someone stuck a lightbulb up your ass."

"Jesus Christ." Luke groaned. "What is wrong with you?"

"So many things," Simon replied. He squeezed Luke's shoulders again. "Will you be introducing Finn to the rest of the Ryan clan?"

"I'd like to." Luke worried his bottom lip with his teeth. "Finn told his parents about me, but I don't know if he's ready for a face-to-face with *my* family."

"He's suggested you meet each other's friends, right? Given how he's already talked to his family about you, I'd say he wants more."

"More what?"

"Of you, Luke. Of your relationship. So, show him your life while he shows you his."

"What if he runs screaming for the hills?"

"Hey, you're the marathon man, Pickle," Simon teased. "Chase him down and throw him over your shoulder. Release your inner caveman!"

Luke scowled. "We agreed you wouldn't call me that in front of other people."

"Do you see anyone else here? Besides, that's bullshit. I'll call you Pickle whenever and wherever I want, just like I always have."

Luke twisted out of his grasp with a laugh. "God, I hate you."

Simon smirked. "You love me and we both know it. I'm a hard habit to break."

A movement at the door caught Luke's eye, and he glanced back to find Finn leaning against the jamb with a smile on his face. Luke's insides immediately turned to goo. *Oh, man, am I fucked.*

"Hey, Doc," he said.

"I wondered where you'd got to." Finn aimed a sheepish glance at Simon. "Gillian wants to know if you plan to share the dessert or keep it all for yourself."

Simon tutted. "Of course she does." He picked up the cake platter and headed for the door. "Will you guys bring the cold brew and creamer when you come back out? They're both in the refrigerator. The glasses and everything else are already upstairs."

"Copy that," Luke called out. He turned to the glasses he'd abandoned on the counter. "This'll just take a second," he told Finn. "Sorry we took so long."

"Oh, no worries. Everything okay?"

"Yeah, why?"

"I don't know." Finn searched Luke's face. "You look stressed," he said at last. "And I wasn't eavesdropping, but it felt kind of heavy in here when I walked in."

"Oh." Luke went to the freezer for the ice bucket. "Simon was just listening to me whine. Sometimes, I need to throw things against the wall and see what sticks, and he's good at helping me get it all out."

"Got it." Finn paused while Luke filled the glasses with ice. "Anything I can help with?" Despite his light tone, Luke swore he saw hurt flash in Finn's eyes.

Shit.

Maybe Finn wanted to be the one Luke turned to for advice. Maybe Luke wanted that, too. He needed to figure out how to do it without tipping his hand, though. Finn liked him—Luke knew that. However, Finn had no idea Luke's feelings had changed and moved well past 'like' toward something bigger.

"I think there is something you can help with. Do you mind if we table this for another time, though?" he asked. "There are a few details I need to work out before I can take any next steps."

Finn said nothing, but he looked puzzled. He seemed to shake it off when Luke leaned in to kiss his cheek.

"Of course." Finn smiled. "I'm ready to listen whenever you're ready to talk."

* * * *

"What do you call a cow who plays violin?"

Peter pondered Ella's joke for several moments and finally shook his head. "I give up."

"A moo-sician," Ella replied, her tone so smug Luke let out a snort.

Peter's expression appeared unimpressed in the chat window despite the amusement dancing in his eyes. "Jeeze, El. Where the heck are you getting these?"

"Milk cartons at school," Luke replied.

"And friends, too," Ella added. "But Luke finds the most jokes."

Peter eyed his brother. "Get any from the guy you've been seeing? Because Ella told me you got yourself a boyfriend."

Luke stared at Ella, and she stared right back. "I've been dating, yes, but no, he doesn't give me jokes," he said for his brother's benefit. "The guy's name is Finn, which you no doubt know already, and we've been seeing each other about six weeks."

Ella rolled her eyes. "He's your boyfriend," she said, her tone far too dry for any ten-year-old, ever.

"I never said that."

Peter's expression shifted from curiosity to amusement when Luke turned back to the monitor. As always, he appeared fit and hearty, but there were lines of fatigue on his face, and Luke could see a streak of grease or dirt or God knew what on the shoulder of his green T-shirt. The buzz of other voices rose and fell in the background, and Marines passed behind Peter on occasion, though he seemed not to notice.

"Six weeks, huh? That's a pretty good chunk of time," he said. "You sure he's not your boyfriend?"

"He totally is," Ella cut in.

Luke ignored her. "No labels yet. Finn works in trauma medicine and his schedule is different from mine but almost as weird, so we're taking our time getting to know each other."

"Sounds pretty grown up," Peter said, his smile wide and genuine. "When can I meet him?"

"Soon." Luke turned to Ella. "Finn met Simon and Gillian today, and I met some of his friends on Friday. I'd like you and your dad and Gram and Pops to meet him too, El. Like next weekend, if Finn can swing it."

Ella pushed her curls over one shoulder. They'd pulled her hair into a side ponytail this week and Luke couldn't help noting how mature the style made her appear. Ella's attitude as she glanced at her father left something to be desired, however. "Told ya," she said to her dad.

"She said you wouldn't introduce us to someone *unless* he was your boyfriend," Peter said in answer to Luke's questioning look. "And that you didn't think it'd be worth it unless you planned to get serious about a guy."

Luke exhaled through his nose. Well, Ella had been listening to him at least. "That sounds like me. And, yes, I want you guys to meet him."

"Sure, whatever," Ella said, her tone flat. "He can't have dinner with us on Friday, though."

"Why not?"

"Because he's your friend, not mine. Simon's okay, and Melissa of course, but I don't want anyone else."

"All right, then." Luke worked hard not to react to the dismissal. "Gram and Pops are taking you to Tanglewood next weekend, so I'll check with Finn and see if he's free on Saturday morning."

"Sure." Stone-faced, Ella turned back to her father, who eyed her for a moment before he spoke.

"Honey, I need to talk to Luke about a couple of things."

"Okay. BBL." Ella glowered at Luke before she stood, and her obvious irritation pricked at him.

Peter watched her go and turned wide eyes to Luke. "What the hell was that?"

"BBL means 'be back later.' She and her friends use chat acronyms all the time."

"No, not *that*. I meant the mega attitude she showed you, Luke. Ella was kind of channeling Carly just then, and I won't lie, it's freaking me out."

"Oh, man." Luke ran a hand over his chin. "Well, this is probably a good time to tell you Ella's not jazzed about my dating. It's obvious she disapproves, but she hasn't come out and said it."

"Any idea why?"

"No. Gillian thinks she might feel threatened by the idea of having to share me with someone. I've been effectively single as long as she's known me and this is new for her, not to mention for you." Luke aimed a pointed glance at his brother. "You've been single since Carly left, too, and I think Ella will show some attitude when you start dating."

Peter scowled. "Well, that's something to look forward to. Has she said anything? About sharing us with other people, I mean?"

"No. Finn and I see each other mostly when she's at school because his schedule is crazy and I'm tied up most nights," Luke said. "We go out if Ella's got a thing going herself, like a sleepover, but the only reason she knows Finn and I have been out is because I tell her."

Peter ran a hand over his hair, the dark coils cut regulation high and tight. "Don't get me wrong, but is telling her the best idea?"

"Seems better than lying by omission." Luke shook his head. "I don't want to hide who I am, Pete, not when it comes to people who mean something to me."

A knowing look spread across Peter's face. "It's like that, huh? Love, Luke Ryan style?"

"Mmm, maybe. Someday." Luke dropped his eyes and cursed the heat that licked its way across his face. He wanted to crawl under the table when Peter hummed low.

"Luke." Peter waited until Luke raised his head. "You're serious about this guy, aren't you?" he asked.

"I want to be," Luke admitted. "We haven't been seeing each other very long, but I like him. A lot."

"Good for you, bro. I can't wait to meet him." A weary smile graced Peter's lips and he waved at his surroundings. "So to speak, anyway."

"Me too." Luke missed his brother so much his chest hurt. "You, uh, got any advice for how to make this thing with Ella easier?"

Peter's expression sobered. "Keep being honest with her. You're right about that. She needs to know that nothing has changed between you and her just because you've got a man. I know you love her, Luke, and Ella knows it, too. She'll understand you've got enough love to go around."

* * * *

After Ella went to bed that night, Luke logged ten miles on the treadmill in the basement and rehearsed in his head what he wanted to say to Finn. After he'd stretched and showered, he grabbed his water bottle and dialed Finn's number. Given the hour and knowing Finn was in the middle of a shift, Luke expected to get his voicemail. He blinked in surprise when Finn picked up instead.

"Hey, handsome!" Finn's smile was perfectly audible.

Luke's stomach gave a happy flip. "Hey, Doc. Got a minute?"

"I've got five, actually—my break's almost up." Voices rang out in the background.

"Busy night, huh?" Luke asked.

"Mm-hm. Must be a full moon because this place is hopping like a jackrabbit on crack."

Luke laughed. "These obscure metaphors you pull out of nowhere give me life, you know. I'll make it quick. You feel like having lunch with me tomorrow? I have a proposition for you."

"Ooh, I'm intrigued. And yes to lunch. There's a burger place near your office I've been meaning to try, and I'll meet you there on one condition."

Luke bit his lip against a grin. He'd noticed Finn's mood turned playful any time strange things were afoot in the ED. "Okay, shoot."

"Explain to me why Simon calls you Pickle."

"Oh, boy." Luke tipped his head back and cackled. "You heard that, huh?"

"I heard it and, no lie, I kind of love it."

"Finn, no. You cannot co-opt that terrible nickname!"

Finn's quiet laugh sent delight curling through Luke. "Oh, I don't want to co-opt it, but I do want an explanation."

"Ugh." Luke covered his eyes with one hand. *I am going to nail Simon's ass to the wall tomorrow.*

"C'mon, baby." Finn's bantering tone turned on a dime, going deep and rumbly and, oh man, Luke liked that. "I think you owe me one, considering you've kept that *fantastic* nugget of information from me all this time."

Luke blew a noisy breath out through his nose. He liked it when Finn played dirty. "Okay. It started with a joke about a deer and a dill pickle."

Chapter Twelve

Finn climbed the steps of the brownstone Luke called home and tried to ignore the way his insides trembled. Standing before the building's glossy black doors, he clutched the bag of bagels he'd bought on his way over and tried to find his chill. Goddamn, he was nervous. Hardly surprising given he was about to meet Luke's family.

The nerves weren't all bad, though. Finn hadn't hesitated to accept Luke's invitation to brunch with the Ryans, and he genuinely looked forward to meeting more of the people Luke loved. However, he hadn't changed his mind about taking his time getting to know Luke, and the idea of splitting Luke's time with a ten-year-old girl still boggled his mind. Finn thought he was up to the challenge, though. He just wished his heart would stop trying to beat its way out of his chest.

He rang the doorbell for Number 4 and shifted his weight from one foot to the other before the speaker crackled.

"Dr. Thomason, I presume?" Luke asked, his voice booming.

"The one and only," Finn called back and smiled when the lock buzzed open.

Once inside the foyer, his eyes went wide. He stared at the enormous, ornate spiral staircase that snaked around the building's interior toward the upper floors and, glancing up, spied Luke at the halfway point. Luke waved at Finn and trotted down another flight.

"Holy shit." Finn's voice rang through the space. "Those must be an absolute bitch with shopping bags."

"Even worse if you're drunk," Luke called back.

"Oh, man." Finn walked forward to meet Luke as he hit the landing and Luke wrapped him up in a hug. "Sorry I'm late. The line at the bagel place was nuts."

"You're fine."

I am now.

Finn reveled in the strong arms around him. His hospital shifts had made it impossible for him to see Luke all week, but every bit of tension and overwork melted away as he pressed his nose against Luke's shoulder and breathed him in.

Luke hummed low in his throat. "You smell nice. You stop at home after your shift?"

"Yes, to feed Daisy," Finn said. "She didn't even bother getting off her ass to greet me."

Luke chuckled. He pulled back and caught Finn's eye. "Aw. How are you doing otherwise?"

"I'm good. Glad to see you."

Luke gave him a soft smile. "Me too. Doesn't seem fair you got stuck working two doubles in a five-day stretch."

"Eh, it happens. I have the next two days off. That means I'll have plenty of time to catch up on lots of things."

Finn held his breath at the emotions that flashed in Luke's eyes, all fondness and longing and something intense he couldn't put a name to. Then Luke kissed him and every rational thought in his brain fled.

Finn didn't have an addictive personality. He'd smoked his share of weed and he still enjoyed alcohol in moderation, but he'd never been interested in anything harder. He was addicted to Luke Ryan's kisses, though. As potent as any drug, they soothed Finn's fatigue, melted the aches in his muscles and lit a fire in his belly. He clutched at Luke without even thinking.

Luke smiled against Finn's lips. "Mmm. Easy, Doc."

"Oops. My bad." Finn bit back a laugh.

"S'okay. If we were alone, I'm not sure we'd make it up the stairs." Luke gave him another squeeze and let go. "C'mon. Let's go up before I do something I won't regret but may be hard pressed to explain."

A soft smile on his face, Luke scanned Finn from head to toe. He straightened Finn's collar and smoothed the hair off his forehead, those touches easing the rough edges of Finn's nerves.

They caught up as they climbed the stairs, though neither mentioned the elephant in the stairwell, namely the rest of the Ryan family's plans to go out of town. Luke's parents were taking Ella to Lenox until Sunday and if Finn thought about what he and Luke could get up to in that time, he'd maul the man where he stood, family and bagels be damned.

Luke stopped outside his apartment door, a shy smile on his face. "Thanks again for doing this."

"You don't have to thank me, Luke."

"I know. I want to, though. And, hell, you may change your mind about it after you get to know them. Pops is easygoing, but Mom may give you the third degree. Ella, too, probably. Ugh." He took Finn's hands in his. "I should apologize in advance."

A sweet, mellow pleasure thrummed through Finn. "Don't worry about it. Between my mother and Paul, I've been through my fair share of interrogations. Just relax for me, okay?"

The next fifteen minutes passed in a blur for Finn, punctuated by smiles and greetings and hugs from Luke's mother. Brad and Joanna were in their late fifties, both fair-haired and fit, with a bright energy Finn recognized in Luke. Ella was a quieter presence in the hubbub of activity, and while she shook hands and almost smiled at Finn, her sharp gaze never left him.

"I'll take those, Finn." Joanna gestured for the bag of bagels in the crook of Finn's arm. "I'll stick them in the warming oven while we finish up cooking. There's coffee if you'd like some, and a pitcher of virgin Bloody Mary if you'd rather avoid caffeine."

"I make it a habit never to avoid caffeine," Finn said, and Brad clapped a hand on his shoulder.

"Good man," Brad replied. "I'll be right back with your cup."

Finn's nerves kicked up again as he turned to Ella. He rarely interacted with children outside of the ED, and those were instances already outside of ordinary, to say the least. Ella stood tall and willowy in a peasant blouse and jean shorts and, yep, was still watching him. She'd arranged her dark hair in a series of knots that formed a kind of stylized Mohawk and made her appear more grown-up than Finn had expected. However, her features still held the soft, baby roundness of a child, and he felt stodgy and ridiculous while they made small talk.

"I've heard a lot about you, Ella." He sensed a barely suppressed eye-roll, but Ella simply nodded.

"Yeah, same—Luke talks about you all the time. He was nervous you wouldn't make it."

Luke scowled. "I wasn't nervous."

"Yes, you were." Ella stared at her uncle. "You told Simon at dinner last night."

"I said Finn might be too *tired* to make it. His schedule's been tough all week, and sometimes a person needs sleep more than breakfast."

"Oh, breakfast first," Finn said. "I can't sleep on an empty stomach, no matter how tired I am. That said, I usually stick a protein bar in my face and hope for the best."

Ella wrinkled her nose. "Protein bars taste like flavored chalk."

Luke laid one big palm over her forehead. "Who's the one who keeps emptying my supply of CLIF Bars?"

Trapped in Luke's grip, Ella slid her gaze sideways to his and grinned. "CLIF Bars are different!" she protested.

"Yeah, *different* because they're mine." Luke let her go and tweaked one of her buns with his fingers. "Why don't you go see if Gram and Pops need help with breakfast while I show Finn around?"

Finn's stomach rumbled loudly enough for all of them to hear.

"Damn." Ella scanned Finn up and down, her eyebrows high while Luke chided her about her language. "Good thing Gram made extra bacon," she murmured before she turned on her heel and headed for the kitchen.

"Way to make an impression," Luke said with a smile.

Ugh.

Finn swallowed down his unease and took hold of Luke's hand. "You'd better give me the tour before I eat one of your throw pillows." His stomach rumbled again and Luke snorted with laughter.

They stopped in the kitchen for Finn's coffee and he sipped it gratefully as Luke led him through the two-bedroom unit. The place exuded comfort and had a very Luke feel, both inviting and polished with splashes of rich color among the warm wood hues. Huge windows bathed each room in light, and a long covered balcony ran the length of the back wall of the building. Finn smiled to himself. He could imagine them spending time together here, provided Luke wanted that. Finn hoped he did.

The one exception to the overall vibe was Ella's domain in the smaller of the two bedrooms. While tidy, it almost pulsated with a rainbow of color. Strings of white fairy lights crisscrossed the ceiling and posters plastered the walls, along with photos and art, and everywhere were signs of a young girl with very definite and varied interests. Finn stood in the doorway, staring at the table filled with LEGO models, the bright turquoise Converse by the closet and a black acoustic guitar on a stand in the corner. He let out a low whistle.

"This is amazing and slightly terrifying."

Luke laughed. "Life with Ella."

"Is that a Storm Trooper helmet on the bed?" Finn asked.

"Yes. That's Captain Phasma's helmet," Luke replied. "Ella's developed a love-hate thing with the character since the new *Star Wars* movies came out."

"Does she watch *Trek*, too?"

"Absolutely. Her favorites are Bones and Beverly Crusher, and she's got a secret soft spot for Mr. Spock." Luke reached past Finn to close the door and they turned back toward the living area. He slipped an arm around Finn's waist.

"I told you before that Ella likes a lot of stuff Pete and I do, but I'm not sure how it's going to work as she gets older." His expression shifted, becoming uncertain. "I guess we'll figure it out together."

Finn nodded. In concept, he understood Luke's concern—Ella's impending teenagerhood was a big deal for her whole family. However, her father was due back in the fall. Peter wouldn't continue leaving her with Luke if he didn't have to. Would he?

"When does your brother's deployment end again?" Finn asked.

"Octoberish," Luke replied. "He shipped out in May and we expect him back before November." He stared at the windows overlooking Beacon Street, his gaze losing focus as it lingered. "Depending on how things play out, of course. And how Pete wants to move forward."

Joanna called them to the table, and Luke gave Finn a smile that made his insides melty.

"C'mon, Doc. Let's get some bacon into that belly of yours."

Talk turned to Finn's job as they all tucked into the big meal. He was pleasantly surprised by the Ryans' interest in his experience at MGH, particularly Joanna's. She'd left a career in hospital administration after she and Brad were given the opportunity to adopt Peter.

"We talked about my trying to balance work and motherhood, and Brad did more than his fair share once Pete came into our lives," she told Finn. "But in the end, I decided I'd stay home for a while. Of course, a while almost turned into forever. The boys were in high school before I re-entered the workforce."

Joanna speared a piece of fruit salad with her fork. "Staying home was the right decision for us, though. Pete was almost two when we brought him home and he had some minor intestinal issues that needed attending to. I didn't feel right leaving him in someone else's care all day, especially since that's how he'd been living for over a year anyway."

"His parents were killed in a car accident not long after his birth, and his maternal aunt took him in," Brad said. He passed Finn a platter of scrambled eggs. "She became ill and had no other family and worried Pete would end up on the street if something happened to her. She surrendered him to the orphanage before his first birthday. Eighteen months after *that*, we got the call about Luke and started down the road to being a family of four."

Finn had little trouble imagining the Ryans as a young couple who welcomed little boys without families into their home. "So Pete and Luke learned to speak English with you?" he asked.

Joanna laughed. "Technically, yes, but we didn't teach either of them much when it came to language. Pete soaked it up like a sponge and Luke was born in North Dakota—he came to us already burbling English words. We had a babysitter who spoke Spanish, but she was more help to Brad and me than the kids. Pete had a knack for languages anyway. He learned French in high school and picked up Italian and Portuguese in college."

"Joanna and I remain terrible at every language but English," Brad said. "Neither of the boys ever had trouble letting us know what they wanted, though, and neither did Ella."

Finn looked over the table at her. "How many languages do you speak?"

"Three," Ella replied. "Dad uses English, Spanish and French around the house."

"He did that at our house too," Brad told her. "Your Gram and I figured we were ready for another Spanish-speaking baby because your dad had it under control, even though he was a baby himself." They all laughed. "Then we got the call about Luke and realized we could all talk to him right away. Naturally, Pete started teaching Luke Spanish on day one."

Finn turned to Luke, who was busy spreading cream cheese on a bagel. Luke rarely spoke about his adoption, and Finn paused before he asked, "You speak Spanish?"

"Some," Luke replied. "I'm not a language nerd like Pete, though, and I need more room in my brain for computer languages than anything else."

Joanna tsked at him. "That's not true, sweetheart, and you know it. He spoke near-fluent Spanish by the time he entered school, thanks to Pete, and continued with it through college," she told Finn. "I'm certain he's still pretty fluent, though he'd deny it."

"He uses Spanish with me when he feels like it," Ella said and laughed at Luke's scowl. "Dude, you're busted."

"Don't call me dude." Luke wrinkled his nose at her then turned his focus on Finn. "How much room do *you* have in that big brain for languages, Doc?"

"Oh, not much," Finn said. "I learned some Latin as part of my medical training, and I passed enough Spanish classes to meet my undergrad core requirements. I speak a little Spanish with my patients when I need to, but I'm far from fluent."

Luke smiled at him. "Well, you know how to put people back together again, so you get a pass. Don't worry, your secret's safe with us." He turned to Ella with a gleam in his eye. "Oh, man, this doctor talk reminds me that I have a joke. How do you take a pig to the hospital?"

Ella narrowed her eyes at him for a moment before her face lit up with a grin. "A ham-bulance!"

Finn sipped his coffee while the others laughed, struck by what he'd seen. No one had batted an eyelash when Luke changed the subject away from adoption, not even Ella, and she clearly enjoyed needling him about almost everything. *What is that about?*

"Finn?"

He jumped slightly and snapped back to the conversation. "Sorry, I lost the thread there for a second."

Joanna smiled. "No worries. I asked about your family back in Chicago and whether you planned to go home for the holidays this winter."

"I don't have any firm plans at the moment," he said. "I'm the new doc, which means my hands are tied when it comes to scheduling."

"Living halfway across the country from your family can't make things easy either," Brad said.

"In the sense I can't pop by to see them on my day off, that's true, yes. But my schedule's been unpredictable for a long time, and they're used to it."

"Do you think about moving back?" Joanna asked. "Your whole career is ahead of you, after all, and I'd imagine the hospitals in Chicago would be glad to have you."

Finn exchanged a grin with Luke. They'd had a very similar conversation only minutes after he'd asked Luke out for the first time. "I'm still getting to know Boston and I'm happy here," he said. "Of course, it's shortsighted to say I'd never move back to Chicago, or anywhere, really."

"Never say never, Doc," Luke teased. His eyes gleamed with mischief as he stole a piece of Finn's bacon.

Finn batted at him playfully and the conversation shifted again, so it took him a few minutes to notice a change in Ella's demeanor. The vivacious girl he'd glimpsed had stopped talking and a hardness lurked in her eyes when she glanced Finn's way.

Uh-oh.

Finn gently chewed the inside of his cheek. As the conversation around the table rose and fell, he attempted to engage her several times but she met each attempt with monosyllables. She seemed fine with her grandparents and Luke, though, and Finn could tell from Luke's expression that he'd noticed the shift, too.

After everyone rose to clear the table, Finn found himself alone with Ella in the kitchen, and he tried once again. "Luke told me you're going for your yellow belt in taekwondo class next week. He's pretty excited to watch your test."

"Uh-huh." Ella placed a platter on the counter beside the sink. "Simon's invited too."

And you're not.

Finn heard her unspoken words loud and clear. Simon being invited came as no surprise—he was one of Luke's oldest friends and an assistant uncle of sorts to Ella. Finn hadn't forgotten the snippet of conversation he'd overheard the weekend before at Simon's party, however.

'I hate you so much,' Luke had said with a laugh.

'You love me and we both know it,' Simon had shot back. *'I'm a hard habit to break.'*

A bubble of resentment rose inside Finn. How could he establish a rapport anywhere close to the one Simon had built with Ella if she dismissed Finn after only a couple of hours? More importantly, why did he even care? Ella wasn't Luke's daughter, and soon her dad would be back and everything would change. Finn didn't need to become best friends with this kid—if she didn't want it either, what was the point?

Finn lowered the plates into the sink. "Well, good luck. I'm sure you'll be great."

He forced himself to smile while Ella simply watched him, her brow furrowed. She lingered for a beat, then left the kitchen without a word. Finn shifted his focus to the dishes and quelled a sigh.

Ugh.

Chapter Thirteen

With the brunch dishes cleared and Ella gone to her room to gather her things, Luke realized Finn had remained behind in the kitchen. Intent on stealing a kiss or two, Luke sought him out and was struck by the sight of Finn at his sink rinsing plates and placing them in the open dishwasher.

I like him here.

Luke's heart beat faster at the thought of Finn feeling at home in this space. Unfortunately, Finn's tense posture didn't speak to comfort just then. Luke thought that if Finn turned around right now, his pretty eyes would be troubled. Luke suspected a certain ten-year-old girl was the cause, too.

He exhaled quietly. He'd deal with Ella after he made things right with his man. Stepping forward, he pressed his palm between Finn's shoulder blades.

"Hey, Doc," he murmured.

Finn relaxed under Luke's touch. "Hey. Where are the others?"

"Mom's helping El get her stuff together and Pops is nerding out over the GPS app on his phone. What are you doing out here all by yourself?"

"Just making myself useful," Finn replied. The words carried a weight Luke didn't like. As far as he was concerned, Finn didn't need to be anything but himself, no matter where they were.

He dropped his hand to the small of Finn's back. "You don't have to do this, you know."

"I don't mind."

Luke knew Finn meant it. Washing dirty dishes was easier than dealing with Ella's moods. Cleaning didn't top Luke's list of *Fun Things To Do With Finn Thomason*, however.

When Finn's hands were empty, Luke gently took hold of his wrists and guided them under the running water to rinse away the soapsuds. He let Finn go and turned off the faucet, then grabbed a towel from the hook by his hip. Finn stayed quiet while Luke dried their hands, and Luke's heart ached a little at the unhappiness on his face.

Luke put the dishtowel aside. "I'm glad you're here."

Finn gave him a small, crooked smile. "Me too." The smile grew wider as Luke slipped his arms around Finn's waist.

"I like seeing you here," Luke said, "and I hope you'll come to like it, too."

"I *do* like being here." Finn's expression grew almost painfully earnest. Clearly, he had something to say, and while Luke worried those things could hurt, he reminded himself to listen.

"I want to be here, Luke, but I hate the idea of making trouble for you."

"You're not making trouble for me, Finn, I promise. I'll handle Ella."

Finn grimaced. "No, I didn't mean anything by that—"

"I know," Luke cut him off gently, "but I need to anyway. This thing with her has been brewing for a while."

"Really? But she just met me today."

"She's been hot and cold about my dating pretty much since the beginning. And by hot and cold, I mean subzero most of the time."

"Damn." Finn's face fell slightly and he leaned back against the sink. "Why didn't you tell me?"

"Because there was nothing you could do about it. Besides, I'm allowed to have a personal life, regardless of what Ella thinks." Luke shrugged. "And she hadn't met you and I didn't want to be an alarmist."

Finn shot him a dubious look. "Good call?"

Luke chuckled. "She'll learn to deal with it. She's going to have to, Finn. Her dad's not planning to stay single forever either, and there's no reason he should." Luke paused when Ella hollered his name. "Lord, what now?" he muttered before he hollered back. "Be right there!"

He focused on Finn again. "I know we're not done here. But right now, I want to get Ella and my parents on the road and out of our hair. You have no idea how much I've been looking forward to this, and not only because I plan to hide your clothes to keep you from leaving."

Finn's stony expression cracked. "You're such a weirdo. Go on," he said and turned Luke loose. "Call if you need backup."

Luke's smile faded as he made his way out of the kitchen. Ella had been in an unearthly mood for days, by turns snappish and snotty, and far more emotional than he was accustomed to. Luke recognized part of it was rooted in her reluctance to meet Finn, but he still didn't have a clue *why* Ella felt that way and he fucking hated it.

Then again, he didn't much like the sight that greeted him in Ella's room, either. She sat on the floor, her face set in a pout and the contents of her overnight bag spread around her. Luke could tell she was seconds from losing her cool and quickly glanced at his mother in hopes she'd clue him in.

"Ella wants to pack something different for the concert tonight," Joanna said, her tone serene and the tiniest bit amused. "Not that the outfit you picked out together is in any way lacking, of course."

"Right." Luke rubbed his hands together. "I've got this, Mom. Why don't you go make sure Pops isn't trying to arm wrestle with Finn?"

Joanna chuckled. "It wouldn't be the first time he tried that trick with a friend of yours. I swear that man flirts more than any woman does. Ella, it's almost eleven-thirty," she added. "Your Pops wants to get on the road soon, so please don't give your uncle too hard a time."

The tips of Ella's ears went red, but her voice sounded meek when she replied. "Yes, Gram."

Luke waited for his mother to leave the room before he squatted down in front of Ella. "Decided against the dress, huh?"

"I don't like *any* of my clothes," Ella muttered. She glowered at the garments spread on the floor, all of which she'd liked perfectly well the night before.

Luke restrained himself from pointing out that very thing. Then Ella glanced at her closet and he knew he had to act fast. Otherwise, she'd be tearing everything apart in a fruitless search for something she deemed worthy.

"What about those purple jeans you made me buy?"

Ella's gaze snapped back to Luke's. "You said the jeans were for back to school."

"They are, but you and Gram and Pops will be sitting on a lawn listening to classical music. You think you could manage not to kill them if you put your mind to it?"

Ella sat up straighter. "Yes, dude. I mean Uncle. Yes, Uncle."

"Oh, so *now* I'm Uncle." Luke wrinkled his nose. "Go on and get them out of the closet while I pack up the rest of your crap."

"Hah, you said crap."

"Yeah, but I didn't say shi — oops."

Luke smiled as Ella's fit of brattiness dissolved into giggles, then eased himself onto his knees so he could re-pack the bag. He sat down when she returned with the coveted purple jeans.

"What's going on with you today, El? It's not like you to be rude to a friend."

Ella's nostrils flared and she pushed her lips out, both typically signs of bad temper. The irritation in Luke's chest faded as she sat, however, because Ella twisted her hands in her lap and he understood that she was stressed out rather than angry.

What the fuck?

"Finn's your friend, not mine, remember?" Ella asked, and damn, but she looked forlorn.

Luke's mood sank some more. *How in the world had things gone so wrong over eggs, bacon and bagels?* Carefully, he scooted over the floor and around Ella's overnight bag so he could sit beside her. He made sure his knee met hers.

"You're right," he said. "Finn is my friend. I'd like it if you made friends with him, too. Or at least got to know him."

Ella sighed. "Why?" Her dejected tone hurt to hear.

"I know it's selfish, but I want to share my time with both of you," Luke said. "I'm not saying the three of us will hang out together every day, and no, I won't invite Finn to Friday night dinner if you don't want him there, but I'd like to spend some time with both of you, *together*."

He wanted to wince at the unhappiness in Ella's face. "I won't lie to you, El—I'm going to keep seeing Finn for as long as he's interested. That means you'll see him from time to time, too. I don't want the only times I see him to be when you're not around."

"Seems like that's been working fine," Ella muttered and Luke fought the urge to roll his eyes.

"Up to now, sure, but I can't section off different parts of my life on a full-time basis. I don't want to, and Finn deserves better than to be my backup plan." Luke ran a hand over his head. "We can figure this out, but I need your help to do that, okay?"

Ella studied him, her face solemn and her lips pressed tight. She stayed quiet long enough that Luke started to wonder what the fuck he'd do if she flat-out refused to even consider his request. Then she nodded, the movement small, and relief flared in Luke's chest so sharp it ached.

Dating and unclehood? Still happening.

* * * *

An hour later, near-silence reigned over Luke's apartment and he felt wonderfully, thoroughly relaxed. He'd seen his family off on their road trip—after Ella had made a point of saying a polite goodbye to Finn—then he'd gone to the fridge for two beers.

"Come watch the pregame," Luke said. He beckoned to Finn and patted the space beside him on the couch. "I'm not asking you to love the Red Sox, but you have to tolerate watching the occasional game with me." He froze then, startled by his own words. "I can't believe I said that."

Finn laughed. He took the beers from Luke's hands and put them on the coffee table in front of them, then slid his arms around Luke's neck. "Neither can I. Guess you like me, huh?"

"Of course I do, you silly man," Luke replied. He smothered Finn's laughter with a kiss.

Luke truly did love baseball *and* the Red Sox, and he'd been relieved to learn Finn was a diehard Chicago Cubs fan. However, the baseball and beer were just a pretense for snuggling on the couch. And to get Finn to rest. Because no matter how much Finn denied being tired, Luke knew he was.

Sure enough, Finn fell asleep as they watched the pregame with the sound off, his bare feet up on the table and Luke's arm around his shoulders. Luke studied his face in snatches and fought the urge to run his fingers over Finn's dark brows and golden skin and the sharp angles of his cheekbones and nose. Luke sat silent instead, satisfaction thrumming through him as Finn snoozed warm and lax against him until Luke's arm went numb.

Midway into the eighth inning, Finn stirred and slowly surfaced.

"Mmm. I didn't mean to fall asleep," he said, his voice hoarse. "You should have woken me."

Luke nuzzled his lips against Finn's temple. "You looked tired. And I don't mind hanging out for once. It's rare I get the chance to just be."

"Okay. But I only have you to myself for a short while," Finn murmured. "I want to spend as much awake time with you as possible while I can." Uncrossing his arms, he slid his left hand along Luke's belly.

Luke's skin prickled at the touch, and he shifted so he faced Finn. But Finn stopped moving and stared at Luke. The silence between them stretched, and Luke knew from the way Finn searched his face that he had something to say.

Luke rubbed a hand over Finn's chest. "What is it?"

Finn inhaled deeply. "Can I ask you a question?"

"Of course."

"Does it bother you to talk about your adoption?"

Wow.

Not in a hundred years would Luke have guessed Finn wanted to know anything about the big, blank spot in Luke's life that he privately called 'the time before'.

Luke blew out a gust of air. "Um. No, it doesn't bother me. Why do you ask?"

Finn shrugged. "Meeting your parents today and hearing them talk about how you and Pete came into their lives made me think, that's all. You and I talk about a lot of things but never about that part of your life. I thought maybe it was too painful or that you were…"

"Embarrassed about it?" Luke guessed. "I'm not. I don't have much to tell, though. I don't remember a whole lot about my time in foster care or before that."

Finn's forehead creased. "Really?"

"Yes. My story is a little like Pete's. My birth mother surrendered me to the state before my second birthday. The records were sealed, though, and I don't know what happened to her or my birth father. I was too young to remember them."

Luke thought for a few beats before he spoke again. "The state placed me in a group home in Rugby. My parents told me about the home when I was older, and I looked it up. It was small, with only five other kids. I was there for a little while because it can take time to find someone interested in an older child." He sighed as Finn's hand went still on his belly.

"You were two years old, Luke."

"Most people prefer infants, and I was already a toddler," Luke said gently. "All in all, I was in foster care about a year. I don't remember anything solid about it. Just…impressions. Probably sounds weird, huh?" Luke bit his lip and thought. "A blue room and other kids. One of the kids had freckles. A tall person who smiled. Someone combing my hair. A smell like…like laundry soap and cinnamon. It was nice. I had something soft to touch. Maybe a quilt or a pillow."

He shook his head, aware all the while of Finn watching him with those big gray eyes. "The way Pops tells it, we kids were all healthy and seemed happy and loved. After he and Mom decided they wanted me, things kicked into gear and, eventually, they brought me to Boston. They changed my name from Louis to Luke and that's who I've been ever since."

A soft expression fell over Finn's face. "You never looked back, huh?"

"None of us did. I mean, I was three years old, you know? I had Mom and Pops and Pete—things were good for me. Really good. I can't imagine having a better family than the one I got or being more loved."

"That sounds like the Luke I know." Finn's chuckle made Luke smile.

"Pops says he and Mom gave me a stuffed giraffe as a gift when I met them, but I just wanted them to pick me up. I'd get mad when they tried to put me down." Heat splashed across his face at Finn's jagged laugh.

"Obviously, they didn't want to let you go either." He leaned up and pressed a kiss against Luke's shoulder. "I'm glad you met them. And I get why you stepped up for Pete and Ella."

"I never considered doing otherwise."

"Of course not. You never would."

Luke ducked his head. He didn't focus much on that big blank past, but he didn't resent it either. It just was. Luke had a great life and he'd known from a very early age how loved he was. He'd been extraordinarily lucky, not just in meeting the Ryans but to have landed in the group home in Rugby, too.

His breath caught at Finn's kiss, and what started out sweet turned deep and dirty. Luke melted against the couch cushions as Finn settled between his legs. Finn grabbed at Luke, fingers pressing into his muscles through his clothes and pulling hungry noises out of him.

"Fuck." Luke's skin blazed.

Finn ground against him and the motion lit up the nerves in Luke's body. Luke worked at Finn's buttons and cursed the pins and needles that flooded the arm that had been trapped under him, but they laughed together when Finn finally yanked at the shirt.

"Careful," Luke chided. He tried to calm Finn's jerky movements, but Finn responded by shoving Luke's T-shirt up and dragging it over his head.

Their ragged breaths echoed in the quiet as they stripped each down. Luke kicked off his shorts and Finn palmed his cock, and the lust that crashed through Luke made him shake.

"Holy shit." He gasped as Finn ran his thumb over the head. "Jesus, Finn, love your hands on me."

"Fuck, yes."

Finn took Luke's mouth in a ferocious kiss. The skin on his face and neck were flushed with color when he drew back again, his pupils blown wide. He watched Luke in a manner both predatory and pleading, as if he couldn't decide between mauling Luke and begging to be touched. He caged Luke's head with his arms, his lean muscles flexing, and his eyelids fluttered as Luke ran his hands over Finn's ass.

"Damn, I missed this." Finn dipped his head to suck at Luke's collarbone. "Missed kissing you, touching you. Love the way you sound when we're like this."

Luke pressed his mouth to Finn's ear. "I missed you, too, baby," he murmured, and jammed his lips together as another set of words crowded onto his tongue.

I love you.

Luke went still. The terrifying ache that took hold of him made his eyes sting and his heart hurt, and it was all he could do not to bolt off the couch.

"Hey," Finn whispered, his touch gentle on Luke's cheek. "You okay?"

Luke drew in a shaky breath. Rarely had he felt so exposed. "Yeah." He forced himself to smile. "Everything's perfect."

He sat up, his mind churning with the need not to think. He desperately wanted to get closer to Finn, but everything in him felt scraped raw, so much so, he couldn't bear to look Finn in the face.

Luke pushed Finn backward until he lay flat, then turned himself to face Finn's feet. He straddled Finn's waist and crouched over him, Finn's dazed approval in his ears. *This I can do*, Luke told himself and grasped Finn's hips with his hands.

Together, they shifted onto their sides. Desire crawled through Luke like a living thing. He eyed the tight abdomen and erection mere inches from his face, his mouth watering to taste Finn again. He pressed his face into the juncture between Finn's hip and groin and kissed the hot skin, tasting a heady mix of soap and musk and man. He bucked helplessly when Finn took Luke in hand and licked him.

Pleasure buzzed through Luke's body. He and Finn feasted on each other, creating a feedback loop of sensation. Finn used his hands to urge Luke to move and Luke thrust down into Finn's mouth, his ears ringing with Finn's guttural moan. Blindly, he brought a hand to his mouth and slid two fingers between his lips alongside Finn's shaft.

Finn pulled off Luke with a gasp. "Oh, you...*fuck!*"

Luke pumped his fingers and goosebumps rose on his skin as Finn swallowed him back down. Once his fingers were good and wet, he slid them along the cleft of Finn's ass. Tension jolted through Finn's body. Luke circled the tight ring of muscle and Finn thrust harder and faster into Luke's mouth, his movements desperate and his needy noises coming nonstop. Luke's groin tightened.

He teased Finn until he trembled, then breached him, sinking one finger deep. He curled it just so and Finn came almost instantly, his shout muffled by the cock in his mouth. Luke's orgasm tore through him with a white roar. He floated in that perfect moment, his body on automatic pilot and his limbs locked tight around Finn as they drank each other down.

Finn whimpered as the continued stimulation on his sensitized skin grew too much to bear. Luke pulled off and shuddered as his own dick fell from Finn's lips. He shifted to unwind his legs from around Finn's torso but couldn't bear to let him go. He pressed his face against Finn's taut belly and hid the emotions that reared up as his body trembled with aftershocks and more.

All the while, the three words Luke longed to say pulsed in his brain in between the beats of his heart.

I love you.

Chapter Fourteen

Finn stepped off the train at Kenmore Station in the midst of a thick crowd, his phone buzzing in his pocket. Baseball fans surrounded him, flocking toward Fenway Park to watch the Red Sox play Tampa Bay, and he waited until he was aboveground before he stepped out of the press of people and checked his messages.

Meet you outside the brewery restaurant place on Brookline Ave, Paul had written at six-thirty.

Why not inside? Mick had asked a minute later.

Because the music there is shit, Paul had replied. He'd included a poop emoji in his message and Finn snorted in disbelief at the exchange of messages that followed, every one featuring increasingly larger numbers of smiling cartoon poops.

Finn moved past Paul and Mick's poopy thread to the most recent message, which was from Luke. The words soured Finn's mood.

I'm really sorry.

It's okay, Finn typed before he pursed his lips and backspaced over the words. He wasn't okay with Luke canceling on him. Just like he wasn't okay with Luke canceling their last several dates.

I know. I'm sorry, too, Finn wrote.

He stuffed his phone back into his pocket and forced himself to ignore it when it buzzed again almost at once.

Dammit.

From their first coffee date, Finn had known meshing his schedule with Luke's would be complicated. They'd taken care to connect several times a week, meeting between work hours and when Ella was busy with friends or activities or her grandparents. All their careful planning had gone right out of the window after Ella returned to school.

Now, the sleepovers and evening play dates were gone. That time was instead devoted to homework and class projects, and the weekends disappeared in a whirlwind of soccer games and taekwondo. And as Finn didn't have a place in that part of Luke's life, he saw Luke less and less.

But that's what you wanted – to keep Luke's family stuff separate from your time together, Finn told himself.

He bit back a frustrated sigh as he walked up Brookline Avenue. Much as Finn hated to admit it, sectioning himself off from parts of Luke's life had become a problem, even with Luke trying to bridge the gaps. He showed up at Finn's door for lunch, when time would allow, where he first fed Finn then wrestled him into bed. He'd scored tickets from a client to tonight's Red Sox game to celebrate Finn's first six months in Boston, too. Finn had looked forward all week to visiting the historic ballpark in Luke's company, but now they were across town from each other while Luke did something that had nothing to do with Finn. As was typical.

A piercing whistle cut through Finn's moody musings. He glanced up and caught sight of Paul and Mick on the opposite side of the street, standing outside the restaurant Paul had mentioned somewhere among the poop messages. Quickly, Finn stepped out of the stream of Fenway Faithful and waited while his friends crossed the road.

Paul and Mick were wearing Sox caps and custom jerseys, and Finn cracked a smile at the oversized red foam finger on Paul's hand, emblazoned with the team's logo.

"You let him out in public with that thing?" he asked Mick when they drew near.

Mick huffed out a laugh. "You try prying it away, son."

Paul jerked the foam finger out of reach of Finn's outstretched hand. "No touchy." He checked Finn over and smiled. "I like a man who'll wear a Cubs hat into enemy territory."

Paul used the finger to poke at the bill of his weathered, much loved Cubs cap until Finn batted it away. "Did you guys eat already?" he asked. "Or would you rather grab food inside?"

"Grab food inside, duh. I'm in the mood for overpriced hotdogs and beer! Who's with me?!" Paul shouted and waved the finger over his head as cries of agreement echoed all around them.

They were still laughing when they stopped outside of Gate A, but Finn's good humor faded as Paul glanced around.

"Hey, where's Luke meeting us?"

"He's not coming," Finn replied. "He canceled this morning."

"What? Why?" Paul asked. "He's the reason we have tickets at all!"

"I know." Finn knew he sounded sulky. "He had a thing to do with Ella, and their babysitter couldn't cover. For what it's worth, he seems pretty bummed out about the whole thing."

"I'm sure he is," Mick said. "Luke wanted to see this game with you, Finn."

Finn's stomach tumbled. Luke had said the same thing and while Finn believed him, he'd been short when they'd spoken, in part because he'd been juggling patients but also because he'd been really fucking disappointed. Now Finn was at the ballpark feeling shitty, Luke across town and probably feeling just as bad, and they wouldn't have a free night without Ella again for God knew how long.

So make a free night with *Ella.*

Finn wanted to roll his eyes at himself. A free night with Ella wasn't built for romance. There'd be a lack of adult foods and Ella would probably eyeball Finn while she and Luke slogged through her homework. Finn would fall asleep like he did any time he'd been on duty and sat on Luke's couch for too long. Any fooling around he and Luke got up to would happen in secret and oh, so very quietly. And Finn would be out the door before eleven because he was working nights all week.

Still, he and Luke could be together for a while, and wasn't that the point?

They'd managed just fine over the summer and Finn hadn't cared what they'd done—dinner out or a night in—he had fun if Luke was with him. Finn had spent regular time around Ella, too, because they'd kept up the habit of meeting for Saturday brunch at Luke's. Those afternoons weren't Finn's idea of dates, either, but he'd enjoyed himself. He got to know Peter through the little video chat windows that kept the family connected. Finn and Luke took Ella to meet friends at the park in fair weather or watched movies if it rained, and Finn nearly always caught a catnap as he lazed by Luke's side.

Ella still acted wary of Finn, but he'd made peace with that. He'd stopped expecting more—like an invite to the weekly Friday dinners at Two Men and a Grille, for example—and concentrated on just getting along. Gradually, Ella had grown accepting of Finn's presence, and every once in a while, it was almost as if she forgot she'd decided she didn't like him. Finn would do or say something that brought a small smile to her face and he'd feel a bubble of satisfaction before she blinked and went back to looking bored. But if she tolerated Finn because Luke asked her to, Finn figured it was fine because Luke's interest in him hadn't wavered.

"I'm sorry, Finn." Paul squeezed his shoulder and Finn shook his head to clear it.

"Yeah, me too," he said. "I need to do something nice for Luke to say thanks."

"I'm sure he's not expecting you to, but that's a good idea," Paul said. "What did you do with the extra ticket?"

"Well, I asked around at work, then started calling friends." Finn shrugged. "Chad was the first person I spoke to who didn't already have plans."

He watched, mystified, as Paul tipped back his head and laughed. "What?"

"Chad hates sports," Paul replied. "Including baseball. The only reason he'd sit through a game is to spend time with you, darlin'."

Finn shrugged. "That's nice, but he knows I'm seeing someone. I told Chad all about Luke the last time I saw him."

"Like that'd make a difference," Mick muttered, and the scorn in his voice made Finn smile. Mick and Luke had become friends, and Finn knew they messaged regularly.

Finn elbowed Mick. "If it makes you feel better, you and Paul can take the two middle seats, and Chad and I will sit on either side."

"Again, like that'd make a difference," Mick repeated, though this time he laughed. "I hope you know what you're getting yourself into, boyo."

Finn's reply died on his tongue as an arm curled around his waist and the smell of Chad's expensive cologne filled his nose.

"Greetings, handsome friends!"

Chad grinned brightly at them. His tight-fitting golf shirt and popped collar made him look overdressed, and he wore a Red Sox cap too pristine to be anything but new. Still, the unguarded good humor in his face lightened Finn's mood. Chad had eased off trying to get

Finn in the sack and become much less of a pain in the ass to be around.

"Hey, Chad. Glad you could make it," Finn said.

"I try to get to at least one game a year." Chad aimed a haughty glare at Paul, who snorted.

"Relax, buttercup. Finn knows you're lying through your teeth."

Chad narrowed his eyes. "Only because you'd have told him so, but that's fine. Unlike you, I don't live and die with the Red Sox. I *do* enjoy coming out to the odd game, however. They make for excellent people watching, especially after the game's done and everyone is beerified and raring to go out."

Mick's lips twitched into a smile. "Can't argue with that. Speaking of the game, it's time to find our seats."

Two hours later and with a belly full of processed meats and beer, Finn found he appreciated the Fenway vibe. Their seats were fantastic, located almost directly behind home plate, and the fans were energized by the home team's strong performance against the Rays. The September weather stayed warm after sunset, which lent to the crowd's party-like mood and made for a gorgeous night to be at a ball game.

Even so, Finn fingered his phone in his pocket and fought a mixture of irritation and disappointment at Luke's absence. Over the summer, his connection with Luke had changed and blossomed into more than great sex and easy banter. Finn liked that change, even though it made his heart ache in lovely, scary ways.

He liked watching Luke with their friends and with Ella, his hands in the air and his eyebrows moving wildly as he told a story. The way Luke focused totally on his work and his fingers flew over his keyboard while his eyes narrowed with concentration. That Luke always sensed when Finn's shift had been tough, and that he'd pull Finn down onto the couch and rub his shoulders, pushing heat into Finn's sore muscles with his big hands. Luke was the first person Finn thought to share news with or turn to if he needed an encouraging word. And Finn really, really liked waking up beside Luke, their arms and legs entwined, Luke's quiet breaths gusting across Finn's skin as he slumbered.

Finn quelled a sigh. He stood to let Chad and Mick pass by, and pulled his phone out to read Luke's last three messages.

I'll miss you, too.

I'll make it up to you guys, I promise.

Tell your boys I'll buy first round the next time we all go out.

"Whenever the hell that is," Finn muttered to himself. He immediately felt like a jerk. Luke couldn't help being needed elsewhere. Finn's grumbling didn't make the Luke-shaped absence beside him any less noticeable, either.

Thank you again for the tickets, he wrote back. *We owe *you* the next several rounds for these amazing seats.*

No worries – glad you finally got over there. Tell Paul that foam finger has seen better days.

Finn stared at the phone for several seconds before a grin spread across his face.

You can see us?

Turned the game on 10 mins ago and, yep, there you are in the middle of my screen. Hi, Finn.

A waving hand emoji popped into the next message bubble and Finn chuckled. He stole a glance in the direction of home plate, his cheeks warm at the idea of Luke watching him. A sudden thought had him tapping at his phone again.

You just got home?

Unfortunately, yes. Long, boring story – I'd much rather ogle you instead.

Finn aimed another quick glance at home plate. *How long have you been doing that?*

For the 10 mins the TV has been on, der.

I see...so what are you wearing? Finn laughed outright at the pink bikini emoji Luke sent next.

"What's got you so smiley all of a sudden?" Paul called from two seats over. "As if I couldn't guess."

Finn grabbed his beer and scooted over to sit beside Paul. "Luke's watching from home and says he can see us," he explained. He laughed when Paul blew a kiss in the direction of home plate. "He also says you should shove that stupid foam finger up your ass."

Paul immediately poked Finn in the nose with it. "Bullshit. Luke would *never* advocate for the desecration of Red Sox paraphernalia."

"What's this about Luke?" Mick asked as he and Chad made their way along the row toward them, both carrying cups of beer in each hand.

"He's watching from home and can see us on TV," Finn replied. They all burst out laughing when Mick stopped and turned to shake his ass in the direction of home plate and, by extension, Luke.

Finn stood to swap places with Mick, but Chad sat down in the seat that had been Finn's.

"Hey, that's my spot," Finn joked, but Chad merely shrugged.

"Not anymore."

Mick grunted and slid past Finn. He handed Paul a beer and stepped over his legs to get to Chad's vacated seat, which left Finn in the remaining spot between Chad and Paul.

"Luke's the guy you told me about, right?" Chad handed Finn a beer. "The architect?"

"Software programmer and designer."

"Ooh, la la. He gave you these tickets, right? So why the hell am I here instead of him?"

"He couldn't get a babysitter." Finn winced at the obvious horror on Chad's face.

"Honey, why on earth are you dating a breeder?"

"Luke is the kid's uncle, not her father," Finn replied. "He helps out when Pete's not around to take care of Ella."

Chad blinked. "Who the hell are Pete and Ella?"

"Hah, sorry. Pete is Luke's brother. He's in the Marine Corps and a single dad to Ella, who is the kid, obviously."

"The kid Luke is home with right now instead of here watching the game?"

Finn nodded. "Correct."

"His loss," Chad replied. "You're okay with spending time with her, too?"

"Sure, it's fine. I usually see Ella once a week, and she's old enough to entertain herself," Finn said. "Gives me more time with Luke, if you know what I mean."

"Ah, yes, I see — *together* being in bed, of course. That's fun that you have a code word for sex."

"That's not at all what I meant," Finn replied with a laugh.

"Oh, whatever. I get it — you have a man in your life and that's why you're never around. Too busy playing boyfriends to hang out with me, hmm?"

"Um. We don't really throw labels around." Finn wanted to curse the heat that crawled up his neck. "And what do you mean, I'm never around?"

"I haven't seen you in weeks, Finn," Chad said. "Ever since you introduced the Marrieds over there to your boy, none of you have time for a single guy like me."

"My schedule is unpredictable, Chad, you know that. Just like Paul's." Finn frowned at him. "We don't have nine-to-five gigs with every weekend off, and if you don't see us, it's probably because we're holed up in the hospital or sleeping."

Chad flapped a hand at him. "You and I both know there's more to it than that. We saw each other at least twice a month when you first moved here."

"That's because Mick and I used to force Finn to come out with us," Paul said, and Finn and Chad turned to look at him. "He'd have never left the house otherwise."

Chad cocked his head. "You don't do that now?"

"Well, he's not at our place anymore, so it's not like we'd know what he gets up to. Plus, he's got Luke to get him out of the house." Paul focused on Finn. "Now that I'm thinking about it, though, Mick and I haven't seen much of you and Luke lately either. What's that about?"

"Luke's busy with Ella back in school." Finn licked his lips. "We're trying to find time to hang out like adults, but we've been coming up empty."

"And why is that?" Mick asked.

"Lots of stuff going on with her projects and sports and that kind of thing."

Paul nodded. "So, what, you guys are doing kid stuff with Ella?"

"No." Finn sniffed. "Luke's free time has kind of evaporated since the end of the summer. I go over to his place on Saturday and we hang out. Otherwise, we see each other around my shifts during the week."

"So you're basically waiting around for Luke to have time for you?" Chad appeared confused. "That's weird, isn't it?"

"That's not—no, that's not what's going on." Finn wanted to squirm in his seat. Chad's words held a grain of truth, but they also seemed very wrong. "Luke and I make time to see each other during the day because of *my* schedule, too. Luke works business hours, but depending on my shifts, I'm asleep while he's at work and vice-versa. We try to go out when our schedules line up, but sometimes that's in the middle of the day."

"We saw you guys a lot over the summer," Mick said.

"Right, and that's because school was out," Finn said. "Ella had her own things going with friends and her grandparents, so Luke had more free time to himself. But everything changed when Ella went back, I guess? I have no idea." Finn shrugged at his friends' laughter. "Anyway, her schedule changed, which means Luke's did, too. I figure we'll work out something new eventually."

"And you're okay with that?" Chad made a face. "Living around other people's lives sounds exhausting and kind of shitty, to be honest. I mean, the guy bought you baseball tickets but couldn't make it because something more important came up."

The crack of bat hitting ball split the air around them, and Finn and his friends jumped to their feet with the rest of the crowd to cheer the Red Sox's fifth run of the night. Finn's phone buzzed in his hand and he glanced down to find the screen filled with fireworks and clapping hands. He smiled and fired off a similar reply but caught Chad watching him and his knowing expression curdled Finn's enjoyment.

* * * *

"I should get going," Finn said. He'd drunk more tonight than he would typically and knew it was time to shut himself off. No need to get sloppy.

"Why?" Chad asked. "Neither of us is working tomorrow, so I say we buy another drink."

"It's almost closing time," Finn replied. "In a half-hour, we won't be able to."

"Then let's get an order in before last call."

After the game, Finn and his friends had walked to Wilde's, Mick's favorite bar in the South End, and spent time ogling the hot bartenders over burgers and a round of unbelievably delicious boozy milkshakes. Having sensed danger in their potency, Finn had switched to beer after he'd eaten, but then Paul and Mick had gone home and that had left no one to argue the side of moderation. However, to Chad's point, Finn had the next day off and no special plans — who cared if he had another drink and slept in?

Order placed, Chad turned to Finn. "Tell me more about what you've got going with this Luke. No offense, but I still can't wrap my head around you doing a stepdad thing with his kid."

Finn held up a hand. "Whoa. That's *definitely* not happening. Ella tolerates me pretty well, but in no way is she looking for me to act dad-like."

"What do you mean by 'tolerates me pretty well?'" Chad asked. "She doesn't like you?"

Oops. So much for not getting sloppy.

"She doesn't love me, no," he replied, "and given a choice, I doubt she'd choose to spend time around me. But mostly, she's cool, and we can all hang out together in peace."

"That's cute, but why the fuck even bother?" Chad smiled as Finn broke up laughing. "I'm serious, man! I wouldn't willingly subject myself to any child, let alone one who hated me."

"I don't think Ella *hates* me." Finn sipped his beer. Ella's vibe wasn't so much '*I hate you*' as '*why are you here?*' and it was obvious she held back around him. "And I'm pretty sure you would bother if the kid in question belonged to a guy *you* liked and wanted to spend time with." He waited for Chad's reluctant nod.

"Maybe. Frankly, I'm not sure I'd get started with a guy who had a kid. That's not what I want in my life."

"Fair enough. I didn't want that either," Finn admitted, "or at least not yet. But I got to know Luke, and his guardianship didn't seem like a big deal. To me, I mean. Taking care of Ella is a big deal for Luke, but he's still *him* outside of all that."

"And you like him."

"I do," Finn replied. "He's great and we have a fantastic time together."

"Even with the asshole kid?"

Finn nearly choked on his beer. "Dude. C'mon, she's ten years old."

"So? Kids can be assholes too."

"I know, but I'm the one who spends time around her. I'd rather not hear your voice in my head saying 'there's that asshole kid' whenever I see her."

Chad tipped his head back and cackled. "Point taken. When are you seeing him again?"

"Saturday for brunch. Kid included."

"And look at how happy you are about it." Chad poked at the corner of Finn's mouth with one finger. "Why don't you guys try spending more time together during the week, whether the kid's there or not? That'd make you less pouty, right?"

"I've been thinking along those lines, too." Finn sipped and swallowed beer. "Not sure how Ella will like it. Obviously, I'd prefer alone time with Luke, but I'll take what I can get."

Chad grimaced. "So romantic. Why don't you invite them over for dinner tomorrow?"

"Can't. Luke's got a standing dinner date with Ella and a couple of friends every Friday night." Finn stayed silent at the understanding that crossed Chad's face.

"A standing date to which you are not invited?" Chad let out a low whistle. "Damn. Then my original question stands. You like this guy enough to put up with the kid hatin' on you?"

"Yeah, I do." The bartender stepped up with their fresh beers and Finn paused to settle the tab. He met Chad's gaze head-on once the bartender moved away. "Like I said, I didn't plan to get involved with a man who has a child in his life, but that's how it worked out. Spending time with Luke is worth a little hate."

Chad set his empty glass down. "Okay. So Luke's schedule's been pretty shitty lately, huh?"

"Yeah. I know he's got a lot going on, but it kind of sucks."

"I get you." Chad's lip curled. "I don't know, Finn. Are you really good with always being second priority? Because to someone outside of the situation, that's how it sounds. Almost like you're the other man even though you're the *only* man, right?"

Finn grimaced. "Yeah, that's sort of how I feel. I know it's ridiculous because everything Luke's doing is for the good of his family, but I can't help feeling shitty."

Chad studied his glass of beer for a moment before he spoke again. "So Luke doesn't know? That you feel this way, I mean."

"No." Finn ran his fingers over his lips. "You're the first person I've talked to about it." Despite his and Luke's promise not to hold back on the awkward with each other.

A sly smile lit Chad's face. "Oh? I can't help feeling flattered."

"You would," Finn replied with a snort.

"But are you going to tell him? Seems like Luke should know he's making you feel bad." Chad rolled his eyes. "Wait, what the fuck am I doing giving you relationship advice? The last thing I should do is help you get along with that jackass!"

Finn couldn't help laughing despite the ache in his chest. It was a relief to voice his insecurities about Luke, even if doing so didn't solve anything.

"I don't know, Chad. I'm not sure I *can* tell him. Luke's had trouble in the past balancing the different sides of his life—guys get impatient that he has other priorities."

"Well, gee, I wonder why that is?"

"I know, I know. But I don't want to be another one of those guys who disappears on him if things get complicated." Finn shook his head. "I don't want to disappear on him at all."

"So don't. Doesn't mean you should suffer in silence either. Not when you've got someone like me around to entertain you when Luke can't get his head out of his ass." Chad waggled his eyebrows at Finn like a cartoon villain.

Finn winced. "Look—"

"Yeah, yeah, you just want to be friends. I get it."

"You'll think this is cheesy, but it's not you, it's me. Luke and I don't throw titles around, but I've never been much of a player. If I like a guy, I'm happy being with him and only him."

"It's a shame for me you're not slutty, but I can deal with it." Chad knocked his shoulder against Finn's. "Besides, I like hanging out with you. You're a good guy. Plus, you need someone to remind you to be selfish on a regular basis. It's okay to put yourself first once in a while, Finn. You should try it sometime."

Finn thought back to something Paul had said earlier in the summer after Finn and Luke had started seeing each other.

'You deserve happiness for yourself, and it's on Luke to make sure he's giving that to you.'

Finn picked up his glass and tapped it against Chad's. "Putting myself first sounds nice. So here's to being selfish."

Chad swallowed down a healthy mouthful of beer and set his glass down with a *thunk*. "When's the last time you went out to a club?"

"Fuck, I don't know. Since I moved here, I think."

Chad uttered a long-suffering sigh. "That changes tomorrow, doll. You are coming out for dinner with me, and I'm not letting you go home until the sun comes up or we need to call for bail money."

Finn laughed. "Oh, God. What have I done?"

Chapter Fifteen

You're fucking this up, a voice in Luke's head whispered. He glared at the line of code he'd been testing and tried to clear his mind, but the words looped round and round his brain like an earworm he couldn't shake. The little voice was right, too — something was off with Finn and Luke didn't know how to fix it.

This past summer had been the best Luke'd known in a long time. He'd gone on actual dates, as in staying out past ten o'clock and acting — mostly — like an adult. He'd made new friends in Paul and Mick and had watched Simon and Gillian draw Finn into their circle. And every day, whether he saw Finn or not, he'd fallen deeper in love and his desire to have Finn in his life intensified.

Unfortunately, the happy Finn-bubble Luke had been living in since June was cracked. His time for dates was gone, swallowed up by Ella's class schedule, activities and lessons outside of school. Not that Luke minded being there for Ella. He *wanted* that. Ella deserved

Luke's attention and presence, and he knew she counted on him in Peter's absence.

Luke's project load at GLS had also increased, and most nights, he logged back in to the office after he'd put in his miles on the treadmill. He still managed to connect with Finn on Saturdays with Ella, but otherwise, the only time alone he could count on involved meeting Finn in between his hospital shifts. But while Luke looked forward to any time they could get, Finn seemed less than happy with the arrangement and Luke in general.

Why can't I get this right?

Luke rubbed his eyes as a headache built behind them. He couldn't be in two places at once, but fucking hell, he was doing a terrible job of being a man in love.

"Hey, Luke?"

Simon's voice snapped Luke back to the present. "What's up?"

"I thought I'd head over to the Park Plaza early for our meeting at three, maybe grab a coffee on the way. You wanna walk with me?"

"Sure." Luke saved his work and put his computer to sleep. He slipped it into his bag and grabbed his phone but found Simon watching him, a quizzical expression on his face.

Luke rose and picked up his jacket. "What?"

"Are you okay?"

"Sure. Why?"

"I don't know. You've been quiet this week. Like, hardly making any noise whatsoever, and that's not like you."

Luke settled the jacket over his shoulders. He didn't feel in the mood to talk about anything serious unless it had to do with software applications.

"Aren't you the one who's always telling me to stop muttering to myself?" he asked.

"Yes, but that doesn't mean I don't notice when it's not happening, you bozo," Simon said, and they turned toward the door. "We've been sharing work space for the better part of our adult lives and a part of me will always expect to hear you talking to yourself while you code."

Luke wanted to laugh at his friend's words but a lump rose in his throat instead.

Oh, hell.

He moved ahead of Simon toward the exit and waved at Gillian when she called out a 'good luck'. He and Simon were outside the building and in the middle of the sidewalk when Simon took hold of Luke's elbow.

"Hey."

Luke bit back a groan "Simon, I don't —"

"Yes, well, I do."

Simon moved to stand in front of Luke, effectively blocking his way. The genuine concern in his eyes made Luke feel even worse.

Simon sighed. "Pickle, what's going on?"

"Nothing. I just have a lot on my mind."

Luke wasn't lying. Between work and life, he had an enormous amount on his mind. Nevertheless, while he didn't feel like talking, he recognized the determined gleam in Simon's eye. Gently, he pulled his arm free of Simon's grasp.

"Can we not do this right now? I don't... We can talk later, but right now, I need to focus on the work."

Simon pursed his lips. "You're okay, though, right?" he pressed. "You and Pete and Ella? I don't have to, you know, worry about any of you?"

"Yes, we're okay. Pete and Ella are fine." Luke took hold of his friend's hand and squeezed while relief filtered over Simon's face. "I promise. This is just me thinking too much and getting moody."

"Okay. But I'm coming over after dinner with Ella tonight and feeding you beer until you talk."

"Good thing I'm out of beer," Luke muttered.

Simon's lips twitched into a smile. "I'll pick some up on the way back to your place."

"And just a heads-up, Pete and Ella will be chatting."

"Awesome. I feel like I haven't talked to Pete in forever!" Simon let Luke go and his worried face smoothed out. "C'mon, let's get that cup of coffee."

* * * *

Luke focused on the work and slowly turned his afternoon around. Then, as he left to pick up Ella, Finn messaged and that put a real smile on Luke's face. The words in their little speech bubbles progressed from flirty to filthy, and by the time they met Simon at the diner, Luke felt literally hot under the collar and a lot less stressed about his relationship fizzling out like a used-up bottle rocket.

"El, are you finished?" Simon asked, his voice light.

Luke smiled. Simon was eyeing the remains of Ella's plate of mac and cheese, just as he did nearly every Friday.

"I think so," Ella said. "Do you want the rest?"

"Seems a shame to waste it." Simon shrugged. The gleam in his eye belied his nonchalance though, and Luke saw Ella's next move a mile away.

"Tell you what—I'll trade you my leftovers for a joke." She flicked one long braid over her shoulders while Simon stared at her for a good ten seconds. He actually appeared alarmed.

"I…don't know any jokes that aren't dirty, Ella. Every one I can think of is at least R-rated."

"Tell me!" Ella exclaimed, and Luke held up a quelling hand.

"Nope. You repeating Simon's dirty jokes is the last thing any of us needs." Luke nudged Ella gently with his elbow when she pouted. "How about I tell one in Simon's place and he does me a favor later?"

Ella thought about it for a moment. "That's fair," she said at last and turned a beady eye on Simon. "It has to be something really nice, you know, even if it's not a thing you like."

Simon made a face. "Ugh. Maybe this isn't a good idea after all," he began, but Ella's attention had already shifted back to Luke.

"Okay, go."

Luke schooled his expression. "What animal goes 'Ooooooooooo?'" He kept his face straight while Ella racked her brain. Finally, she shook her head.

"Tell me."

"A cow with no lips."

"Oh, my God!" Ella burst out laughing. Her eyes sparkled and she pushed her plate toward Simon, who managed to appear both irritated and amused even as he thanked her. "Remind me to tell that one to my dad tonight," Ella told Luke.

Simon grumbled. "How did this terrible joke habit begin again?"

"I don't know." Luke hummed. "It started after Ella learned to read, that much I remember. She memorized some jokes from the milk cartons in school, and I learned some as a form of retaliation. Honestly, they're a nice break from harder questions."

Simon narrowed his eyes. "Harder questions?"

"Like how come you don't order your own plate of mac and cheese?" Luke replied brightly.

"Or how come you never bring a boyfriend to dinner?" Ella added. She laughed at Simon's scowl.

Luke chuckled too, though the question made his heart burn. Ella and Finn had reached an accord in their interactions, but he was still not welcome to their Friday night dinners.

"One, I don't want a whole plate of pasta—a quarter plate is plenty," Simon replied. "Two, while I am seeing someone right now, I haven't decided if he's special enough to invite to dinner with you." He gave Luke a crooked grin across the table. "Besides, Luke and I used to go out about a million years ago, and on nights like this, it's almost like we're boyfriends."

Luke shook his head. "No, it's not."

"So not the same thing," Ella agreed. "How come you guys broke up anyway?"

"Simon wasn't in love with me." Luke raised his hands at Simon's theatrical gasp. "You weren't, dear, and we both know it. Besides, we're much better suited as friends than boyfriends."

"That's true." Simon smiled at Ella. "I love Luke in my own way and that's why he's been my *best* friend for longer than you've been alive."

Ella's jaw dropped. "Holy shit, you guys are *old*."

"Ella!" Luke groaned as she and Simon burst into giggles, but he didn't mind the wisecracks. Ella and Simon's uncomplicated fun was a balm for him after having been so caught up in his head for the last several days.

Luke soaked up their continued antics after they left the diner to walk home. He wandered slightly ahead and stopped at the curb where Stuart Street intersected with Clarendon Street while he waited for the others to catch up. The sound of laughter caught Luke's ear and he glanced to his right in time to see a familiar figure on the next block. Gladness flashed through him until he understood what he was seeing.

Finn and another man were headed in Luke's direction, both immersed in conversation and watching each other instead of where they were going. Finn's fine black clothes spoke of plans for a night out, and his handsome face was animated. He looked happy, Luke thought, and about a thousand times more at home with the man at his side than he ever did at Luke's.

Oh.

Everything inside Luke clenched. He knew that man. He'd been at the baseball game last night with Finn. He'd taken Luke's ticket and his place. Luke froze, right there in plain sight of Finn and his friend, with nowhere to hide. But the man from the baseball game stopped walking before either of them glanced Luke's way. He pulled open a door and gestured Finn inside with a smile, then they were gone, leaving Luke still standing on the sidewalk, his hands stuffed in his pockets and his whole world changed.

* * * *

The next several hours passed in a strange, numb kind of vacuum for Luke. Back at his place, he and Ella whipped up a pan of brownies while Simon bought beer, then the three of them played Crazy Eights while the brownies baked and cooled. He didn't have to force a smile during the video conference with Peter because Peter told them he'd be back in the States by mid-October. He couldn't give them an exact date, but Ella's skyrocketing excitement had been contagious and lifted even Luke's heavy spirits for a time.

However, once Ella went to bed, Simon immediately retrieved the six-pack from the refrigerator and jerked his head at the hall leading to Luke's bedroom.

"Let's talk, Pickle."

The cold, tight feeling inside Luke broke apart as they climbed out of his bedroom window to the balcony. Simon handed Luke a beer, and if his 'thank you' sounded gravelly, Simon didn't mention it. They sipped in silence for a while, watching the traffic below on Storrow Drive and the boats on the river beyond.

Luke inhaled the cool evening air and wondered how to begin. Now that the time to talk had come, he wanted to, even though he knew it would hurt once he got going. In the end, Simon simply leveled his eyes at Luke and words started bubbling out of him without his even thinking.

"I saw Finn out with another man tonight." Luke blinked, surprised by what he'd said, and his stomach twisted at the umbrage that streaked across Simon's face.

"You *what*?"

"Wait, no." Luke closed his eyes. "Fuck, that's not how I wanted to start."

"Okay. How did you want to start? And when the hell did this happen?"

Luke opened his eyes and found Simon frowning. "After dinner on our way back here. I don't know what they were doing, but it looked like a date." Luke grimaced. "Fuck, for all I know, he's been seeing this guy all along."

Simon rested his elbows on the railing. "Explain that to me, if you would."

"I never asked Finn if he was seeing anyone," Luke said. He felt stupid and sad as he said the words, and his heart ached. "I just assumed he'd stop if he were because I am an entitled asshole."

"No, c'mon." Simon reached over and brushed the knuckles of one hand against Luke's. "I think the two of you got your signals crossed, is all. You should talk to him about it, Luke."

"How? 'Hey, I know it's never come up, but I think it'd be cool if you stopped sticking your dick in other people.'" Luke winced at Simon's bark of laughter.

"Okay, wow."

"The worst part is knowing I don't have a snowball's chance in hell of competing with another man anyway. Not with Ella and Pete and...fuck, everything." Luke waved vaguely at the apartment behind them. "I can't keep up with someone who doesn't have so many constraints on his time."

Luke ground his teeth when Simon shook his head. "I'm not wrong, Simon."

"I think you are. You just need to figure out how to make the time you do have work better for you."

"What do you think I've *been* doing?" Luke asked, his voice strained. "I haven't been able to keep a date with Finn for weeks, unless it's meeting at his place to fool around in the middle of the afternoon."

"I don't understand why you say that like it's a bad thing," Simon mused. "Most people would be envious of the way you spend your lunch hours. I know I am."

"It's not a bad thing at all, but it's the only thing I'm capable of the majority of the time, and that's not fair to Finn. He was going out to dinner tonight, probably somewhere very nice. I'll bet he had great food and wine and is *still* out there because it's Friday night and that's what single guys who aren't me do."

"Not all single guys. I'm here with you, aren't I?"

"Yeah, but you're not *my* boyfriend—you're seeing Miles," Luke protested. "And we both know you're only here because you pity me and you're trying to get me drunk so I spill my guts."

"I don't pity you, you jackass—I pity *me* for having to listen to you whine." Simon groaned. "Besides, my plan is working, right? Hell, you haven't even finished one beer and you're already blabbering out of control."

Luke smiled but the knots in him didn't loosen one bit. Somehow, Simon guessed as much.

"Luke, the first time we talked about this, I told you not to write off the good doctor without giving him a chance," Simon said. "That hasn't changed. It's a mistake to assume your responsibilities with Ella are going to drive him off."

"I'm not assuming anything," Luke said, his voice soft. "It's started happening, Simon. You forget—this is something I've seen before. I can *feel* him pulling away. And I'm not sure there's anything I can do to stop it."

Simon watched him for a moment and slowly nodded. "Okay. Explain it to me. But first, give me two minutes to get something from inside." He set his beer down and headed for the window.

"Where are you going?"

"To grab the bourbon and some glasses from your liquor cabinet." He flashed Luke a grin. "I have a feeling this conversation calls for more than beer."

Chapter Sixteen

"Hey, Ella?" Finn tapped her shoulder as they set the table for brunch on Saturday morning. "Is Luke okay?"

Luke sure didn't seem okay. He looked pale and tired and as far from relaxed as a person could be. Every time he met Finn's gaze, a crease appeared between his eyebrows followed by a quick grin that didn't warm his eyes.

Ella glanced toward the kitchen where Luke was holed up, her expression troubled. "I think so, but... I don't know," she said. "He's been working late a lot, and he had a headache this morning. He seems tired. I think he's stressing because my dad's coming back soon, too, and we have lots to do to get ready."

Finn smiled. "Hey, that's great. About your dad coming back, I mean."

"I know." Ella beamed at Finn. She seemed genuinely happy, and he watched, amused, as she bounced on her toes.

"Excited?"

"I can't wait!"

Neither can I, Finn thought. He didn't feel even a little guilty. He was all for Luke's brother getting back home safely, especially if that meant Luke got a personal life back and had more time for Finn.

Ella ambled off once they'd finished setting up, and Finn went to the kitchen to check on Luke. Luke stood at the stove, wrangling a skillet of scrambled eggs and somehow looking more stressed than ever.

"Hey."

Luke started and almost spilled the contents of the pan, and Finn's trickle of concern sharpened. He moved swiftly to Luke's side. "Whoa, you okay?"

Luke set the heavy skillet back on the stove with a grunt. "I didn't hear you come in."

Finn slipped his arms around Luke's waist. "What's the matter?" he asked. He gave Luke a gentle shake when Luke pushed his lips into a thin line. "C'mon, handsome. Talk to me."

Some of the tension leaked out of Luke's frame. "Sorry. I know I'm kind of a mess."

"Maybe more than kind of." Finn smiled as Luke looped his arms around Finn's neck. "What's going on with you today?"

"Got a lot on my mind, I guess."

Finn hummed. Non-answers weren't like Luke at all. "Ella told me her dad's coming back soon," he prodded and Luke's face lightened slightly.

"She did, huh?"

"She seems pretty stoked."

"Everyone is. You have no idea." Luke pressed his forehead to Finn's and closed his eyes. "We talked last night and went through logistics and timing for mid-October. That could change, but I'm just relieved he'll be on the same continent again."

He sniffed. "I'm, um, also hungover."

Delight bubbled up in Finn's chest. "Wait, *what*? What the heck went on during dinner last night?"

"Simon made boilermakers *after* dinner and after Ella went to bed." Luke wrinkled his nose. "I only had two and a half, but clearly, they were enough to hurt my brain."

"That half will always get you." Finn smoothed the hair off Luke's forehead with one hand. Luke leaned into the touch and the corners of his lips twitched up. "Ella said you had a headache."

"Meh. Serves me right. I'll take some ibuprofen after we eat and that should fix me up." He opened his eyes again and, though his smile faded, the affection in his expression did not. "Thanks."

"You're welcome." Finn pulled him in for a quick kiss, mindful as always of Ella in the rooms beyond. He went still when Luke's hold on him tightened.

Finn let Luke take the lead, and his insides heated. Luke lengthened the kiss, and while it was slow and careful and still relatively chaste, it carried a sweetness that tightened Finn's chest. His heart was pounding by the time Luke pulled away, and the way his eyes shone made Finn feel about ten feet tall.

"I'm glad you're here," Luke said. He let Finn loose and turned back to the pan of eggs. "I know it sounds ridiculous considering we ate lunch together on Wednesday, but I missed you."

Finn watched Luke's shoulders tense again. *What the hell is going on?* he wondered.

"That's not ridiculous at all," he said, then stopped when Ella dashed in.

"Hey, Luke!"

"Hey, Ella."

She held up a black USB key embossed with an orange GLS logo. "I found this on the floor and I think it's Simon's."

Luke peered at the key over his shoulder. "You're right. I'll bet it fell out of his pocket when he got changed last night." He scraped the eggs onto a platter. "Will you ask him if he needs it before Monday? My phone's by the couch and it's unlocked, so you can use it."

"Okay."

"Don't call anyone else."

"I won't," she said over her shoulder, already on the move. "BRB!"

"I mean it, Ella!"

"I know, Jeeze!"

Why would Simon get changed here?

Finn's gut curled but he forced himself to smile. "BRB?"

"Be right back."

"Ah. And Simon stayed over?"

"Yeah." Luke chuckled. "I didn't want him risking life and limb on the stairs after the bourbon. Besides, it was the least I could do after he listened to me bitch about my problems all night."

"That seems fair," Finn replied. He kept his tone light. Knowing Luke had turned to Simon again for support, though…that stung.

Finn held his hands out for the platter of eggs. "You can talk to me, too. You know that, right?"

Luke paused in his movements. "Yes, I do." He met Finn's stare and handed over the eggs, then turned to the counter. "I figured you were busy last night, that's all."

Discomfort wormed its way through Finn. He'd been busy, yes, enjoying dinner and drinks and a night out dancing with Chad. Not that he had anything to be ashamed of. He deserved time to unwind, too. Finn had needed a break from thinking about why this thing with Luke suddenly seemed so complicated.

He sighed. That was part of the problem—he didn't know *what* he and Luke had together. Their light and flirty fun had matured and now, nearly four months later, Finn was attached. He thought Luke was too, but what if Finn was wrong?

Luke scooped up the plates loaded with sausages and the bagels Finn had brought, and Finn followed him out to the table. Once their hands were empty, Finn took hold of one of Luke's.

"I had dinner with a friend last night," he said. "But I'm here now if you want to talk."

A softness stole over Luke's face. "Okay. How about after we eat?"

Ella slid over the floor in her socks and almost crashed into both of them.

"Oops." She snickered. "Simon said you can give him the USB key on Monday but *not* to look at it because it's full of incriminating photos," she said, enunciating the last two words with care. "What does that mean?"

"That Simon is a punk with a weird sense of humor," Luke said. "Though, knowing him, he's probably telling the truth." He squeezed Finn's fingers a final time before he let go. "Come on. Sit down and get your brunch on with me."

Finn and Luke did talk after brunch and caught up after having missed each other during the week. More than once, Finn caught a glimpse of something he couldn't place on Luke's face—something raw and intense. Then Luke would reach out and touch Finn and the flash of emotion would disappear.

Luke also surprised Finn by inviting him over for Sunday dinner. The evening went much as Finn had expected, and he enjoyed himself thoroughly. They ate lasagne and salad, then watched *Star Trek* re-runs while Ella worked on a color theory project for school. She was friendly toward Finn, and even told him one of her many terrible jokes. He dozed off beside Luke on the couch around seven-thirty and Luke let him sleep, which left no time for fooling around before Finn had to go to work. Luke kissed him for a long time at the door, though, and gave Finn's ass a squeeze. His gray-green eyes were filled with promise as they said goodnight.

He showed up at Finn's door every day for lunch after that, armed with takeout and an impish smile. The food went uneaten, however, because Finn couldn't resist him. Not that he tried very hard because he wanted that closeness with Luke, and Luke seemed so eager. The sex was amazing, incendiary even, but the quiet times afterward spoke to Finn's soul. Times like right now when they both lay boneless and content and told stupid stories to make each other laugh until Luke went back to work.

Finn put his hand over the arm Luke slung around his waist. "You need any help getting ready for Pete's homecoming?"

"I don't think so, no." Luke kissed Finn's shoulder. "I'm having dinner with my parents on Sunday and we'll divvy up tasks, like his cell phone and car insurance, and restock the stuff he needs."

"Where does Pete store his car? In your parking space?"

"Nope. He stores his Chevy Silverado in my parents' garage, much to their dismay." The humor in Luke's voice made Finn laugh even more than the idea of Luke's parents driving a big pickup.

"That's a whole lot of truck," he mused. "Do your parents mind giving up the space?"

"Nah. They mind that Pete won't let them drive it while he's gone. Well, Pops minds. He's obsessed with Jennie and it kills him that he can't touch her."

Finn blinked. "Your brother named his truck Jennie?"

"Yes, he did."

"Okay." Finn laughed. "I can't imagine Brad behind the wheel of a pickup at *all*, by the way."

"I know!" Luke rolled up on his elbow. "I have no idea why the old man wants it so bad, but he's been talking about Jennie ever since Pete drove her back from Quantico before he shipped out."

"I'm surprised he doesn't just do it. It's not like your brother would ever know."

"Aha, he can't. Pops doesn't have the keys, and neither do I." Luke's eyes twinkled merrily and he rolled again, this time away from Finn to sit up. "Pete leaves his keys with Simon along with a list of who is and is not allowed to claim them."

Simon again. That figures.

Finn tucked his hands under his head. "This gets better and better. Are you on the list of privileged few?"

"Of course," Luke scoffed gently. "Though it's Ella who's on the list—I'm only the driver. I don't take advantage of the privilege much, though. I'm just not that into Jennie."

"Oh?" Finn scooted over and pressed a kiss to Luke's hip. "Too much woman for you?"

Luke hummed and carded his fingers through Finn's hair. "Afraid so. I don't even have a car. I just rent a Zipcar if I need one."

"Who parks in your space?"

"My downstairs neighbor. I rent it to her cheap since I don't need it." He yawned. "Anyway, Simon's got a couple of weeks to make sure Jennie's running okay while my folks figure out the insurance. He's probably already started, but I help out, too."

Finn suppressed a sigh. He didn't like talking about Luke's best friend while naked. Truth be told, he didn't care to talk about Simon much at all these days, something he knew was terribly unfair. Finn liked Simon. He was excellent company and a good friend to Luke, not to mention an important part of the Ryans' lives. Unfortunately, his presence in Luke's world had grown so large Finn sometimes felt it ate up any remaining room for other people. People like Finn.

Finn closed his eyes as Luke bent down and pressed another kiss to his shoulder. His breath warmed Finn's skin when he spoke. "You around tomorrow?"

"Mmm, no. Working tonight and a weird midday shift tomorrow." Finn grumbled. "I'll probably resurface sometime late Friday afternoon."

"Right in time to start the weekend."

Finn opened his eyes and found Luke watching him. He traced one of Finn's cheekbones with a fingertip. "What about Saturday? My parents have Ella for the afternoon and I thought maybe you and I—"

"I can't," Finn cut in quietly. "I've got a work thing on Saturday. There's a golf tournament in Rhode Island—a fundraiser—for the Cancer Center at the hospital. The ED and trauma docs put their names into the lottery to play and I won."

Finn licked his lips. He'd never expected his name to be picked. He hadn't thought to mention it to Luke, either, whom Finn had assumed would be unavailable to play anyway. Besides, Finn ate brunch with Luke and Ella every Saturday unless he was working— missing one occasion didn't seem like a big deal in his mind. Now, as Luke's sunny expression clouded, Finn wondered if he'd miscalculated.

He stroked Luke's waist with his fingers. "I meant to tell you before today, but it slipped my mind. I'm sorry."

"Don't worry about it," Luke replied quickly. He smiled but that crease was back between his eyebrows. His expression had grown worried again, even as he ran his hand over Finn's hair. "I didn't know you were a golfer."

"I played in high school and during my time as an undergrad, but that all stopped after I started med school. I maybe play once or twice a year now. I'll be lucky not to embarrass myself."

"I doubt that." Luke leaned down for another kiss then got to his feet. "You'll be great."

The silence that followed seemed heavy and awkward in a way things never were with Luke. Finn lay still in the bed, watching Luke gather his clothes, and frowned when he started dressing. They'd wiped each other down after sex, but Luke typically showered before returning to work.

"No time to get wet today?" he asked. He meant to tease but the words fell flat, and Luke just looked apologetic.

"I'd love to, but I've got a meeting at two." He smoothed his tie down with both hands. "I need to get back and prep."

He eyed Finn and ran his teeth over his bottom lip for a moment before he moved back to the bed. The uncertainty in his face had Finn sitting up.

"What's up?"

"Would you mind if I came by on Sunday? If you're not going to be busy, I mean." The tips of Luke's ears turned red. "Monday is a school holiday and I have a road race in Salem that morning. With the way our schedules have been lately, I may not see you again before next weekend."

Finn stared at his lover. Would he mind if Luke came by? He loved that Luke wanted to see him, but the idea of another beautiful, golden afternoon followed by more waiting for Luke to have free time again... Slowly, Finn shook his head. It didn't feel right.

"I don't know, Luke," he said.

"What do you mean?"

"I don't think these afternoons are working for me anymore." He pursed his lips. "I mean, you and I have such a good time, but more and more, it's like this is all we can manage instead of a full evening together.

"I'm not trying to give you shit about Ella," he said hastily. "I know she needs you and I respect the hell out of you for being there for her, but I don't see much of you at all these days. We got together over the weekend, but outside of that, the only time you're around is at lunch when you want to fuck."

Luke paled. "That's... Is that what you think this is? Why I'm here?" he asked, his voice hushed.

A hollow feeling fell over Finn. "No. Maybe. Damn it, I'm not saying this right." He sighed, his frustration rising.

Why is this so hard?

"I like spending time with you, I really do. Fuck, it's more than like. These afternoons are the best parts of my day! But they don't feel like enough for me anymore." Finn ran his hands through his hair. "I see you, what, maybe once a week outside of this room? We don't get any time to be with each other anymore, and I miss it. I don't know. I want to feel closer, you know? Connected. To know I'm not just a distraction. I'm sure that sounds sappy, but it's true."

He scratched his head at the distress on Luke's face. "I'm not trying to make you feel bad and I don't even know if I'm making sense. But things have changed for me."

"You are absolutely making sense," Luke replied. "There's nothing sappy about what you want, but God, I wish I knew how to tell you how *wrong* you are about the way I feel." Hurt flashed in his eyes and he held Finn's hand tight between his own.

"The time I spend with you isn't a distraction, Finn. I love it. I love being with you and around you, and I wish I could offer more than Saturday brunch or burgers and reruns while Ella does her homework."

Finn's heart sank. Luke wasn't getting it. "No, that's not what I mean—"

Luke plowed on. "Any time I get to spend with you means a lot to me. I know it could be better, but my schedule's so weird, and I thought that coming here like this would help keep things from…"

Abruptly, he let go of Finn and put the hand over his face. "Fuck. I'm so bad at this." Misery was plain in every line of his body when he dropped the hand again and Finn wanted to kick himself.

"Shit, Luke, I'm sorry."

"Don't." Fire filled Luke's eyes. He grabbed hold of Finn again, this time his touch so soft it bordered on tentative. "This is on me. *I'm* sorry, Finn. I never meant to make you feel bad or think I spend time with you just for sex. God, I'm so embarrassed that—" He stopped and pressed his lips thin. "I'm gonna go."

Startled, Finn stood when Luke did. He dragged the sheet around himself. "Luke, wait—"

Luke's phone chimed and he gave Finn a pained smile. "Let's, um, table this for now, okay? I need some time to think. To figure out how to make this work better and stop fucking up all the time."

Finn caught hold of Luke's wrist and pulled him in. Luke's body was wound tight like a bowstring set to snap, and Finn ached as he carefully gathered him close.

Damn, I really hurt him.

"You're not fucking up," Finn murmured. The slow shake of Luke's head told Finn he didn't believe it. "You're not, Luke. I don't want you thinking that at all."

"I know," Luke whispered. "But I am, Finn."

Finn sighed. He knew Luke well enough to feel certain he'd spend the next several days beating himself up over this. "I have time off next week," he said. "Let's talk, okay? I'll bring dinner for you and Ella and we'll talk it all through, okay?"

Luke stayed silent while Finn rubbed circles between his shoulder blades with one hand and held him. Luke's body relaxed a fraction. He rested his hands on Finn's waist and kissed his cheek. He went still, as if he meant to speak, but his phone chimed again and he stepped away. He didn't look back as he made his way to the door.

Finn wished he'd held on tighter.

Chapter Seventeen

"I have a joke for you," Ella announced as she and Luke walked away from her after-school program.

"Oh, yeah?" Luke cast a sidelong glance down at her. "Hit me."

Ella's eyes gleamed. "What do penguins eat for breakfast?"

"Hmm." Luke pretended to think. When they stopped at an intersection to wait for the traffic flow to change, he shrugged. "I give up."

"Ice Krispies."

"Ugh. That is terrible."

"I know!"

Luke's lips twitched into a semblance of a smile at Ella's gloating. "Make sure you tell your dad that one the next time he calls."

"Oh, yeah." Ella skipped beside him. "I'm gonna tell Simon at dinner, too."

"Simon's not coming tonight." The traffic signal changed and Luke held his hand out to Ella. "He went out of town with Miles, the guy he's been seeing."

"Oh, right—he told me last week. Humph." Ella grasped Luke's fingers as they stepped out onto the crosswalk, her lips pushed into a pout. "He's coming to the race on Monday, though, right?"

"As far as I know, yeah. He and Miles went to a party at a friend's house on Cape Cod, but he said they'd be back on Sunday night. That should give Simon time to meet us for the race. If he wants to be there, anyway. He and Miles may just stay at their friend's house another day instead."

Ella let go of Luke's hand once they were safely across the street. "So it's just you and me tonight, huh?"

"Yep," Luke said. "You feel like sharing a vanilla frappe with me at dinner?"

Ella smiled. "Um, yes, please. But can we get chocolate instead?"

"Mmm, okay. Guess I'll have a burger."

"Aw, poor you."

"I know." Luke rubbed his hands together, more for effect than out of any real desire to eat. "What are you having?"

"Banana pancakes," Ella replied without hesitating.

"Really?"

"Uh-huh. I like the pancakes at the diner."

"I know you do," Luke replied. "Guess I'm used to you ordering the same thing every Friday night. You're kind of blowing my mind, kid."

"Well, Simon's not here to 'help' me eat my dinner" — Ella made air quotes with her fingers—"so I thought I'd eat something different."

Luke processed her words for a moment. "You don't order the mac and cheese for Simon, do you?"

"No way." Ella shook her head. "I love it. I save some for him, though, because I know he likes it too. Besides, that way I have room for dessert."

"So smart. Simon complained about you always ordering the same food, you know."

"He did?"

"Yes," Luke replied, with utmost solemnity.

Ella tsked. "He's so weird."

"You have no idea how right you are, honey."

He held his hand out again at the next intersection and this time, Ella kept hold of it after they'd crossed the street. They talked as they strolled, discussing her day at school and the apple-picking outing she had planned with her grandparents, as well as things left to prepare for Peter's return home. Luke thought Ella had forgotten all about Simon's absence, and she caught him off guard by circling back to the topic.

"Were you invited too?" she asked. They were a block from the diner and Luke stared at her while he parsed the question.

"Invited where?"

"To the party with Simon and Miles."

"Oh. On the Cape, you mean? No, I wasn't. I haven't met Miles' friends," Luke said.

"I thought maybe you were but couldn't go because of me and I felt kind of bad." Ella looked dissatisfied. "How come you're not invited? Simon's your friend, and Miles is Simon's friend. Isn't Miles your friend, too?"

"Not exactly. I've met him a couple of times and he seems cool, but we don't know each other very well yet." Luke shrugged. "That'll change if he and Simon keep seeing each other and I get to spend more time with him." He thought Ella seemed oddly concerned.

"You don't mind, right? That you weren't invited, I mean."

Luke gave her a small smile. She was worried his feelings had been hurt. "No. Simon and Miles are getting to know each other. It's good for Simon to have some time away from work and, well, me."

Not to mention I'd be the only single guy in a house full of pairs. No thanks.

"I have other things to do anyway, like hang out with you," Luke said aloud.

Ella nodded. Her expression remained thoughtful, however, and Luke braced himself for more probing questions. To his relief, they didn't come. He'd never shut Ella down, but he didn't feel like talking about much of anything and hadn't since his disastrous lunch with Finn on Wednesday.

A familiar sense of grief and shame fell over him as he and Ella entered the diner. Luke had gone to Finn's that afternoon resolved to get them back on track. He'd even had a pair of tickets for Saturday's baseball game at Fenway Park in his jacket pocket. Unfortunately, Luke hadn't had a chance to ask Finn about the game before everything had gone to utter shit.

If Luke had been able, he would have gone home after leaving Finn's apartment instead of back to the office. He would have locked himself in the bathroom and, for the first time in more than a decade, shed tears over a man. The luxury of a pity party hadn't been an option, of course, so Luke had shoved his emotions down instead, put on his game face and forced himself to keep moving. Luckily, Simon and Gillian had been working offsite all week and hadn't been around to witness his dark mood.

Finn had reached out several times since Wednesday with both phone calls and messages, but his late shifts had made the exchanges rushed. They'd been stilted and devoid of their usual flirting, too, and Luke blamed himself. His confidence had taken a real hit and now he dreaded doing or saying the wrong thing so much he went nearly tongue-tied any time they spoke.

Luke kept all those thoughts to himself while he and Ella were seated, and they talked about upcoming movies they wanted to see after placing their orders. He caught Ella watching him a couple of times with a puzzled kind of expression on her face, but the stack of pancakes she'd ordered soon provided an excellent distraction.

"What time are Gram and Pops picking me up tomorrow morning?" she asked around a mouthful.

"Gram said to be ready by eight," Luke said. "Pops is craving French toast and he found a place outside the city he wants to try."

"Why don't we eat brunch with you and Finn? It's not like there won't be a ton of food."

"I'm not making brunch tomorrow." Luke fixed his focus on his plate and half-eaten burger and worked at keeping his face straight. "Finn's working and you'll be with Gram and Pops—doesn't seem any point in making all that food for one person."

"Well, that stinks," Ella grumbled. "You want to come to breakfast with us instead?"

"Nah, that's okay. I have stuff to do around the house."

"Uh-huh." Ella smirked without missing a beat. "You want to spend time with Finn after he gets out of work. I see how it is."

"Of course you do." Luke didn't bother correcting her assumption. He didn't want to go into why Finn wasn't coming by for brunch, or whom he'd be spending time with playing golf. Luke had a good idea of who that was because he knew Paul and Mick were already busy. They'd be at Fenway Park, using the baseball tickets Luke had wanted to give to Finn.

* * * *

The next day, Luke functioned mostly on autopilot. His alarm woke him and he got Ella out of the door with his parents. He put in an easy two-mile run along the river and spent some time doing yoga to stretch. He got his race bag together and absolutely didn't think about Finn and what he might be getting up to with a handsome dark-haired someone. After lunch, Luke stretched out on the couch with a book, but the next thing he knew, he was waking up in an almost dark room.

Luke blinked and sat up. He heard the front door open and checked his watch, and his stomach sank when he saw it was already six. He'd slept away the entire afternoon and didn't feel any less weighed down by fatigue.

Ugh.

He blinked again as the overhead light came on.

"Luke? Honey, are you okay?"

Luke's mother crossed the room toward him with a brown paper bag in her hands. Ella followed close behind, a cloth tote no doubt filled with apples looped over one shoulder.

"Guess I fell asleep." Luke got to his feet and faked a sheepish expression. "Sorry about that."

Joanna cocked her head at him and hummed. "You look exhausted. Are you here by yourself?"

"Uh, yeah, why? Here, let me get that." Luke held his hands out for the paper bag.

"Well, Ella thought Finn would be here," Joanna said, then chuckled. "I didn't know what to expect with the lights out."

Luke met Ella's searching gaze before he glanced back to his mother. "Got it. Finn has a work thing today, actually. What's this?" he asked and held the bag up.

Joanna smiled. "Pasta from that place you like in the North End."

"Nice. Are you staying to eat? Where's Pops?"

"He's downstairs with the car. We're having dinner with Jeanne and Bobby Lutz and should get going if we want to be on time." Joanna replied, then paused. "Are you sure you're okay? You're a bit pale. You didn't overdo it training today, did you?"

"No, ma'am. Two miles and stretching, that's all." Luke held up one hand in a fair approximation of a scout's salute and put on another smile for his mother. "I took it easy, I swear. Thank you for the dinner, and for taking Ella with you today. El, you said thanks, right?"

"Of course she did," Joanna said before Ella could speak. "We had a great time and the only person who ate too many apples was your father."

"He looked a little green," Ella agreed. "He didn't barf, though."

"Almost." Joanna laughed. "You were too busy scaling that tree with the other kids to notice when your old Pops disappeared for a good ten minutes."

Ella grimaced. "Gross. I'm gonna go pretend that didn't happen now. Bye, Gram. See you guys tomorrow."

Luke walked his mother out and locked up, then headed for the kitchen. He handed Ella the takeout bag and went to the cabinet for plates.

"How many apple desserts will we be baking in the next week?" he asked.

Ella smiled at him over her shoulder. "So many. Gram thought we could make some of those vegan oatmeal muffin cup things you like and bring them with us to Salem."

"That's a good idea."

Luke stopped by the flatware drawer before he carried everything over to the table. He noticed then that the order included three of everything: three containers of pasta, three side salads and servings of bread, even three chocolate chip cookies wrapped in paper glassine bags. He stared at the spread for a moment.

"Are you feeling extra hungry tonight?" he asked Ella.

"I thought Finn would be here, too," she said, "so we ordered enough for three."

Oh.

"I see." Luke managed a smile. "That was thoughtful of you. What did you order for Finn?"

"Some bacon and tomato thing with penne. I thought it kinda sounded like a BLT sandwich. He told me you bought him one the first time you went out for coffee, and he's liked them ever since."

"That's true—he can't get enough of them." Luke swallowed against a sudden swell of emotion. Quickly, he cleared his throat and focused on their food. "Thank you, honey. Finn would appreciate this."

They put the extra dinner in the refrigerator and took the rest to the living area where Luke put on a movie. He and Ella rarely watched television during mealtime, but he felt like zoning out in the Marvel Cinematic Universe for a couple of hours with a plateful of carbs. Their dishes were empty and Ant-Man was battling Yellowjacket when Ella's head came to rest against Luke's shoulder. He glanced down at her mass of dark hair.

"You tired?"

"Nah." She tilted her head and stared up at Luke. "Can I ask you a question?"

"Of course."

"How come you weren't with Finn today? I thought you guys were going to a baseball game."

"He had a golf tournament for charity," Luke said. "Hard to argue against raising money for the hospital, you know? Even I know that's more important than a baseball game." He worried his lip with his teeth. "Don't tell Pops I said that."

"I won't." Ella smiled faintly. "Is Finn coming to watch you run on Monday?"

Luke shook his head. "He's working nights this weekend. He could still be sleeping by the time we get back to Boston." Luke raised a hand and gently fingered one of Ella's braids before he shifted his focus back to the movie. "We could ask if he has time for dinner next week, if you like."

"Okay. Like, before Saturday brunch?"

"If he has time," Luke hedged. He didn't even know if brunch with Finn was on the table anymore. Ella sat up straight and the open concern in her face prompted Luke to run his palm up and down her arm.

"What's wrong?"

"If we don't see Finn before brunch next week, that'll be two weeks since he was here."

"Almost, yeah. Sometimes, our schedules make it tricky to line up time together." Luke weighed his next words and kept his tone light. "Don't take this the wrong way, El, but it never occurred to me you'd mind not seeing him."

The tips of Ella's ears flushed pink. "I've gotten used to him being around, I guess. And I know you like spending time with him."

"Sure."

Ella rolled her eyes. "I know you do, Luke. You don't have to lie about it."

"I'm not lying—"

"Is this because of me?"

"What do you mean?"

"Is Finn staying away because of me?" Ella asked. The question threw Luke for a loop and he sat up straighter in his seat, too.

"No, it's not about you at all. Finn likes you fine."

"But he doesn't come over more because of me."

"That's not true," Luke said earnestly. "Finn and I wanted to spend time getting to know each other on our own first. To do things that aren't always related to school and homework and rainbow-striped food, if you know what I mean." He licked his lips.

"Finn is aware you don't much like him, though. I get that you probably think that's no big deal. Why should Finn care, right? But he has feelings, just like you. He wasn't super jazzed to know you banned him from our Friday night dinners, for example."

Ella grimaced. "You told him?"

"He asked about joining us, and I didn't want to lie, so yeah, I told him. He mostly understood. Finn knows I love you and that I want you to be happy, but I don't want him to think I'd stop seeing him because he's not your favorite person, either."

"Would you do that?"

The insecurity in Ella's voice cracked Luke's heart. "I hate to think I'd have to, honey. You're my family, and I would do anything to keep you safe and happy. Finn means a lot to me, though, and I've been trying hard to make sure I don't *have* to choose. I'm not doing a very good job of it, unfortunately."

"What do you mean?"

Luke ran a hand over his mouth. How could he explain something to Ella that he had trouble understanding himself? "I tried to do things with Finn to make him feel good...special. But the opposite happened."

Ella frowned. "How?"

"I made him feel bad instead and like I don't care about him." Luke jammed his lips together in a tight line. "I didn't mean to, but it seems I'm flat-out terrible at being someone's boyfriend. Not that Finn and I really got there."

Ella stayed silent for a long moment. "Did you break up?" she asked at last, her voice small.

"No. But I'm not sure what's going to happen next."

She nodded slowly. "That's why you've been sad."

"Damn, I thought I did a good job of hiding it." Ella's somber demeanor shifted to withering and Luke chuckled past the ache in his chest. "Yeah, okay. That's why I've been feeling down. I told you Finn is important to me. It hurts to think about losing him."

Ella said nothing, and he could almost see the gears turning behind her eyes. "What about when he moves back to Chicago?" she asked.

Luke enfolded one of her hands in his own. "What makes you think he'd do that?"

"He told Gram he could move back there someday."

"Yes, he did," Luke said. "That doesn't mean Finn has any real plans to move, though. He just moved here this past spring and he has a really good job at the hospital. Finn likes living in Boston, too. He could go back to Chicago someday, sure, because his work could take him to anywhere, but I hope he doesn't anytime soon. Just like I hope you and your dad stick around Boston, too."

Ella frowned. "Huh?"

"After your mom left, your dad wanted you to have a place you could call home instead of moving with him to a different Marine base if his orders changed. He knew I didn't have plans to go anywhere, so you came to live here. Your dad could take you with him instead, though."

Ella blinked slowly. "I never thought about it that way. What if *you* wanted to move?"

"Well, we'd have to figure something out. But I don't see that happening anytime soon, El." Luke shrugged. "I have a lot of things keeping me here in Boston. My friends are here, my business, not to mention you and your Gram and Pops."

"What about Finn?"

Luke chewed the inside of his cheek as he struggled to understand. "What about him?"

"If he asked you to move to Chicago with him, would you?"

"I've never thought about it. I'd be surprised if Finn has, either." Realization struck Luke like a slap of cold water. "Is that what you've been thinking? That Finn would leave and I'd go with him?"

"I know you like him, Luke. Maybe you even love him." Ella's lips tightened when Luke moved his head in a jerky nod. "So if Finn moves, you'll go with him, right?"

"I don't have an easy answer for that." Luke gestured at the room around them with his hand. "Leaving here would be something I'd have to *know* was right before I could do it. I wouldn't pick up and leave simply because a man asked me to. No man I'd want to be with would ever ask that of me without talking it through, either."

"Would Finn?"

"If the right thing came along and he thought it was a good time to move, he'd talk to me about it. If we were still together, I mean. But Finn would want to find the best solution for everyone, not only himself."

Ella nodded, and her eyes were suddenly bright with tears. "I got scared," she said. "I thought if you liked him enough, you'd leave, too."

"Is that why you don't want him spending time here?"

"I thought if you didn't see each other a lot, you wouldn't fall in love."

Luke's eyes stung. "Oh, El. Love doesn't work that way. You don't have to spend a lot of time with a person to fall for them. Besides, I'm pretty sure I started falling for Finn the second he opened that silly umbrella for me." *Maybe I'm an insta-love kind of person after all*, he thought.

Luke rubbed Ella's back. "What made you think I'd move away?"

Ella let out a long sigh. "My mom left. And my dad. I thought... I didn't want you to leave, too."

The weight of Luke's sadness nearly overwhelmed him. Ella had always been a happy child. She shared her father's sunny, can-do attitude toward life and was one of the most open and loving people Luke had ever met. Even so, her mother's desertion and the upheaval that marked her early life had left scars behind. They broke Luke's heart any time they showed themselves.

He squeezed Ella's hand. "Your dad is coming back, honey."

"But then he'll leave again!" Ella's tears brimmed over and fell onto her cheeks. She dashed at them with her free hand. "He stays for a while, then he goes away, and it keeps happening over and over again, and I *hate* it."

"Your dad goes away because his job takes him to other places," Luke said, pitching his voice low to soothe her. "You could go with him, if that's what you wanted, and live on base instead of here with me. You're older now and maybe you don't need Gram and Pops or me as much. You and your dad can change things if that's what you want."

"But I do still need you and Gram and Pops. If I didn't live here, I wouldn't get to see you or them."

"You'd see your dad every day, though." Luke hauled in a big breath. The idea of Ella leaving Boston hurt like a physical blow. "I know how much you miss him, and he misses you the same. I hate that you have to spend time away from each other."

Ella wiped at her tears. "Do you want me to go live somewhere else?"

"Never." Luke smiled sadly. "But this isn't about what I want. It's about you. And what *you* need to be happy, El. Your dad, Gram and Pops, me — all we want is what's best for you."

"I don't want to choose," Ella croaked. She sobbed once as Luke pulled her into a hug. "I miss my dad so much, but I don't want to leave here either. I want to stay here with you and Gram and Pops *and* Dad. Can that happen?"

"I don't know." Luke rubbed circles into her back and swallowed his tears. "But let's talk to your dad when he gets home. I know he'll want to make this work better for you and I'll bet he'll have a ton of ideas about how to do that. And let me tell you right now that you can always, always talk to me, okay? No matter where we go or how old we get. Even if we live apart, and even if we hate each other's boyfriends. Or girlfriends, if it turns out you like girls."

"I don't hate Finn," Ella murmured. "He's pretty okay."

"Yeah, he is." Ella sniffled against Luke's shirt. "You're making a mess on me, aren't you?" he asked.

"No, I'm not."

"You're lying. I can tell." The soft laugh that followed eased some of Luke's hurt. "It's okay," he said and gave Ella another squeeze. "I've never cared for this shirt anyway."

Chapter Eighteen

Finn took a seat at the nurses' station in the Emergency Department early on Sunday morning, his body fatigued and his mind distracted as he updated patient notes. He'd spent the previous day tooling around the links and had eaten an excellent dinner afterward with the charity organizers and participants. After driving back to Boston with Chad, he'd dropped off his Zipcar and come straight to the hospital for a lively night shift that only now was beginning to mellow. Through it all, his mind continued circling back to Luke.

Luke had gone too quiet in the last several days. He responded when Finn reached out but didn't initiate texts or calls himself, and Finn heard hesitation in his voice whenever they spoke. Luke sounded anxious and sad, too, and uncertain in a way Finn had never known him to be.

Finn hated that he'd had a hand in that. Hated that he'd made Luke feel awful the last time they were together and still hadn't done a thing to make things right again. He and Luke needed to sit down again and *really* talk, interruptions and the world be damned. More to the point, Finn needed to tell Luke he cared about him. Even if Luke didn't feel the same way, he deserved to know.

Finn rubbed a hand over his face. *Fucking hell, I want to see Luke. Ella too, for that matter, and isn't* that *just the craziest thing?*

"You missed a hell of a ballgame yesterday." Paul took the seat beside Finn. "Though the way you look now makes me wonder just what kind of golfing you were doing. Did you play drinking games in between holes, Finn?"

"Shut up. And, no." Finn chuckled, his eyes still on the monitor. "I probably had three beers all day."

"Then why do you look like hammered garbage?"

"Because I stayed later than I should have in Newport and didn't nap before coming here," Finn replied. "It's my own fault. I should have skipped the dinner and come back to sleep."

"Aw. At least the photographers at the event got your good side. Not that you have a bad side."

Finn paused his work and faced his friend. "What are you talking about?"

Paul eyed him for a moment then drew his phone from his pocket. "You and Chad are on the front of the Arts & Leisure section in today's *Globe*," he said as he tapped the screen. "I figured you'd seen it already."

Finn blinked, sure his friend *had* to be joking until Paul handed him the phone. Sure enough, among other photos taken during the tournament, there were Finn and Chad standing side-by-side, faces rosy from sun exposure and smiles wide.

"I thought the photos were for the MGH newsletter and website," Finn said, mostly to himself. His mouth nearly fell open when he read the caption: *Finn Thomason, MD, with his partner, Chad Lawry.* "What the hell is this?"

Paul shrugged. "Mick and I figured they meant 'golf partner' and didn't really think about how it would read in print." He paused. "Unless you and Chad have something you want to tell us?"

Now Finn's jaw really sagged. "Why would I have anything to tell? You know Chad and I are just friends."

"Sure," Paul agreed, though the tightness around his mouth belied his easy words.

"What, you don't believe me?"

"No, I do," Paul protested. He held his hand out for the phone. "You haven't seemed happy about things with Luke lately, that's all. You've been spending a lot of time with Chad, too, and—"

"So you assumed I'd start screwing around and lie to you about it?" Heat flashed across Finn's cheeks. "Chad's single and easy to hang with, *without* anything else going on. I'm capable of being friends with a guy I'm not sleeping with, you know."

Paul's face fell. "Well, of course. And I didn't say you weren't."

"Then what are you saying?"

"*Nothing*, Finn. Okay, yes, I wondered if things had changed between you and Chad, especially after seeing Luke the other night, but—"

Finn held up a hand. "Wait, what? When did you see Luke?"

"Friday after work, for a few minutes. He stopped by on his way to pick up Ella and gave us the tickets to the game after you said you couldn't go. He seemed down."

"What game?"

"Yesterday's baseball game at Fenway," Paul said slowly. "I sent you photos."

"Yeah, I got them, but I didn't know Luke gave you the tickets."

"I don't understand. Luke said he asked you first and you backed out because of the golf tournament."

"Luke asked me—" Finn paused and thought about his last real conversation with Luke. His stomach fell to his feet. "Luke asked me if I had plans for Saturday and I told him about the golf thing. Shit. I didn't even let him finish his question, Paul. I just told him I was busy."

"Maybe he figured he shouldn't bother asking once he heard you were doing the charity thing." Paul's expression grew troubled. "Luke knows you were golfing with Chad, right?"

"No, but they've never met. I'd be surprised if he had any idea who Chad was."

"I don't know." Paul shook his head. "You brought Chad to the game a couple of weeks ago, remember? Luke had to have seen the two of you flirting on TV while he watched from home."

Finn remembered. He hadn't been flirting with Chad, but he'd never thought about how their interactions might appear to someone on the outside looking in, either. Say, through the filter of a television screen. Hell, if Paul and Mick were questioning Finn's relationship with Chad, who knew what Luke might be thinking? And if he'd read the Arts & Leisure section today ...

Quickly, Finn pulled his phone out, intent on calling Luke, but paused when he noticed the time. It wasn't even six in the morning and Luke was probably still sleeping. He didn't need Finn's messages about another guy. Another guy who wasn't even *that* kind of guy to Finn.

Ugh.

Finn rubbed his face again. "I think I fucked up."

Paul reached over and patted his knee. "Maybe not. Talk to him. You're both off tomorrow, right?"

"Yeah, but he's racing and I'll be sleeping off my shift. I'll pass out on Luke if I go over to his place this afternoon."

"Just don't sit on a couch. Or, fuck, pass out on him! Luke already knows what you're like after a long shift and I doubt he truly minds. Maybe he'll fall asleep with you." Paul waved a hand at Finn. "You're off for a couple of days after tomorrow, so take your man out for dinner and talk it out. *Make* him dinner if he can't get a sitter. No one says you can't be romantically delicious just because there's a kid around, Finn."

"The kid's name is Ella," Finn replied. He imagined Ella's expression at Paul's words and smiled. "She would spurn your romantic advice so hard, you know."

"That's only because she hasn't met me yet."

"She could." Finn shrugged. "Ella'd probably like you. I know she'd like Mick."

"Everyone likes Mick." Paul turned back to his terminal with an exaggerated sigh. "Why don't you and Luke set that up? I'll baby proof the apartment and hide the remote control for the DVR before you bring her over."

Finn barked out a laugh. "Ella's ten, Paul, and her uncle is a tech nerd. Odds are she understands how to work your DVR better than either you or Mick."

Paul's answering laughter soothed him. Finn liked the idea of Ella meeting his friends. Obviously, he and Luke needed to talk first and smooth out the wrinkles that had formed between them over the last several weeks. But Paul had a point. Finn could still romance his man with Ella around — that was what he should have done all along. Separating himself from Luke's family had worked when they were still getting to know each other and Finn had wanted Luke all to himself. However, things were different between them now and it was time to erase the line he'd drawn to separate himself from the rest of Luke's life.

That's why Luke's been coming over, Finn thought abruptly. The afternoon visits to Finn's were Luke's way of staying close while giving Finn what he'd asked for. No wonder he'd looked so crushed by the things Finn had said last week. *Man, I really messed things up.*

Finn glanced down at his phone again and this time didn't stop himself from tapping out a message.

I'm done at 8 today. Can I bring you breakfast?

* * * *

Once more, Finn's insides were a nervous mess as he climbed the winding staircase to Luke's door. He felt charged up, too, like he'd been chugging Red Bull instead of patching people up all night. That energy deflated once Finn stood face to face with Luke and got a good look at him, however. There were shadows under Luke's eyes and he looked pale and fretful in his dark jersey and joggers. Still, he gave Finn a small smile as he closed the door.

"Hey, Finn."

"Hey."

Finn set the bag of bagels on the floor and wrapped Luke up in a hug. Luke went stiff for a moment, but then his arms came up and Finn closed his eyes.

God, it felt good to be near this man again.

"I'm sorry things got so fucked up the last time we saw each other," Finn said, his voice low. "I didn't mean to hurt you, Luke, and I said some things —"

"It's okay." Luke sighed against Finn's neck. "I mean, it's not *okay* but I get why you weren't happy with the way things have been going between us."

"No, you don't." Finn drew back and scanned Luke's face, and he almost winced at the sorrow he read there. "I didn't get a chance to say what I wanted to that afternoon and that's not like me. It was like my brain shorted out and all my filters failed, and I'm so damned sorry that I hurt you." He rubbed Luke's shoulders with his hands. "Can we talk? I'd like a chance to make sense this time, if you'll let me."

"Of course. I'm okay with talking." Luke gave a helpless little shrug. "I'm glad you're here. After the other day, I didn't know what to expect anymore."

What a mess.

Finn stooped so he could grab the bag of bagels from the floor. He slipped an arm over Luke's shoulders after he'd straightened back up. "C'mon. Let's eat so my brain works while we talk."

Luke didn't look any happier. "Finn, no. This can wait until you're rested."

"Yeah, but I'd rather not," Finn said. "I don't like how we left things the other day and I don't want to wait anymore to talk about it." He glanced around then, struck by the apartment's silence.

"Are you here by yourself?" he asked. "Where's Ella?"

"She's out with my parents doing some food shopping for the overnight in Salem," Luke said. He led the way to the kitchen and went straight to the cabinet for coffee cups. "Pops is making club sandwiches for dinner tonight and, of course, I don't have the right kind of turkey, cheese *or* bread."

They discussed Luke's race strategy over bagels and cream cheese with fresh fruit from Luke's pantry and a carafe of coffee. Finn knew they were running on borrowed time — Ella and her grandparents would soon be back and they'd all head north to Salem. Still, Finn hesitated talking about the heavy topics for a while longer so he could simply enjoy being around Luke again.

Luke had different ideas, of course, and soon pushed back his empty plate. He met Finn's eye. "Who is that guy from the baseball game?"

Finn set down his coffee cup. "Chad is a friend of mine. Well, a friend of friends, to be more accurate. I met him through Paul and Mick."

"You're seeing him, right?" Luke exhaled through his nose. "We never talked about seeing other people and that's fine. I guess I'd want to know about it, though. Is that weird?"

"No, but —"

"I saw you with him on the street a couple of Fridays ago near Two Guys and a Grille. I recognized him from the game." Luke said. His expression grew flinty, as if he were bracing himself for bad news. "You guys looked friendly, then the paper today... Well, I wondered who he was to you."

Oh, wow.

Finn almost checked to make sure the floor hadn't dropped out from under his feet. "Why didn't you say something before now?"

"You didn't mention him, and I didn't know what to make of that. I had no idea how to bring it up without coming off like a possessive asshole." Luke ran a hand over his mouth and lowered his gaze. "It didn't feel right getting in your face over someone we'd never even talked about."

"Damn, I'm sorry." Finn put his hand on Luke's arm where it lay on the table. "Chad's a friend, Luke. It never occurred to me I'd need to tell you about him specifically because he's just a guy I know and sometimes hang with. He's unattached and doesn't work weird hours, and that makes it easy." Finn swallowed at Luke's nod. "We're friendly, but there's nothing going on between him and me."

Luke met Finn's eyes and everything about him screamed of weariness. "I started thinking you'd gotten tired of waiting around after I canceled on you so many times."

"No." Finn frowned. "It sucked that you didn't have time for me, but I understood why it was happening. As far as waiting around, okay, I didn't love feeling like that. That's what I tried to tell you the other day. I wanted to talk about it, though, not stop seeing each other. It'd take more than some canceled dates for me to ghost."

Luke pursed his lips. "I know I shouldn't have assumed, but I couldn't help thinking about what happened with other guys I dated and seeing it happen with you," he said. "Every time I canceled, you seemed to slip a little further away."

"I know what you mean," Finn said. "I felt like we were slipping too and I didn't like it. I should have done a better job saying that the other day. I wish you'd told me how you were feeling, though. About Chad and how you felt about the way things have been going between you and me." He worked at keeping the hurt out of his voice. "I know you have Simon, but I want you to talk to me too, Luke."

"What do you mean?"

"You go to Simon with the serious stuff, and I get that. He's your best friend, and his opinion is important to you."

Luke furrowed his brow as he considered Finn's words. "I go to Simon because I need advice about *you*, Finn. He and Gillian listen and try their best to keep me from going off the rails and usually do a pretty good job," Luke said. "I'll bet Paul does that for you when you need it, right?"

Finn blinked, caught by the observation. "Actually, yeah. I never thought about it that way, but he's always there for boyfriend advice." He bit back a smile at the way Luke's cheeks pinked.

"Right." Luke cleared his throat. "There's nothing I'd tell Simon that I wouldn't tell you. As long as you wanted to hear it."

"What does that mean? Ella-type stuff? You can talk to me about that too, Luke." Guilt prickled at him as uncertainty flickered over Luke's face. "You can. I wasn't super enthusiastic about being the third wheel in the beginning, and I know Ella hasn't exactly been a fan of mine, but I'm good with all of it now."

Luke's face fell. "You've never been a third wheel, Finn. I'm sorry you thought that you were." His soft voice made Finn ache.

"I think I did it to myself, to tell the truth." Finn scooted his chair closer and slipped his arms around Luke. "I wanted distance from that part of your life because I wasn't ready for it, and you tried to give that to me. I don't feel that way anymore and things are different now. *I'm* different. And I'm ready for more. I think we both need more than lunch and sex when our schedules line up, too. Which I *love* having with you, by the way, so please never stop." He smiled at the gleam in Luke's eye.

"I like those afternoons too," Luke said. "But you're right. Things are different now for both of us. So let's work on it together and figure out what we want."

"What, right now?" Finn's heart lightened at the way Luke narrowed his eyes at him.

"No, you nerd. Not right now, but going forward." He paused again and his expression became melancholy.

"Ella's okay with you, Finn, I promise," Luke said. "More than okay, I think. Pretty sure she actually likes you, though she might not admit it." He ran his fingers over his coffee cup. "We've been talking about some of her feelings the last few days. She's been struggling with Pete being away, and my meeting you threw her for a loop. Not because she didn't like you, but because she didn't know how to handle you. I told you once that sometimes Ella needs more from us because of the things she went through when her mom left, and some of that stuff has come into play here."

Finn nodded. Though his heart grew heavy for Ella, he couldn't help feeling relieved Luke was talking to him about it and sharing some of the weight of responsibility. Luke carried that burden alone far too often.

"I can't say I understand, exactly, but I'm listening," Finn said. "I hear you, Luke. And I want to figure this out. Or start over again from the beginning, if that's what it takes."

Luke's lips quirked up. "We already started over, Finn. Is a third do-over even a thing?"

"Totally a thing if we need it to be," Finn said. "We can start over as many times as we need to get it right. I'll even take you across the Common and stand under the awning at Paul and Mick's again, though that's going to have to wait a couple of days. I'm too fucking tired to walk over there today."

He smiled at Luke's laugh and couldn't resist kissing him. He raised his hands and cradled Luke's face in his palms, each brush of their lips soothing. Lazy pleasure lapped through Finn when they came up for air.

"What do you say?" he asked. "Think we're worth starting over again? Because I do."

Luke flashed a brilliant smile. "Yeah. I do, too."

Finn moved in for another kiss but the front door opened, so he settled for a quick peck instead. He and Luke exchanged wry smiles at Ella's hollering.

"Luke!" She rushed into the kitchen and her eyes went round when she caught sight of Finn. "Oh, hey! I didn't know you were coming over."

"I didn't know myself until about an hour ago," Finn replied. He and Luke sat back and a lovely, fond feeling came over Finn at Ella's smile. "How're you, Ella? Want a bagel? There's a cinnamon crunch one with your name on it and honey cream cheese."

Ella's face lit up. "Zomahgod. Yes, please, and thank you," she said, her tone fervent.

Finn felt more than a little smug at her unbridled delight, but Luke's satisfied gaze when he caught Finn's eye warmed him even more.

Finn chatted with all the Ryans while Ella ate her bagel, and he couldn't help noticing how closely she watched him and Luke. Ella's expression was gentler than usual and she didn't roll her eyes at him or turn away or any of the things she might have done to let him know his presence was an afterthought.

By the time Luke and his family headed out for Salem, Finn felt lighter than he had in days. He'd promised to come back the next day — after his next shift and Luke's race — so they could eat dinner with Ella and he and Luke could keep talking and putting things back together.

Finn's Sunday night shift passed in a blur of patients and surgeries, and the sun had risen by the time he headed home to sleep. He'd have driven to Salem in a flash if he could, but he settled for sending a message to Luke instead.

Rock your race, big guy.

He smiled when his phone buzzed almost immediately with Luke's reply.

Thanks, Doc. Ella says hi.

It was almost two in the afternoon when Finn dragged himself out of bed. He showered and dressed in jeans and a navy cable-knit sweater, but he was still bleary-eyed as he contemplated shaving. Finn's desire for coffee was so strong he almost ignored his phone when it buzzed on the nightstand. However, Luke's name on the screen put a grin on his face and he scooped it up.

"Hey, I was just thinking of you! How'd it go today?"

A strange pause followed. Finn heard bursts of background noises that sounded oddly familiar, and as the pause stretched out, he drew breath to speak again. He fell silent as an unexpected voice spoke on the other end of the line.

"Finn?"

Finn went still. "Ella?"

"Can you come here?"

"Where?" A nameless dread crept over Finn. "Where are you, Ella? Where's Luke?"

"We're downstairs where you work? A car hit us and, um, the ambulance brought us here. Luke says this is your hospital."

Goosebumps rose on Finn's skin. Ella's voice sounded small compared to the buzz around her—noises Finn recognized as hospital staff at work—but he heard her. She sounded scared.

"I'm coming." Finn's drowsiness disappeared utterly. He grabbed his hospital ID and wallet from the dresser and dashed toward the door, stopping only to slip on his running shoes. "I'm across the street at my place and I'm coming right now. Are you and Luke okay?"

"Luke got hurt. He hit his head and there's blood. The ambulance guys put a thing on his neck."

Cervical collar, Finn thought and swept his keys from the hook on the wall. Collars were standard protocol for trauma victims transported from a scene, but it had to look alarming to someone with no understanding of EMS.

"That's to keep Luke from moving too much," Finn told Ella. He rushed out of the door and locked it behind him with a shaky hand.

"Um. That's what the nurse said, but I…it looks like it hurts him."

Finn pressed his lips together at the waver in Ella's voice. He took off running for the front gate and kept his voice easy. "I know it looks weird, but it's not hurting him, I promise."

He kept up the chatter as he moved, as much to center himself as to reassure Ella. Finn covered the distance it normally took ten minutes to walk in five, even with afternoon traffic, and he was still talking breathlessly when he dashed into the ED. He headed for the section reserved for acute care.

"I'm here, Ella. Looking for you guys now." He scanned the glass-fronted triage rooms and spotted a small figure in a purple jacket and dark jeans almost at once.

There.

Ella stood outside the door of a triage room not far from Finn. She seemed dwarfed in size by the ebb and flow of personnel moving around her and something in Finn's chest twisted.

"Ella!"

He cut off the call the instant she turned toward him and he ran to her side. Ella lowered the phone as Finn squatted down to her level. Her eyes were wide, the color gone from her cheeks, and she looked spaced out and lost. Finn reached over and grasped her free hand.

"Jesus, Ella. Are you okay? Have you seen one of the doctors or nurses yet?"

"M'okay." Ella curled her fingers tight around Finn's. A rusty smudge above her lip and several spots on her jacket told Finn she'd recently had a bloody nose. "One of the ambulance guys checked me after they got us out of the car. He said I was okay and could ride with him and Luke."

"Thank God."

Finn cut a glance at the triage room and his chest went tight. Luke lay on the bed, his face pale above the bulky neck brace and bloodied from a laceration on his left temple. A nurse was cutting his shirt off to allow the doctor to perform an exam and his eyelids were at half-mast. Luke's focus fixed on Ella, as if he were afraid to look away. After several blinks, his attention shifted to Finn and his expression changed immediately, becoming almost pleading.

"She's okay, Luke. Ella's okay," Finn called out, his voice pitched loud enough to cut through the din. He knew he'd answered Luke's unspoken question when Luke clenched his eyes closed.

"Finn."

A familiar voice tore Finn's attention from Luke, and he noticed only then that Paul was the doctor palpating Luke's torso. Finn gave him a quick nod and turned back to Ella.

"That's my friend, Dr. Gallagher," Finn told her, "and the nurse's name is Salena. I'm going to go and talk to them for a second so we know how Luke's doing, okay?"

Ella eyes went even wider. "Can I stay?"

"Of course you can," Finn replied. Carefully, he guided her to the left side of the doorframe. "Stay here by the side so no one bumps you. I will be right over there and I'll come back for you." He waited for Ella's nod and gave her hand another quick squeeze before he stood.

Finn crossed the triage room in two steps, his focus on Luke's pained expression. He jammed his phone into his pocket and took hold of Luke's hand. "Hey," he said, his voice as calm as he could make it.

Tears stood in Luke's eyes when he opened them. "Hey," he croaked and clutched at Finn's fingers.

Finn's pulse thundered in his ears. "I know, baby," he murmured. He bent and gently cupped Luke's cheek with his other hand. "Take it easy for me, all right?"

"Is she okay? I can't—" Luke clamped his lips shut. His chest hitched and Finn shushed him as the tears slipped down the sides of Luke's face.

"Ella is fine, Luke. She's totally fine. EMS checked her out before they brought you in." Finn wiped at Luke's tears with his fingers and forced himself to focus on Paul. "What have we got?" he asked.

"Vitals are steady, and no sign of fractures or internal bleeding," Paul replied. "Ella needs an exam, but EMS said the impact to Luke's vehicle was focused on the front driver's side and that's why he's a lot more banged up."

Finn glanced back down at Luke while Paul continued.

"Beyond the facial lac, he's groggy and emotional and had some difficulty focusing during the cognitive assessment. No loss of consciousness, but EMS found vomit at the scene. He's also suffering from vertigo."

Finn licked his lips. Luke blinked at him blearily, trying to focus despite the haze that clouded his eyes. "Concussion?" Finn guessed. He knew the signs as well as Paul.

"Yes." Paul waited until he had Finn's attention again before he continued. "I'll suture the lac and we'll keep him under observation."

"I'll get someone to give Ella an exam," Finn said. "Salena, see if you can find Luke's wallet when you get him changed, please—we'll need his insurance info for the paperwork." He glanced back to Luke when he made a plaintive noise. "What's wrong?"

"You do it," Luke said, his tone weary. "You do the exam, okay? Ella knows you, Finn, an' you'll take care of her."

Finn nodded at once, even though a tiny part of him balked at leaving Luke. The idea of letting him go for even a few minutes made Finn's insides squirm. He understood then that Luke could only be going through the same thing right now, looking at Ella and not knowing if she was okay. Worse, Luke couldn't even sit up, let alone walk over to check on her himself.

Finn squeezed Luke's fingers. "Okay. I'll do that while Paul stitches you up."

"We'll do that right now." Paul asked Salena for lidocaine to numb the wound and a suture kit, then turned back to his patient. "I'd try not to screw up that sexy hair of yours, but I'd say that deed's been done. You're a mess, girl."

The fear weighing Finn down lightened as Luke's lips twitched in a tiny smile. Finn ran a thumb over his knuckles. "We'll come right back, okay?"

A familiar worried line worked its way between Luke's eyebrows again. Finn knew from the way he pursed his lips that Luke wanted to say more. He waited, unsure if he should push, but Luke stayed quiet and the silence dragged out for several moments before he nodded. "Okay."

The apprehension in Luke's eyes followed Finn as he turned back to Ella, but the moment Salena twitched the privacy curtains closed, Ella's tense expression crumpled.

Finn pulled the glass slider shut behind him and got down on one knee, taking her hands in his. "Hey, what's wrong? Are you hurting?"

"No," she whispered. "What's wrong with Luke? Is he okay?" Finn's heart dropped. Ella was trembling from head to toe, no doubt from plain old fear on top of one hell of an adrenaline crash.

"Ella, Luke is doing just fine. The cut on his forehead needs to be closed up, and Dr. Gallagher and Salena are taking care of that right now. Once they're done, we can go back in there, all right?"

Ella nodded, but the dam had broken and her emotions got the best of her. Finn climbed to his feet as she burst into quiet tears. Without a word, he led her into the next empty triage room and guided her to a chair. He found some tissues on the supply cart and squatted down beside her, talking softly and rubbing Ella's back while she put her face in her hands and cried. Her tears tapered off after a few minutes and when she raised her head, her expression was tired but much calmer.

Finn held up a tissue. "Better?"

"Yeah." Ella sighed and blew her nose. "It felt like my head was gonna explode."

"I hate that." Finn's heart hurt in a nice way at her almost-smile. He handed Ella another tissue so she could wipe her eyes some more.

"Is Luke really okay?"

"Yes." Finn took her hand again. "I told you that Dr. Gallagher is my friend but he's Luke's friend, too. He'll take good care of him."

"I've never seen Luke cry before." Ella swallowed and Finn's heart squeezed. Watching Luke fall apart had taken a toll on them both.

"I know that must have been scary," he said. "Dr. Gallagher and I think Luke has a concussion. That can happen when a person hits their head hard enough to shake up their brain. The concussion is making Luke dizzy and it probably made him cry, too. If you want, you can help us keep an eye on him after he's stitched up and make sure he's okay."

Finn smiled at Ella's eager nod. Giving her permission to help with Luke's care was exactly what she needed.

"Luke asked me to look you over and double check the EMS guys did their job right," he said then. "You okay with doing that while we wait to see him?"

"Yeah, okay." Ella glanced around the triage room. "In here?"

"Yes." Finn tipped his head toward the bed. "Wait right over there and I'll ask one of the nurses to help us. I'm going to close this curtain so you can change into a gown."

Ella groaned. "Oh, crap. I'll get my own clothes back, right?"

"Is there anything weird on them? Besides the little bit of blood I saw?"

"Well, my shirt says 'Stay Weird'…so, yes?"

Finn chuckled. "That figures. Don't worry—you'll get them back."

He took a few minutes to request help at the nurses' station, then hunted down the attending physician on duty to give her a heads-up he'd be performing the exam. Ella was seated on the bed in a pediatric gown and red striped socks and chatting with Ashley, one of the nurses, by the time Finn returned to the triage room. She looked relaxed as Ashley measured her blood pressure, but relief streaked across her face the moment she caught sight of Finn.

"How is Miss Ryan, Nurse?" Finn asked. He made his tone grave and winked at Ella's snort of laughter.

Ashley smiled. "Vital signs are good, Doctor."

She handed the chart she'd started to Finn, which he scanned and set aside. Finn carefully pushed Ella's hair back over her shoulders so he could palpate her neck.

"How's your head feel, Ella?" he asked. "Any aching?"

"Not really," she replied. "Kind of tired from all the emotions."

Finn nodded. "I feel you." He pressed her trapezius muscles where the neck met the shoulder. "Sore here?"

"A little. Kind of like the time I went to Six Flags and rode everything twice."

"Gotcha. C'mon down from there for a sec so I can see how you move." Finn helped Ella off the bed, then checked the range of motion of her neck, back and extremities and was pleased to note she moved with ease.

"You had a nosebleed earlier, right?" He helped Ella back onto the bed. "How'd that happen?"

Ella grimaced. "I smacked myself in the face with the seatbelt when the firemen came to get us out."

"Yikes." Finn traced a faint bruise on the right side of her nose with his fingers. "Did that take a long time?"

"Yeah. Luke made me wait in my seat because there were too many people and cars around."

"I see." Finn fought off a chill at Ella's words. He held up an ophthalmoscope and switched on the light in the instrument. "I'm going to check your eyes."

"This always makes me see spots," Ella complained. She went quiet as Finn examined her pupils and checked the optic nerve for swelling.

"Looking into your eyes like this gives me good info about your health," Finn said. "Plus, I can see your brains." He smiled as Ella cracked up.

"Get out!"

"Pupils equal, round and reactive, fundus background normal," he said to Ashley.

Ella sniffed. "Finn, how come your hair is wet?"

Finn blinked and brought a hand to his hair. *Oh, yep, still damp.* "Um. I was in the shower right before you called and I ran over here. I forgot all about it." His cheeks heated when Ashley caught his eye and grinned.

"It doesn't look too bad," Ella said. She sounded amused. "Nothing like Luke's in the morning."

"I'm more concerned with making sure you guys are okay than the way I look, anyway." Finn patted the pillow. "Lie down for me, please. Let's make sure the seat belt didn't hurt you."

"Is Luke going to have to stay in the hospital?"

Finn put a hand on Ella's back as she stretched out. "I don't know," he said. "With a concussion like his, we watch and wait to make sure the patient's symptoms don't get worse."

"And Dr. Gallagher does a good job?" Ella snickered when Finn palpated her belly. "No tickling!"

"Sorry, my bad. Yes, Dr. Gallagher does a very good job. If I were sick, I'd want him to treat me."

Ella hummed. "I think you're both pretty good."

Fifteen minutes later, Ella was dressed again and scarfing down water and a protein bar from the stash in Finn's locker. She appeared a whole lot steadier by the time he brought her to see Luke, but Finn couldn't say the same for himself. He'd never been in this position before, with people he cared about under ED treatment. Examining Ella had soothed some of his stress, but he felt useless being unable to doctor Luke, too.

Relief flooded through him as he scanned Luke. The cervical collar had been removed and his face cleaned of blood, and a neat white bandage covered the laceration on his temple. An IV line was running into Luke's left hand, and though he was far too pale over the blue and white hospital gown, Finn thought he was the most beautiful thing he'd seen in a long time. Luke's smile at seeing them brought a lump the size of a boulder to Finn's throat.

He'll be okay, Finn told himself and worked hard not to totally lose his shit.

Chapter Nineteen

"Hey. C'mere, girl." Luke held out a hand. Every inch of him hurt, but seeing Ella eased the crush of fear in his chest. He swallowed when she moved to clamber up on to the bed. "Um, wait a sec—"

"It's okay," Finn said.

Ella shot him a questioning look. "Really?"

"Really." Finn flashed her a small smile. "But do me a favor and be gentle, Ella. I'm sure he won't admit it, but I'll bet Luke's head is killing him." Finn helped Ella up onto the bed, then closed the privacy curtains while she gave Luke a long, careful hug.

Luke bit his lip against another swell of tears. The effort sent a terrible ache through his head and made his stomach roil, and he blew out a shaky sigh after Ella finally sat back. She held Luke's hand tight and he knew just from looking at her that she'd been crying. He sought out Finn's gaze again.

"She's okay?"

"Yes." Finn rested a hand on Luke's shoulder. "Nurse Ashley and I checked Ella out. She's bruised from the seatbelt and sore from being tossed around but perfect otherwise. I'd like to write an order for Tylenol. Ella said she's not allergic and she'll feel even more sore soon."

"Yeah, absolutely." Luke grimaced. He thought he and Ella had been talking about lunch when things had gone all to hell, but his head was all muzzy. "We didn't eat."

"I had a snack while we were waiting for you," Ella piped in.

"She ate my last chocolate CLIF Bar." Finn made a sad face in Ella's direction and she giggled. "I can go over to the cafeteria and grab her a sandwich, too."

"Okay." Luke's stomach lurched again. A chill passed over him and though he tried to hide his shiver, Finn laid the backs of his fingers against Luke's neck.

"What's wrong?" he asked.

"Still feel sick." Luke closed his eyes. "Paul said maybe I'd need a CT."

"What's a see-tee?" Ella asked.

"CT is short for computed tomography, and it's a special kind of X-ray," Finn replied. His voice sounded tenser now, and Luke sensed he was trying to keep things light for Ella. "Dr. Gallagher may want to take one of Luke's head to make sure everything's okay in there. You don't want his brains running out of his ears, right? Because ew."

"I see you've got everything under control, Dr. Thomason." That was Paul's voice.

Luke opened his eyes as Paul stepped around the privacy curtain.

"You must be Ella," Paul said with a friendly smile. He stepped up beside Finn and extended a hand to her. "I'm Dr. Gallagher, a friend of your uncle's and Finn's."

"Yep, Finn told me who you are." Ella shook his hand, then put it back over Luke's.

"Great!" Paul beamed. "I'm going to ask Luke some questions so we can see how he's doing."

He asked Luke to identify the day of the week and the year and to repeat the words 'table, dog, green,' all easy tasks that somehow made Luke's head hurt.

"What city are you in, Luke?" Paul asked.

"Boston."

"And what hospital?"

"Finn's."

Paul's lips twitched. "Can you be more specific?"

Luke sighed. "Mass General."

"That's right. What were you doing before you were brought to the hospital?"

"I ran a race today. And I was driving." Luke swallowed down a bubble of fear, and his voice wavered when he spoke again. "We had an accident." Finn rubbed his shoulder gently.

"That's right," Paul said. "Can you tell me the president's name?"

"Not without swearing."

"Fair enough." Paul chuckled. "Do you remember the three words I asked you to repeat earlier?"

"Um." It was a long moment before the simple pattern came back to Luke. "Table, dog, chair. No, wait. Table, dog, green." His stomach churned again and he swallowed.

Paul nodded. "Good. You seem steadier than when you were first brought in, so let's see how it goes for now."

"Okay." Luke licked his lips. He'd already learned that gritting his teeth against the nausea just made him vomit quicker and sitting up was out of the question.

"Ella, I wanted to tell Finn and you that we may need to take Luke upstairs to get a look at the inside of his head."

"The computed tomography thing?"

"Yep, the computed tomography thing. He vomited again while you were examining Ella," Paul said to Finn.

Finn nodded and Luke thought he went a little pale. "I figured as much." He exchanged a glance with Paul, who quickly rounded the bed to help Ella down.

God, Luke hated being stuck in this bed. And throwing everything at Finn all at once...*so* not what he'd had in mind to give Finn and Ella more time together. Luke's breath hitched and Finn bent close.

"Can you take Ella with you to the caf?" Luke asked.

Finn took hold of his hand around the IV line. "You sure?"

"Yeah. I don't want her to watch if I hurl again." Luke blinked. The edges of the world went soft as a powerful fatigue slipped over him.

"Shit, okay." Finn sighed, his whole face tight and unhappy. "I'm sorry you feel so bad."

"Me too."

"Who should I call for Ella? Your parents? Simon because he's closer?"

Luke stared, thrown by the question for a moment, but then he understood. Ella couldn't just hang out here while Luke was under observation. She looked stressed and, no wonder, with Luke such a wreck. *Why didn't I think of that?*

"Mom n' Pops were stayin' over in Salem, but yeah, they need to know," he said and tried to pull his thoughts together. "Um. Simon drove back ahead of us. He can help if he's home."

"Okay. Ella still has your phone. We'll make some calls while we eat." Finn went still when Luke squeezed his fingers.

"Ella's okay, right?" Luke whispered. He knew he'd asked that more than once, but the car was smashed and Ella had cried and Luke was too fucked up to comfort her.

Finn cupped Luke's cheek so gently. "She was worried about you and stressed out from the accident," he said, his voice low. Of course, he knew what Luke was asking. "I let her cry for a little while until she felt better." Finn smoothed Luke's hair off his forehead, and that careful touch eased Luke as much as Finn's words. "I'll get some more food into her and explain everything so she doesn't feel like she's in the dark."

"Okay. She'll like that." Luke blinked against another wave of exhaustion and held Finn's hand tight. "Thanks, Finn. I'm sorry to dump all this on you."

Finn's throat worked. "I'll take good care of her," he promised.

Ella came around the bed to stand beside Finn and Luke gave her a smile. "Finn's gonna get you something to eat."

"What about you?" she asked, her faced pinched.

Luke saw spots of blood on her jacket and suppressed another shiver. "I'll be here when you get back, El. I'm not going anywhere."

Finn gave Luke's fingers a final squeeze then straightened up. He and Ella exchanged a glance and the weight on Luke's heart lightened some more at their shared smile.

"Let's go grab some food, kid," Finn said.

* * * *

"Luke."

Someone squeezed Luke's shoulder, the touch light compared to the fierce ache in his head.

"Can you open your eyes for me, Luke?"

Not someone. Finn.

Luke peeled his eyelids open with a soft groan and squinted against what seemed like way too much light. The light made his head hurt more. He'd been right, though. Finn bent over him, his smile sweet.

"Hey, handsome," he said, his gaze sharp as it moved over Luke's face. "How're you doing?"

"Hurts," Luke mumbled.

"I'm sorry." Finn leaned over Luke and touched something on the mattress beside him. "You fell asleep while Ella and I were eating, and Paul held off medicating you in favor of rest. I'll talk to your nurse about getting you some pain relief. Keep your eyes open for me, all right?"

"M'kay. Where's El?" Luke tried to keep the tension out of his voice. He knew Finn wouldn't have left Ella alone. But she was nowhere to be seen, and a ball of worry formed in Luke's gut. "She okay?"

"Yep, she's good." Finn rubbed Luke's shoulder. "She fell asleep after lunch and woke up when Simon got here. He took her to change her clothes and stretch her legs, and I told them I'd wake you up. They should be back pretty soon."

He leaned over Luke again, and this time came back with a small plastic cup. It occurred to Luke that his mouth was unbearably dry. He raised his hands for it, and grimaced when the IV line pulled. Finn's fingers on Luke's wrist steadied him as he brought the cup to his lips.

"Go slow. I don't want you throwing up again because that will hurt like a bitch."

Everything already hurts, Luke thought. Even his hair hurt, for God's sake, and his head throbbed with an intensity that made him want to cry. Still, the water cooled his throat and Finn's voice sounded nice as he encouraged Luke to take small sips.

The glass door behind him slid open and a cute, dark-haired woman wearing purple scrubs came to stand by the bed. Luke thought he knew her when she smiled. "Hi, Mr. Ryan. I'm Salena, and I'm sorry I ruined your shirt earlier."

Luke managed a faint grin. "That's how I know you." She'd cut off his jersey and helped Paul get Luke out of his shoes and joggers and into a hospital gown. No great loss—Luke was sure there'd been blood and worse on everything.

Finn gave Luke's shoulder another squeeze. "Luke's ready for some pain relief," he said to Salena. "He's had about six ounces of water, and kept it down so far."

"That's good." Salena moved to check Luke's chart.

She said something else, probably to Finn, but Luke lost the thread of their conversation because the door slid open again and Ella appeared with Simon right behind her. Her bloodstained clothes were gone and she was wearing a pink and black tracksuit, and her face brightened with a big smile.

"You're awake," she exclaimed, her voice quiet.

Luke's heart squeezed so tight it hurt. Ella glanced at Finn, who waved her in, and crossed the room. Simon gave her a leg up onto the bed and leaned over to kiss Luke's cheek, his features worried.

"Jesus, Luke. Are you okay?" Simon's eyes were red when he pulled back.

"Yeah," Luke squeezed the hand Simon slipped into his.

"What the hell happened?"

Luke shook his head once and stilled as his headache bloomed, growing exponentially worse. He closed his eyes. "Ow," he whispered. Simon's fingers tightened around his, and Ella's warm palm came to rest on his chest. Luke's stomach lurched.

"Shh." Finn rubbed his fingers along the side of Luke's neck. "Salena's going to give you some Tylenol, Luke, just hang on. Are you going to be sick?"

It took Luke a moment to answer. "No."

"Okay. Breathe for me, nice and easy."

He sensed movement around him—hushed voices and rustling—and he heard the slider open again. But Luke did as Finn told him and worked on breathing in and out.

"On a scale of one to ten, how's your pain, Luke?" That was Paul again, his voice softer than usual.

"Um. Eight." Luke didn't know how to put a number on what he was feeling, but fucking hell, his head ached.

Slowly, slowly, the throbbing eased. Luke slit his eyelids open and found Finn and Ella watching him, their tension evident, while Paul made notes on Luke's chart. Salena was working at one of the carts and Simon hadn't moved from Luke's other side. He looked close to losing it.

Paul glanced back up at Luke. "Better?"

"Getting there," Luke muttered. He aimed a weak smile at Ella. "Sorry."

"That's okay," she said. "Finn and Dr. Gallagher said you'd have a headache when you woke up."

Luke checked her over carefully and saw she looked tired but otherwise okay. "You feel all right?"

"Yup. Finn gave me some stuff after lunch. Same as you, but pills."

"You're in much better shape than your uncle," Finn told her. He turned an apologetic look on Luke. "Obviously, it's your family's decision, but I think Ella's fine to go to school tomorrow. I'd like her to take a day or two off from anything sports-related, though. She may experience some muscle soreness and while the Tylenol will help, she needs rest."

"Okay." Luke stopped himself from nodding at the last second.

Finn turned to Simon. "I wrote everything down for you and Luke's parents. And you can take some more pills later tonight and tomorrow before school, as needed," he said to Ella.

Paul stepped forward to examine Luke, which meant Finn had to move away, and Luke immediately missed his touch. The headache thumped behind his eyes, but he answered Paul's questions again and tried not to wince at the poking and prodding, though he almost balked when Paul shone a light at him.

"Outside of what I'm sure is a spectacular headache, you're improved from a couple of hours ago." Paul folded his hands in front of him. "I'd like to keep monitoring you for a while longer. I know you're not eager to eat, but you need something in your system. The IV's kept you hydrated, but you expended a lot of energy racing today and your body needs to refuel."

Luke stifled a yawn. "Okay. I can do that."

"I won't admit you overnight if you keep improving," Paul said, "and Finn wants to keep an eye on you if you are released. You should plan to take several days off from work and take it easy after you go back. The nature of your work puts stress on your brain, and you'll need to limit your thinking activities. Right now, rest is your main priority."

"We'll make sure he does that," Simon said, his tone firm. Luke saw him exchange a glance with Finn.

"I'll be back to check on you," Paul told Luke, then smiled at Ella and stuck out his hand again. "I hope I see you again very soon, Miss Ella, and definitely *outside* of this hospital."

The little room seemed hushed after Paul and Finn stepped out and closed the slider behind them, but Simon drew the guest chair over to the bed and sat. His blue gaze was almost too intense.

"What can I do?" he asked Luke.

"You're doing it," Luke replied. "Thanks for being here."

Simon sighed and took Luke's hand again. "Don't be dumb. Where the hell else would I be?"

"Having fun with Miles on your day off?" Luke smiled at Simon's snort, but he couldn't help feeling guilty. He didn't have time for days off right now and being forced to stay home would create work for the people in his life. "You and Gilly are gonna get stuck with a lot of extra projects, Simon. I'm sorry."

"We'll work it out," Simon replied. "You concentrate on keeping your head in one piece and let us handle the rest."

"Okay." Luke closed his eyes again. "Thanks for bringing El some new clothes."

"Of course," Simon said. "Finn told me she'd want to change. I, um, told your parents to take their time coming back after he said you were okay, too. Didn't want them speeding." He paused and Luke squeezed his hand. "They said they'd be here by dinnertime," Simon continued after another beat, "and they'll bring food to your place. Probably so I don't stuff Ella full of pizza and Coke."

Luke opened his eyes at Ella's grumble.

"I love pizza and Coke."

"Too bad, squirt. Extra salad for you tonight." Simon wrinkled his nose at Ella and she huffed, but Luke knew from the way her lips twitched it was all in jest.

"I brought clothes for you, too," Simon said to Luke. He gestured to a bag in the corner. "Finn said your clothes were trashed and you'd want more coverage than a hospital gown when you got out of here."

"Thank you." Luke was beginning to feel tired again. "The nurses put everything together over there with my shoes. Fu—crap, I don't know where our stuff from the rental car is. Ella had a bag and so did I," Luke frowned and tried to remember where he'd last seen everything.

"No doubt everything's still locked in the car at the towing yard," Simon said. "Don't worry—I'll track it all down."

"The rental agreement is in my wallet with Finn," Luke murmured. "We were near the Science Museum. We had the light and I went to merge onto Storrow Drive." He shivered and the slider opened and closed.

"We were moving and… I don't know what happened." Goosebumps rose on Luke's skin. A remembered blur of sound and motion washed over him. Ella screaming. A bone-jarring crunch and a fracture web splashing across the car's windshield, and Luke feeling trapped in his seat. His head spinning so badly he didn't know which way was up. "I never even saw the car that hit us," he whispered.

"It was so loud," Ella said. "Just bam and bam and cars beeping. You told me everything was going to be okay and not to worry and to stay in the car." The wonder in her voice made Luke feel sick all over again.

"The first car ran a light," Finn said.

Luke opened his eyes and found Finn watching him, his jaw tense. He rested a hand on Luke's shoulder, and the touch centered him instantly.

"The cops are here to follow up and I talked to one of the officers who processed the scene," Finn said. "The first impact pushed you into a car traveling in front of you and yours ended up sideways. Then the driver behind you couldn't stop in time and plowed right into your door." Finn let out a big gust of air. He appeared shaken, now that Luke was looking. "You okay to answer questions and give them a statement?"

"Sure." Luke licked his lips. "I, um, gotta take a leak."

Finn rubbed his arm. "I'll help you."

Luke dragged his gaze back to Ella's. "How about you go home with Simon, honey? No sense in staying here when you could be comfortable. You'll have more fun with Gram and Pops anyway, and they'll be really happy to see you're okay."

"But what about you?" Ella asked.

"I'll be here," Finn replied even before Luke could formulate an answer. "I'm not working for a couple of days and I don't mind waiting with Luke." He worried his lips with his teeth and glanced back at Luke. "It could be late when we get out of here, though, and the stairs in your building are a nightmare."

The thought of climbing three flights of a winding staircase with a head that felt stuffed full of sawdust and rocks made Luke swallow down another wave of nausea. "Ugh."

"Maybe come back to my place tonight?" Finn asked. "It's closer to the hospital and you'll be tired by the time we get out of here. Plus, no crazy stairs." He turned to Ella. "You think that's okay?"

Luke watched with wonder as Ella's features relaxed and something unspoken passed between her and Finn. She nodded. "Yeah. That's a good idea."

Finn nodded, too. "Call me if you want to talk, and we'll text Simon and your Gram later to let you know what's going on."

"Don't I get a say?" Luke teased.

Ella scoffed. "No way, dude. Not 'til Finn and Dr. Gallagher say you're okay."

She climbed off the bed while Finn took Simon aside to discuss Tylenol doses and exchange phone numbers. Luke noticed Ella's expression growing uncertain, and he wrapped a hand around her elbow.

"What's wrong?" he asked.

"Who's taking me to school tomorrow?"

"Probably Gram. Or maybe Pops if he's feeling his coffee." He pursed his lips at Ella's hesitation. "Is that okay?"

"Yeah. You'll be home tomorrow when I get home, right?"

"That's the plan."

"What about the stairs?"

"I think I'll be okay by then. If not, I'll ask Finn for help." Luke didn't know if Finn would still be with him at that point, but it didn't matter. He'd get home one way or another. He pushed Ella's braids over her shoulders and tried not to fret at the tears that sheened her eyes. "El—"

"I'm glad you're okay, Luke."

With care, Luke guided her into a one-armed hug and swallowed against the lump that rose in his throat. "I'm glad you're okay too," he whispered. "So glad."

* * * *

Time and medication eased Luke's symptoms over the course of the evening and slowly, he felt much closer to normal. Shaking or nodding his head made it pound, and his balance wasn't quite back to one hundred percent. His brain also seemed somehow too large for his body. However, the world no longer slid around every time he got vertical and he managed to eat without being sick, and Luke counted both as a win. He said so to Ella, his parents and Simon when he spoke to them and sent them a blast text after he was released just before midnight.

Even so, a short Lyft ride from the hospital to Finn's put a serious drain on what remained of Luke's energy, and he'd gone woozy by the time Finn locked the door behind them.

"You want anything to eat?" Finn asked while Daisy twined her body around their ankles. "Or maybe take a shower?"

"Not hungry. I'd love a shower," Luke replied, then stopped. Standing under a stream of hot water sounded like heaven, but he honestly didn't know if he could trust his own body to cooperate. He felt ready to drop.

Finn cocked his head. "What is it?"

"I'm so fucking tired." Heat spread across Luke's cheeks at the understanding in Finn's face.

"I'll help you." Finn took hold of Luke's elbow, his grip gentle. "C'mon. The sooner we get you in there, the sooner you can go to bed."

"Hey, hang on." Luke planted his feet and looked at Finn — *really* looked at him — for the first time in what felt like ages. Lines of stress and exhaustion were drawn into Finn's face. His color was wan against his blue sweater and dark circles spread under his eyes. Hell, he'd worked a night shift and spent the day taking care of Ella and Luke instead of sleeping — he was probably more tired than Luke.

Luke pulled his arm free and grabbed Finn's hand. "You don't have to babysit me anymore," he said. "You need sleep as much as I do."

"I'm... Fuck, I'm fine, Luke." Finn smiled, but the angles were wrong on his face. His eyes blazed with an emotion Luke couldn't pin down, but before he could speak, Finn was leading him toward the bedroom.

"Wait a sec," Luke said as they neared the foot of the bed. "*Hey.*" He gripped Finn's hand until he stopped moving, and his insides tightened at the distress in Finn's face. "What aren't you saying?"

"You guys scared the hell out of me today." Finn pressed his lips into a grim line before he spoke again. "Ella called and asked me to come over because a car hit you and, Jesus, Luke, I didn't know what to think. I almost jumped out of my skin when I saw her standing outside of that triage bay. All I could think was thank God she was okay, then I saw you." His big eyes were haunted as he stared at Luke.

"I'm sorry," Luke whispered. He pulled Finn into a hug. "Damn, I'm sorry, Finn."

"What the fuck are you sorry for?" Finn's voice cracked.

"For scaring you." Luke sighed. "And for not telling you I love you before now."

Finn made a broken noise, and Luke drew back to kiss him. Finn raised his hands and held Luke's head in his palms, each movement gentle despite the desperate hunger in his kisses. Luke held him tight against the tremor that went through them both.

Neither moved from that spot for a while, which suited Luke fine. With his secret out of the bag, he had no idea what tomorrow would bring. He couldn't bring himself to care, though. Right now, Finn was what he needed and the rest could wait. He felt dizzy for a completely different reason when Finn pulled back, his eyes shining.

"I know we said we'd talk more, but it'll keep." Luke rubbed the tense muscles between Finn's shoulders.

"We can talk tomorrow," Finn offered.

"All day, if you want. I have doctor's orders to stay home for a couple of days."

"I'm off, too. And we're both so tired we're about to fall over."

Luke smiled. "So let's sleep. Because that's all I want right now. To sleep and hold you until I wake up again. Is that okay?"

"God, yes. I want that, too."

He helped Luke change into a T-shirt and sleep pants, then checked Daisy's water bowl while Luke brushed his teeth. Finn had changed too by the time Luke emerged, and nothing could dissuade him from escorting Luke to bed and tucking him in.

Luke's bones liquefied as he stretched out on the bed. Daisy curled up by his hip on top of the duvet, and a moment later, the mattress dipped under Finn's weight. Luke waited for Finn to settle beside him, and he made sure their bodies touched at every point possible. He laid his cheek on Finn's shoulder, his heart full as Finn let out a quiet sigh.

"Come with me to my place tomorrow?" Luke asked, his voice thick and sleepy.

"Yes, of course."

"El's gonna make you listen to her terrible jokes again if you stay for dinner."

Finn smiled against Luke's temple. "I'll look forward to that." He sounded pleased and almost shy, and Luke had no doubt he meant every word.

Luke spread one hand wide over Finn's sternum. "Thank you for taking care of us today, Finn."

Finn said nothing for a long moment, but he tightened his hold on Luke ever so slightly. When he spoke again, his voice was as gentle as Luke had ever heard it. "You're welcome."

Chapter Twenty

Despite his deep fatigue, Finn slept restlessly. He woke every few hours and stared into the dark silence of the room around him, his heart beating fast from dreams he didn't really remember. *Luke's safe*, he told himself each time. *Luke's fine and right here beside me.* Then he'd count Luke's breaths until his eyelids grew heavy again, and the cycle would start over.

He lay awake with gray light creeping under his window shades when his phone vibrated on the nightstand at six-thirty a.m. He saw half a dozen messages on the screen from Paul, Mick, Simon and Gillian, all asking how he and Luke were doing. The most recent message made him smile, though, because while the number belonged to Joanna Ryan, Finn identified the actual sender easily.

Hi, Finn.

Hi, Ella, he replied. *How're you feeling?*

Finn set the phone down and turned back to Luke, who was sprawled on his belly with his face mashed into the pillow. Finn pressed a careful kiss over the bandage on his temple, then stuck a hand under the duvet and ran it over Luke's back.

"Luke. Wake up, handsome."

Luke stirred under Finn's petting. A sleepy rumble went through him and he looped an arm over Finn's waist. Finn closed his eyes. He nuzzled at Luke's hair until the phone buzzed again behind him and didn't need to check the message to know what Ella would ask.

"Ella wants you."

Luke sighed. "M'kay." He gave Finn a long squeeze before they let each other go.

Finn turned back to the nightstand as Luke rolled onto his back, and the phone buzzed again.

I feel OK but kind of like I fell down 100 times, Ella wrote. *Is Luke there? He's not answering his phone yet.*

"Sounds like she's feeling sore," Finn said. He handed the phone to Luke. "Remind her to take the pain relief if she needs it."

"Okay, Doc."

Finn went to the kitchen with Daisy at his heels and talked to her while he emptied and refilled her food and water. He used his tablet to reply to the rest of his messages, one ear tuned to the low rise and fall of Luke's voice in the other room. Finn's stomach rumbled and he thought about making breakfast, but his eyelids were heavy, and he went back to the bedroom when he heard Luke say goodbye.

He found the bed empty and the bathroom door closed, so he stretched out on the mattress to wait Luke out. The next thing Finn knew, Luke was beside him and drawing the bedding up over them both. He spooned up behind Finn, his broad chest warm and solid against Finn's back and his breaths steady over the nape of Finn's neck.

"Sleep some more," he said, his voice low in Finn's ear.

"Was gonna make food," Finn mumbled.

Luke hummed. "Later, okay?"

"Okay. You all right? You drink some water?"

"Yep. I'm fine."

Finn sighed as Luke dropped a kiss behind his ear. "How's Ella?"

"She's good," Luke replied. "She tried to talk my parents into letting her stay home from school, but her Gram's not having it. I told her we'd be over later."

"M'kay."

* * * *

Finn didn't know how much time had passed the next time he surfaced, but the light behind the shades was much brighter, and Luke was still wrapped around him like a limpet. Carefully, Finn shifted in the bed to face him and quelled the impulse inside him to doctor.

The bruising around the cut on Luke's forehead had spread and blackened his eye, but his face bore no other physical signs of his injury. His eyelids trembled and his breathing changed as he dreamed, and his full lips came together in a pout.

He's okay, Finn told himself for the hundredth time, and this time, he recognized the words as true. Luke really was okay. He was here with Finn, and he'd told Finn he loved him.

Finn's throat ached. A wild sense of joy and near disbelief filled him at the idea that Luke could love him. But Finn knew Luke never said anything he didn't mean. There were things Finn wanted to say to Luke, too, words he'd thought too risky only yesterday, and they would keep until Luke had rested and was ready to put up with Finn's awkward bumbling.

Finn climbed out of bed and went to the kitchen to make something to eat. He brewed coffee and fried a half pound of bacon, and the clock read noon before he heard noises from the bedroom. Luke sauntered in, dressed in Finn's borrowed clothes and his hair a wreck, with Daisy riding on his shoulder like a furry little gargoyle. Finn smiled and used his tablet to snap a photo.

Luke lowered Daisy to the floor. "What's all this?"

"Bacon sandwiches." Finn picked up a roll and slathered it with butter. "There's coffee if you want some, or juice and water in the fridge."

"Can I help?"

"Everything's done, but if you could grab some plates, that'd be fantastic. I haven't had a chance to buy groceries this week, but I figure this'll do since it's lunchtime anyway. Besides, I'm about to eat my hand, I'm so hungry."

Luke grinned. "I hear that."

They chatted over the meal and Finn again tried to refrain from doctoring Luke too much. He couldn't help noticing things that told him Luke didn't feel his best. Luke didn't shake or nod his head, and every once in a while, he'd close his eyes for several seconds, as if centering himself.

"Ella asked me if you were okay when I talked to her earlier," he said as Finn reached for another sandwich. "She said you were really worried about us yesterday."

Finn's cheeks heated. "She doesn't miss anything, does she?" he asked.

Luke smiled at him. He wiped his lips with his napkin. "Nope. She sees everything, even when it seems like she's not paying attention. And Ella likes you, though she might not say it all the time. If you were worried, she'd notice and feel concerned."

Finn swallowed a mouthful of food. "Paul's an excellent physician, but it was hard seeing you all banged up and not be your doctor. Then checking Ella out to make sure she was okay — I've never had to do that for people I care about before."

For people I might actually love, Finn thought. *Jesus.* He swallowed. He wasn't ready to say anything like that aloud. Not yet, anyway.

"So, yeah, I was worried," he said. "And Simon's face when he showed up..." Finn shook his head. "I knew if he lost it, I would too. I guess I didn't do as good a job as I thought of hiding it."

"El said you were great. You even stuck a light in her eyes and she hates that." Luke covered Finn's hand where it lay on the table with his own. His expression grew somber. "I'm sorry we put you through that. And it means a lot to me knowing Ella had someone she could trust when I couldn't be there for her. Thank you, Finn."

Luke's raw gratitude humbled Finn and hollowed him out. "I'm glad I could be there for you both," he murmured. "Ella and I talked a lot yesterday, about all kinds of stuff. She asked me if I'd ever want to move back to Chicago, actually."

Luke nodded. God, he looked so sad. "She's been worried about that. I had no idea, or that she'd want to distance herself from you because she felt a need to protect herself."

"It's okay." Finn turned in his seat and slipped his arms around Luke. "We know now. And I told her I don't have plans to go anywhere. I like where I am."

The corners of Luke's mouth tilted up. "Yeah?"

"Hell, yeah," Finn said. He ran his hands over Luke's ribs through his T-shirt. "I got caught up trying to figure out how I could fit your family into my life, but I figured out I don't need to do that at all. You'll make space for me."

"Yes." Luke pressed his forehead to Finn's and closed his eyes. "I'll give you the room you need, Finn. I need to know what you want, too, though, and make sure you get it. Because with my life and family, there's a ton going on there. It's a lot for any one person to handle."

Finn's chest tightened. Luke really got it. "I know. Thank you for thinking about me." He kissed Luke's cheek. "But I told you on Sunday morning over bagels—I want more of you in my life, no matter what kind of weird shenanigans you're getting up to by yourself or with Ella. The homework and taekwondo practice, heck, even the rainbow foods. You should know I'll probably fall asleep and drool on you after every shift, though, even while you're nerding out over *Star Trek*."

Luke uttered a creaky laugh. "And I told *you* how I feel about you. I can handle a little drool."

Finn's heart felt too big for his chest. He wrapped Luke a little tighter in his arms. "Well, good because you're stuck with me."

Eventually, time forced them to clean up the kitchen and themselves. A somber mood fell over Finn as he helped Luke shower. The bruises on Luke's body were a stark reminder that Finn had come too close to losing moments like these, simply holding Luke close, his nose pressed against Luke's neck while Luke hugged him back. Finn's eyes stung as he slotted his mouth against Luke's and kissed him until the water ran cold.

They dressed and piled their things and Daisy into a Lyft, and while Luke appeared pale and exhausted after the three-flight climb to his apartment, he endured Joanna and Brad fussing over him with a real smile.

"Come sit with me," Finn coaxed after he'd put away their things and let Daisy loose to explore.

"Ella needs to be picked up soon," Luke replied, but he allowed Finn to lead him to the couch.

"Your parents have got it covered." Finn used the remote to turn on the TV, then sat down and patted the cushion beside him. "Joanna said she's making roasted chicken and pasta for dinner, so they'll go shopping first and grab Ella on their way home."

Luke sat down beside Finn with a heartfelt groan. "That's one of my favorite things to eat, you know. Mom makes the pasta by hand, and there're pine nuts and sultanas in this lemon butter sauce. So yummy." He yawned, then winced slightly.

"Headache?" Finn asked. "You can have more Tylenol if you need it."

"Nah, I'm all right." Luke leaned against Finn's shoulder and closed his eyes. "You might be the one getting drooled on in a minute, though."

"I'm sure I can handle it," Finn replied and rubbed his back.

Sure enough, Luke fell asleep in under a minute. He stirred a little as Finn eased him down onto a pillow he'd placed on his lap but was out cold by the time the Ryans came to check on them.

Finn put his head back too and chatted with Joanna and Brad to fill them in on Luke's post-concussion treatment. However, he dozed off himself before they left to do errands and woke to a much dimmer room and Ella curled up in a nearby chair with Daisy on her lap.

"Hey, Ella," Finn said, his voice low.

Ella glanced Finn's way and gave him a small smile that Finn returned without missing a beat. "Hey." She slid a hand over Daisy's fur. "I'm glad you guys are here."

* * * *

Late that night, following some of the best food Finn had ever eaten, after Ella had gone to sleep and Brad and Joanna went back to their own home, Finn woke in Luke's big bed. Luke lay facing him, and a nightlight in the corner cast enough low light to illuminate his features as he slumbered.

He's fine, Finn told himself again. *He's right here.*

Heat curled inside Finn, and though he knew sleep would be better for them both, he needed more. To touch Luke and feel him close, inside and out.

He cupped Luke's face in his hands and kissed him awake, and the embers inside Finn burned hotter at Luke's sleepy sigh.

"Mmm, baby." Luke dipped a hand under the waistband of Finn's sleep pants, the movement eager. Finn shivered.

Slowly, they stripped each other down, exchanging deep, languorous kisses. Lust and an almost overwhelming tenderness thrummed through Finn. *This*, this is what he wanted and needed, Luke warm and pliant against him with nowhere special to be and all the time in the world. Finn rolled on top of Luke, slotted their groins together and rutted his cock against Luke's.

Luke gasped. "God. Need you."

Finn bit his lip at the wanton need in Luke's whisper. Luke wanted one thing when he sounded like that, and normally, Finn wouldn't hesitate to fuck him through the mattress. However, they weren't alone in the apartment and the closed doors between the bedrooms could only muffle so much. The doctor in Finn also knew that no matter what Luke's hormones were telling him, he wasn't ready to be manhandled.

"How's your head?" Finn murmured.

"Still on my neck." Luke grabbed Finn's ass and chuckled at his grunt.

"Feel dizzy?" Finn asked.

"Nope."

"Any pain?"

Luke smiled against Finn's lips. "Nuh-uh."

"That's good. Still not gonna fuck you hard." Finn covered Luke's curse with his lips and kissed him, fucking Luke's mouth with his tongue until Luke whimpered. Only then did Finn break away and reach toward the nightstand for the lube and a condom.

Luke ran his hands over Finn's ribs and back, then down over his thighs, raising goosebumps over Finn's skin. He seemed intent on touching every inch of Finn he could reach. Struck by a need to see him, Finn turned on the lamp and the sight that met him stole his breath.

Every inch of Luke broadcast trust and desire, and his gaze burned with what Finn now recognized as love.

Fuck.

How long had Luke had been looking at Finn like that? Weeks? Maybe longer?

Finn's heart squeezed tight. He bent to kiss Luke, more gently this time, and Luke's eyelids slid closed. He spread his legs wider and made room for Finn to kneel between them. Finn's body pulsed with need.

"Jesus, Luke."

"Want you," Luke told him, his voice deep and growly.

He watched Finn tear open the foil wrapper and stroked Finn's thighs with his big hands, almost petting him. Finn slicked his fingers from the little bottle of lube and rolled the condom on, but then Luke reached down and touched himself, a wicked gleam in his eye. Finn bit his lip. God, but he loved it when Luke put on a show.

"You keep that up and this is going to be over pretty quick," he joked, just to hear Luke laugh, and bent between Luke's thighs.

Luke's smile faded under Finn's teasing fingers. He pressed his head back onto the pillow with a quiet groan and Finn took his time torturing with touches too gentle to get Luke off. Luke fisted the sheets, his gaze wild.

"Finn."

"I've got you."

Finn pulled his fingers clear and crawled over Luke, covering Luke's body with his. His nerves prickled as their mouths met, and when he pushed inside Luke, Finn was lost. He clenched his eyes shut as Luke surrounded him and slid home in a long, slow movement. Luke smothered a moan against Finn's shoulder.

Fire filled Finn's bones. He hardly recognized his own voice as he murmured Luke's name, and his hands shook as he brought his arms around Luke, using them to cradle Luke close and hold him still. Luke's breath hitched as Finn rocked in and out of him, and he gripped Finn's shoulders hard.

Finn swallowed past the tightness in his throat. He wanted to crawl inside Luke and never leave. Lust burned low in his groin and wound its way along his spine.

Luke gasped. He hooked one long, muscled leg over Finn's hip and writhed against him. "Oh, fuck. Christ." Somehow, he slid one hand between them and wrapped it around his cock. "You make me feel so good."

Finn forced his eyes open, intent on watching Luke fly. "That's it, baby," he murmured, his voice hoarse. "Wanna feel you all over me."

Luke's chest heaved. His mouth fell open and his eyes went wide as his cock pulsed and smeared their skin with cum. Finn's control snapped. He grasped Luke tight and thrust over and over until the world tilted around them. Time stretched and everything went perfectly still as Finn buried his face against Luke's neck and came.

He pulled Luke with him when he floated back to earth, and they rolled onto their sides to face each other. Finn knew he should get up to find something to clean them off, but then Luke kissed him, and he lingered instead. He rode the hazy afterglow as the sweat and cum on their bodies cooled, and Luke's heat soaked into Finn.

Not letting him go, Finn told himself, and absolutely nothing about that thought scared him.

Chapter Twenty-One

Luke hurried along Tremont Street and cursed under his breath at the raindrop that hit his cheek. He stopped after several more splashed against his face and ducked through the doors of a movie theater in a bid for shelter. Quickly, he pulled out his phone.

Guess who doesn't have an umbrella?

Finn sent back a frowny face. *Need a rescue?*

Luke glanced out of the glass doors at the rain. His coat had a hood and it was warm for April—he'd be okay if he got a little wet. Not that Luke didn't appreciate the offer. He smiled as he wrote back.

I'm good. On my way.

Luke pulled up the hood and made his way back outside. Traffic clogged the streets of the Theater District, but while rain and other pedestrians slowed his progress, Luke didn't fret. His Friday night dinners with Ella had grown to include many more at the table besides Simon and Melissa, and no one minded waiting if anyone ran late.

The sidewalks were almost empty by the time he turned onto Stanhope Street. Luke broke into a light jog but kept tight hold of his bag and his eyes peeled for any obstacles in the way. He and Mick were running the Boston Marathon in two days and the last thing Luke wanted was to do something stupid like hurt himself running in a pair of lace-up boots.

Two blocks later, he spied a huge umbrella outside of Two Men and a Grille, its rainbow colors cutting through the gray evening air. Finn and Ella stood together beneath it, Finn in the jeans and fleece jacket Luke knew he liked to wear after a shift. Ella was still in her white taekwondo dobok and a jacket, her hair up and out of her face. She brought one arm up, her elbow slightly bent and her fist facing out in what Luke recognized as a high block.

Finn watched raptly. He'd caught Ella's interest in taekwondo and while he attended classes on his own, it wasn't unusual for the two of them to practice forms together when the mood struck them. Thankfully, they hadn't broken anything in either Luke's or Finn's apartments yet. Luke might not care if they did anyway — he liked watching the two of them enjoy each other's company far too much.

Ella caught sight of Luke as he drew closer and her grin redirected Finn's attention, too. However, Finn's happy expression dimmed the moment he noticed Luke's wet clothes.

"You're soaked," he began, but Ella spoke right over him.

"Dude, you're a *mess!*"

"I know, and don't call me dude." Luke laughed. "It's fine. Once I get warmed up, I won't even feel it anymore."

"Let's get you inside then," Finn replied. "You should use the hand drier in the men's room."

"Nah, I'm dry-ish under the coat." Luke dropped his hood as Finn pulled him under the cover of the mammoth umbrella, and Ella made a dash for the door. "Is Simon inside?"

"Yep. He grabbed a table with Mick and Melissa. Paul's working 'til ten, so we won't be seeing him."

No Chad tonight either, Luke thought. Finn wouldn't mention Chad unless he planned to join them and that was fine as far as Luke was concerned. He didn't mind hanging out with Finn's most single of single friends, or that Finn and Chad still had occasional dinners and nights out on their own. Luke didn't love the way Chad stared at Finn when he thought no one was watching, though. Not that it mattered. Finn had made it clear Luke was the only man who held his interest.

Luke nodded. "Gillian said she and Charlie and Shelli might stop by for dessert and Pete's on his way. He should be here by seven."

"Perfect." Finn reached up and smoothed Luke's hair back from his face. "Ella wanted to wait out here after she heard you'd forgotten your umbrella. *Again.*"

Luke hummed. "Doubtful. Pretty sure any waiting outside Ella wanted was more about this circus tent on a stick you've got than me." Luke jerked a thumb at the umbrella over their heads and Finn laughed.

"You know, you could be right." He hooked his free arm around Luke and led the way inside.

To say Luke's life had changed significantly in the last several months was an understatement. Some days, he almost didn't recognize the world around him, but he liked it all very much.

In the weeks leading up to Peter's return home, the brothers had talked a great deal about Ella and how best to care for her. Understanding her separation anxiety was one thing, but dealing with it was another, and while Peter wanted to remain with the Marines, he struggled with being separated from his family. This most recent deployment had really brought that home for him.

'El told me about your headaches,' he'd said to Luke one night over chat. Ella had already gone to bed and though the car accident had already been two weeks in the past, fatigue and worry had been written all over Peter's face. *'You're both okay, right? You'd tell me if—'*

'Of course,' Luke had interjected, his tone gentle. *'We're fine. You know Ella had a wellness check last week and passed everything with flying colors. All things considered, my headaches are normal and nothing some OTC meds won't fix. They've been tapering off, too.'*

As had the bouts of dizziness and blurred vision, symptoms Luke hadn't shared with anyone beyond Finn, Paul and his own physician. He'd downplayed feeling crappy around Ella. She'd been far too worried about Luke's health and no wonder, given her fear of losing people she loved.

Luke had blown a noisy breath out through his nose. *'I'll talk to El about the headaches. But we're good. You guys should be way more focused on the fact you'll be home soon and not my aches and pains.'*

'Believe me, I am laser focused, bro. I can't wait to see you guys.' Peter had chuckled despite the wistful cast in his eye.

Luke's heart had ached for his brother. *'We can't wait to see you, too, Pete. Ella is really, really excited to have you home.'*

'Me too. I missed out on more than I ever imagined possible,' Peter had said. He'd frowned. *'I look at Ella during these calls and it's like she turned into a different person when I wasn't paying attention. Sometimes, it feels like talking to a stranger. Well, until she cracks one of those stupid jokes and everything goes back to normal again.'*

Luke had laughed. *'I get it. I feel like that sometimes too, and I've seen her every day.'*

'It's not just me, huh?'

'Not at all. She's changing and growing up so fast. It's ninety percent surface, though. Inside, she's still the same kid you've always known.' Luke had smiled at Peter. *'She still needs Mom and Pops and me, and she needs her dad even more.'*

Peter hadn't needed persuading to request a change in orders. Life in Boston made his daughter happy in many ways, but she clearly craved deeper stability with him. Before Peter had even gotten on a plane back to the States, he'd reached out to his recruiter to negotiate a permanent duty station swap closer to Boston. He had eventually been assigned to the Marine Corps Detachment in Newport, Rhode Island, less than two hours' drive from Boston.

In addition to his regular duties, Peter hoped to train in Aviation Logistics Tactical Information Systems on the Newport base and further leverage his extensive experience as a pilot. He still returned to Quantico for periodic assignments, and typically stayed in Newport during the week, but the base's proximity to Boston made visits easy for everyone in the family. Peter also tried to attend the Friday night dinner dates whenever he could.

With Peter closer to home, Luke had gotten pieces of his personal life back. While still very involved with Ella's care, he had time for himself again, too, which translated to time with friends and Finn. Finn made things easier simply by virtue of being himself—open, loving and generous, and at home with being a part of Luke's family life.

Warm satisfaction stole over Luke as he shared appetizers with his boyfriend on one side and his niece on the other. They'd built a family together with Peter and made sure it encompassed their circles of friends. They formed an unconventional unit, but a strong one, and Luke thought it suited them all.

He, Finn and Daisy split their time between Back Bay and Beacon Hill depending on where Peter could be and what Ella needed. No matter where they slept, they did a fair amount of juggling to manage both Ella's schedule and their own, but while Finn was new to sharing life with a child, he embraced it without hesitation.

Finn met Luke's smile with one of his own. "What's that face for?"

"Nothing," Luke replied, his voice low. "Just remembered I once promised Ella we could always talk, even if we hated each other's boyfriends. Of course, she'd already decided she didn't hate you, so I lucked out there."

Finn preened a little, and Luke didn't blame him for feeling proud. The night before, Finn had been the one checking over Ella's homework assignments despite the fact he'd just gotten off shift and could have used a nap. Finn and Ella didn't always see eye-to-eye — Luke wasn't sure such a thing was possible with a now eleven-year-old child involved. They were still real friends who shared genuine affection and supported each other without question.

A collective greeting went up from the table as Peter stepped up to join them and Ella patted the chair beside her.

"I saved a space for you!" she got out, her words muffled by a mouthful of spinach dip and pita bread.

Peter sat down and wrinkled his nose. "Girl, that is gross."

"I know," Ella agreed happily. She wiped her mouth on her napkin before she snuggled into a hug with her dad. "I have a joke for you," she said. "I tried it out on Finn yesterday and he said it's one of the worst yet."

Peter laughed. "Okay, go."

Ella sat up straight and looked her father in the eye. "Why can't you hear a pterodactyl go to the bathroom?" Her lips twitched as Peter thought.

"I don't know," he said at last. "Tell me."

"Because the 'P' is silent." Ella beamed as Peter and the rest of the adults broke up laughing.

"Finn is right — that was epically terrible," Peter said. He raised a hand at a passing server while Ella helped herself to more dip.

"Did you drive or take the train?" Luke asked his brother.

"I drove," Peter replied. He looked cheerful and energized in his gray button-down shirt. "I stopped by your place to park the truck and say hi to the cat and left the keys upstairs. You need it over the weekend?"

"Oh, no, I was just curious." Luke sipped his beer. "I figured you'd have it this week since Ella said you have some day trips planned."

"What's happening this week?" Simon asked. "I mean, besides you and Mick voluntarily running twenty-six miles like a pair of idiots?"

Mick choked on his drink and the others broke up laughing. Luke narrowed his eyes at his friend. "It's Spring Break for Massachusetts schools. Pete took some time off to spend with Ella."

"We made a bunch of plans for after Marathon Monday," Ella said. "We have tickets to a baseball game and a whale watching thing." She beamed at her father. "Oh, and a chocolate brunch on Saturday!"

"What on earth is a chocolate brunch?" Finn asked. His eager tone made Luke smile—he'd rarely met an adult with a sweet tooth like Finn's.

"It's a dessert buffet at one of the hotels at Post Office Square," Luke replied. "And by buffet, I mean a whole room full of desserts with a theme like the five senses or Fifties retro. There's even a cotton candy station and a chocolate fountain." He bit back another laugh at the way Finn's eyes gleamed.

Ella leaned past Luke to speak to Finn. "You sure you can't come with us?"

Finn actually appeared pained. "I'd really, *really* love to, El, but Luke and I are flying out of town after dinner next Friday night. Maybe we could all go another time?"

Ella cheered and clapped her hands and Peter snorted out a laugh. "Yeah, like a second chocolate brunch is a hard sell. Where are you guys going anyway?"

"I have no idea because Finn won't tell me." Luke nodded at his brother's wide eyes. "I know, right? The suspense is killing me!"

Simon laid a hand over his heart as if in shock. "I can't believe *you* of all people agreed to a plan you know nothing about, Pickle. Did you hit your head again before Finn asked and forget to tell anyone?"

"Finn asked him to go away last weekend," Ella replied before anyone else could respond. She shrugged at Simon's raised eyebrows. "I was sitting right there when they were talking about it, Simon. We were eating pizza and talking about vacation week."

Luke practically pounced. "Wait, so you know where we're going?"

Ella shook her head. "Nope." She grinned at Luke's exasperated sigh, but any further discussion of the mystery trip paused as their server, Skylar, stopped by the table.

Skylar handed Peter a menu and set a glass of water down in front of him. "I'll give you a minute, hon, but I can start with the rest of the table." She cast a smile around the table. "Everyone else know what they want?"

* * * *

Luke groaned loudly as Finn pinned him against the front door of the Beacon Hill apartment and kissed him. Finn pressed his cock hard against Luke's hip, and they grappled with each other, their movements hungry.

Finn gasped when Luke palmed him through his jeans. "Oh, fuck."

The need in his voice made Luke's dick throb.

After dinner, they'd walked Ella and Peter to Back Bay and picked up Daisy and promised to see each other Sunday for a pre-Marathon dinner at Brad and Joanna's. Neither Luke nor Finn had said much as they headed for Finn's, but Finn had wound his fingers tightly with Luke's and a smile laced with mischief had played about his lips. He'd been on Luke the moment they'd let Daisy out of her carrier and kissed him until Luke thought his bones would melt.

They staggered toward the bedroom, fumbling with each other's clothes and leaving a trail of discarded garments and shoes along the way. Luke slid a hand under Finn's shirt and teased the taut muscles of his stomach, but Finn turned the tables in a flash. He walked Luke backward toward the bed and wrestled him down onto the mattress, each movement sending fire coursing under Luke's skin. He loved bossy Finn.

Finn finally pulled back, and Luke reached up and ran his fingers over Finn's lips, needing that connection. The world around them slowed and a sharp, sweet pain cut through Luke. His heart thundered in his ears.

"Need you," he murmured.

Finn moved his head and pressed a kiss to Luke's palm, then opened his lips to lick Luke's skin. The hot, wet sweep made Luke moan.

"God, Finn."

Finn turned toward the nightstand for lube but kept a hand on Luke, as if reluctant to let go. He only did so to wet his fingers, then tossed the bottle down on the mattress. He reached down and wrapped his fingers around Luke's cock, his eyes burning gray fire.

He ghosted his lips over Luke's. "Love you," he whispered. The intensity in his voice sent a shiver through Luke.

"Love you, too."

Luke wrapped his arms around Finn's neck while Finn jacked him and used his free hand to tease circles against Luke's balls. He reached lower and slipped a finger inside Luke.

Luke shuddered. "Fuck."

"I know. Let me hear you."

Finn squeezed and stroked Luke as he worked him open, and Luke kissed him desperately, lust rushing through him. He fought not to beg when Finn pulled his fingers free only to turn his attention on Luke's chest. He kissed and licked, and each motion drove the fire inside Luke higher. He cried out when Finn's mouth closed over his nipple.

"Finn, please."

Finn shifted back. He pushed Luke's knees toward his chest and ran his hands over Luke's ass, his bottom lip caught between his teeth. Luke hooked his arms under his thighs, but had the presence of mind to notice he wasn't the only one trembling with arousal.

Finn lined their bodies up and pressed into Luke. He slid forward, and Luke's body throbbed with razor-edged pleasure. Luke clutched at Finn as the burn mellowed into a delicious pressure.

Finn rocked in and out, pressing kisses against Luke's face while he fucked him. He pushed deep, his gaze locked with Luke's, and the coil inside Luke tightened. He reached to take himself in hand, but the coil snapped without warning and he came so hard he could scarcely breathe. Luke's world went out of focus in a bright roar, and when he came back down, shaking and gasping, he was clutching Finn so tightly his fingers ached.

Finn stared at Luke with awe. "Fuck," he ground out a second before he came too.

Finn's back arched as he hit his peak and his strangled noise pulled at every tender, loving notion Luke had inside him. Luke gathered Finn up as he fell apart, murmuring soothing nonsense against his cheek, and didn't let go until Finn had calmed.

* * * *

"Are you going to tell me where we're going, or do I have to wait until we check in at the airport? I don't even know what to pack."

Luke popped a strawberry into his mouth at Finn's smirk. They were standing at the kitchen counter sharing containers of fruit while Finn dressed the occasional berry with squirts of whipped cream from a can.

"I'll help you pack. But do you really want to know?" he asked. He fed Luke more fruit. "Because I'll tell you if that's what you want."

Luke studied the warmth in Finn's face. Not long ago, he'd have *needed* to know where they were going so he could figure out a plan and make sure nothing went forgotten if he turned his back for even one minute. Now, though, Luke didn't need to plan anything at all beyond spending time with Finn and getting through his race on Monday. A little added mystery didn't seem like a big deal at all. Especially if it made Finn happy.

"Nah." Luke shrugged. "I don't mind waiting to find out. I trust you."

The smile that lit Finn's face put stars in his eyes. Without a word, he set the whipped cream can and the fruit on the counter and pulled Luke into a scorching kiss yet still managed to hold Luke up when his knees turned to jelly.

"I'm taking you to Chicago," Finn said after he drew back. "I thought you'd like to meet my family in person since you chat with my mom on the phone more than I do."

For several moments, Luke couldn't speak. Sure, he talked to Finn's parents all the time — they were great and so understanding and supportive of Luke and Finn's life in Boston. To meet them, though... Luke hadn't been sure Finn was ready for something like that.

Finn didn't press when Luke stayed silent, though a soft look of understanding filtered over his face. Luke laid a hand on Finn's chest, fingers spread wide over his heart.

This man.

"I would love to meet your family," he said at last. And Luke kissed Finn again because his heart was overflowing with more love than he knew what to do with and just because he could.

Want to see more from this author? Here's a taster for you to enjoy!

The Speakeasy: With a Twist
K. Evan Coles & Brigham Vaughn

Excerpt

Will Martin set down his empty mug and flipped to the next page of the *New York Times*. A familiar profile caught his attention and, despite his better judgment, he read the caption below the photo of two smiling and laughing men in tuxedos.

The year's hottest gay couple cut a fine figure at the Met premiere last night. Riley Porter-Wright and Carter Hamilton are still going strong. The couple appeared oblivious to those around them as they talked during intermission. They were joined by the former Mrs. Hamilton, who seems to have forgiven Mr. Porter-Wright for stepping into her place. Also there was her new paramour, Robert... The ex-Mrs. Porter-Wright was nowhere to be seen. The couple have been spotted at —

Annoyed, Will threw the newspaper on the coffee table. Everywhere he turned there were reminders of his ex-boyfriend Riley's happiness with his new love. Well, long-time love, really. Will had competed with Riley's best friend, Carter, the entire time they'd been together.

But how could Will have competed with a man Riley had loved since college? Riley had left his wife to explore his bisexuality and Carter had ultimately done the same. Will had been foolish for thinking he could offer Riley more than a man who had known him for a decade and a half could.

Will scrubbed a hand through his hair and stood. *I need a change of scenery right now*, he thought and glanced around the living room of his stylish Manhattan condo.

His laptop screen glowed at him from his desk by the windows. He'd planned to take the morning off and enjoy the gorgeous early June weather, but with edits looming over him and reminders of Riley lurking around the edges of his consciousness, relaxation seemed out of the question.

"Fine, fine," Will muttered under his breath. "Work it is."

He filled his cup with coffee, doctored it with cream and sugar and took a seat at his desk. He pulled up his manuscript and scrolled to the place he'd left off — Bernard Schwartz's appointment as Chief Counsel of the House Legislative Oversight Subcommittee.

Half an hour later, Will's phone trilled on the desk and he blinked to clear the haze from his brain. *Riley* flashed across the screen. *Speak of the devil*, he thought, then immediately chastised himself. Riley wasn't the problem. Riley loving Carter instead of Will wasn't even the major issue. Will's habit of falling for emotionally unavailable men then struggling to get over them was something he desperately needed to change.

Not wanting his ex to sense the turmoil in his head, Will made sure to keep his tone pleasant. "Hey, Riley."

"Hey, Will. How have you been?"

"Good. Making solid progress on my book." Will sat back in his chair.

"Oh, that's right, you're not teaching during the summer semester, are you?"

"No, I decided to focus on my writing. I'm in the midst of edits, so I'll be spending the summer cursing at a computer screen while I try not to tear my hair out."

"What a rewarding career," Riley said teasingly.

Will chuckled and relaxed a little. He'd always enjoyed Riley's sense of humor. "I must be a masochist for voluntarily subjecting myself to college students *and* editors." Will taught legal history at New York University and had published a handful of well-regarded books on the topic. He suspected Riley hadn't called to ask about his writing, however. "How's work? Is your father still pretending you don't exist at the office?"

"I think he's hoping I'll leave Porter-Wright Publishing, to be honest. He and Geneva were polite when Carter and I took the kids to the company picnic but I'm sure it's only because they were afraid of looking bad."

"Appearances above all else," Will muttered. He and Riley had always had that in common. Although at least Will spoke to his mother occasionally and kept in contact with his sister, Olivia. Riley's relationship with his parents was far worse. "How are things with you and Carter? And the little Hamiltons?"

"Really good." Will could hear the smile in Riley's voice. "We all spent last weekend in Southampton at the beach house."

Riley sounded so happy every time they talked about Carter and his kids. Will's heart ached, knowing he could never have made Riley that happy, but on the whole he was glad Riley had found the contentment he'd searched for.

"Anyway," Riley interrupted his thoughts, "I called for a reason. You know Jesse Murtagh and Kyle McKee, right?"

"Vaguely. I met them at Carter's birthday and Jesse again at your holiday party last winter."

"Right. Well, they're opening a speakeasy in a week or so."

Will laughed. "A speakeasy? That's intriguing."

"It's basically ready to go, and they've been inviting friends in to see it and try the cocktails. I called to see if you would like to meet me there tonight. I thought we could grab some drinks and catch up."

"Just you?"

Riley hesitated. "No. Carter will be there with Jesse and Kyle. Along with six or eight of our friends."

Will stifled a sigh. "Riley…"

"Hey, I know it's going to be awkward. But it's been six months. You and I are doing pretty well with our friendship. So, stop being a fucker and come."

Will couldn't prevent the laugh that escaped him. "Well, when you word it that way, how can I possibly resist?"

"No, I don't mean to be glib. I know this isn't easy for you, but I don't want to lose you as a friend." Riley sounded earnest. "I'm asking a lot, but I'd like for you to be able to hang out with all of us. And hey, maybe you'll meet the perfect guy there."

Will snorted. "I'm definitely not looking for the last part, but sure, I'll come. What time and where am I meeting you?"

* * * *

Later that evening, Will glanced around Lock & Key, a pub on the edge of the upper West Side in

Morningside Heights, where Riley had arranged for them to meet. The floors were scuffed and slightly gritty under his feet and the tables and chairs had seen better days. The pub was entirely ordinary and not at all what Will had expected.

"Have dive bars become your thing?" he asked, mystified.

Riley laughed and clapped him on the shoulder. "This is not our destination for the night. Someone Kyle used to work with owns Lock & Key. The speakeasy is underneath."

Will raised an eyebrow. "*Under Lock & Key*? Clever."

"What can I say, my friends are punny." Riley grinned. "Come on, follow me." He strode to the end of the bar and opened an unmarked door. Will followed more slowly. At the end of a hallway was an old-fashioned phone mounted on the wall.

Riley picked it up and spoke. "Let me in, you fucker." He fell silent for a moment then tipped his head back and laughed. "That *is* the passphrase, you jackass!"

Riley hung up the handset and turned to Will, merriment clearly written across his face. "Jesse," he said, as if that was explanation enough.

In truth, it probably was. Jesse Murtagh was one of a kind. Part of a powerful media family in Manhattan, he was also pansexual and the biggest flirt Will had ever encountered. Not to mention charming and incredibly handsome—no wonder Carter had been attracted to him. Like Will, Jesse had been left in Riley and Carter's wake once they'd decided to get together, but Will suspected Jesse had been far less affected.

"Are you coming down or what?" A door opened at the end of the hall and Jesse appeared, a smile lighting his face and making his bright blue eyes twinkle. He glanced over at Will and gave him an appreciative grin.

"Glad you could join us tonight, Will. You're looking good."

Will chuckled and stepped forward to offer Jesse his hand. "It's good to see you too." Irrepressible flirt notwithstanding, Jesse had a compelling presence. Broad shoulders capped off a tall, lean body and the closely-cropped beard he sported framed full lips. Not Will's type, but easy on the eyes.

"Think you can manage to not storm off this time?" Jesse asked, raking a hand through his dark-blond hair.

Riley groaned. "Jes…"

Will smiled, despite his stab of discomfort at the reminder of the dramatic ending to his and Riley's relationship six months prior at a Christmas party. Will had finally realized the futility of his feelings for Riley that night and caused a scene in front of a small group of their combined friends, including Jesse and Carter. *Ugh*. It hadn't been one of his finer moments.

"I think I can behave tonight," he said aloud. "So, a speakeasy, huh? What made you decide to open that?"

Jesse held open the door and allowed Riley and Will to precede him down another long, narrow hallway. "Why not? Kyle wanted to open a bar. We looked at a ton of locations and were bored by all of them, but when our friend Matt mentioned the space under Lock & Key, it all fell into place. Who doesn't want to own an underground, secret bar?"

"I can't say it's ever crossed my mind," Will admitted. They reached the end of the hall and Riley pushed open another unmarked door to reveal a stairwell. Although well-lit, the walls were painted black and totally bare.

"This is the problem with you, Will," Jesse said. "You're so buttoned up. You need to live a little."

"Well I'm spending the evening at a speakeasy with you," Will said as he followed Riley down the stairs. "Will that do for now?"

Jesse laughed. "Touché."

Riley pushed open a door at the bottom of the steps and the sight of the bar rendered Will mute.

In sharp contrast to the run-down bar above, the speakeasy was stylish and welcoming. Open shelves on the walls were filled with bottles of liquor. Inlaid floors were topped with sleek leather and metal furniture, and candles in votives glowed on the tables. The mellow music and subdued lighting lent the space an atmosphere of sophisticated relaxation.

Astonished, Will glanced over at Jesse. "This is incredible. I'm impressed."

"You have good taste, I'll give you that." Jesse grasped his shoulder and squeezed. "C'mon, let me get you a drink."

As Will crossed the room to the bar, Riley slipped into a spot beside Carter on the leather sofa. Will tried to hide a wince as Carter reached for Riley's knee and squeezed it without pausing in conversation.

"Wistful or vaguely nauseated?" Jesse asked as he took a seat on one of the bar stools.

Will glanced at him. "Excuse me?"

"Was the look because you wish you had that with Riley or because you're grossed out by two people being disgustingly in love?"

"A little of both, I suppose." Will had nothing against relationships, but they were starting to seem like a pipe dream for him.

A man appeared behind the bar and Will easily recognized him as Carter's friend, Kyle.

"Will, right?" he said, holding out a hand. "Kyle McKee."

"Yeah, hi. We met at Carter's birthday dinner."

Kyle smiled. "It's nice to see you again."

They shook and Will gave Kyle a once-over. Kyle was easily six feet tall, with broad shoulders, thick dark hair trimmed short on the sides, and heavy but well-groomed brows over dark eyes. Unlike Jesse, Kyle was very much Will's type. Except for the suspenders he wore over his crisp gray shirt and his rolled-up sleeves. Kyle pulled them off better than most, but the look screamed hipster too much for Will's tastes.

"Great place you have here." Will glanced around. "I like it."

"Thanks." Kyle's eyes crinkled at the corners when he smiled. "I'm pleased to hear it. A speakeasy wasn't quite what I had in mind when I told Jesse I wanted to open a bar, but I'm glad I decided to go for it."

Jesse grinned. "When will all of you learn my ideas are always brilliant?"

"Probably never." Kyle turned back to Will. "So, what can I get you? We have a wide selection of beer, wine and cocktails." He slid a leather-bound book in Will's direction.

Will perused it for a moment before he closed the cover. "You know what? Surprise me. Make me a cocktail."

"Hmm. I can do that. Anything you particularly dislike?"

"Anything too sweet. And Amaretto."

Kyle scrutinized Will for a moment before his eyes gleamed. "Got it."

Will watched with interest as Kyle pulled a glass out of the freezer and mixed together cognac, Cointreau and lemon juice in a shaker with ice. A few moments later, Kyle poured it into a glass, topped it with a twist of lemon and slid the drink across the bar to him. "Sidecar. Tell me what you think."

Will raised the glass to his lips and took a sip. He found the drink refreshingly cold and a perfect blend of sour and sweet with a fresh citrusy taste balanced nicely by the cognac. "That's delicious."

Kyle grinned. "Excellent."

"C'mon." Jesse picked up a tumbler filled with amber-colored liquid and a large spherical ice cube. It clinked pleasantly as he moved. "Let's go hang out with the guys."

The majority of the patrons were part of Riley and Carter's group, spread out across two leather sofas and a handful of chairs that made a square seating area around a finely crafted wood coffee table. Riley leaned forward and set his martini glass down. Will placed his own drink on a table and pulled up a chair.

"Everyone, this is Will Martin. Some of you met him at Carter's birthday and a few of you met him over the holidays. I'll introduce everyone, though."

Will gave him a brief smile. "Thanks."

"You know Carter, obviously." Carter nodded in greeting and Will returned it. "Next to Carter is his sister, Audrey." A tan blonde woman gave him a smile over a martini glass filled with something frothy and yellow. "And Audrey's husband, Max." An attractive, bearded man with brown hair and light brown eyes raised a pilsner glass in greeting.

Riley continued around the circle. "Gale, Jarrod, Henry and Miles are friends of Carter's." The men waved and murmured their hellos.

"You seem outnumbered here, Audrey," Will said.

She grinned at him. "I'm not complaining. My brother has some very good-looking friends."

Her husband elbowed her. "What am I? Chopped liver?"

"Never, darling. But I see you every day."

Kyle seated himself at an empty chair across the group. "You're a law professor, right, Will?"

Will nodded and took a sip of his drink. "Yes, at NYU. I'm spending the summer working on my latest book."

"What do you write?" Max asked. "I'd love to hear about it."

Will chuckled. "You may regret you asked, but I'm currently writing about the Chief Counsel of the House Legislative Oversight Subcommittee."

"So, political law then?"

"I couldn't totally avoid the family business," Will said dryly.

Audrey frowned. "You have a family member who's a politician?"

"My father." Will made a face. "And a Republican at that."

"How does that work at family dinners?" Audrey asked. "I thought my parents and Carter were bad, but at least they're not pushing discriminatory legislation."

"I haven't spoken to him since college, to be honest." Will took a fortifying sip of his sidecar. "I see my mother and sister on occasion, but never when he's around."

Riley shot him a sympathetic smile.

"Sorry to pry," Audrey said with an apologetic glance. "I've been battling my parents about them shutting Carter out and that's difficult enough."

"Ancient history." Will waved off her apology. "What do you do, Audrey?"

"I chair several philanthropic organizations. And I recently got involved with PFLAG." She exchanged a look with her brother.

Jesse leaned forward. "Beautiful *and* socially aware? Be still, my beating heart. If Max hadn't met you first..." Jesse took a sip of his drink. "That goes both ways, Max."

Max chuckled and Carter rolled his eyes. "We've had this discussion before, Jesse. No hitting on my sister *or* my brother-in-law, please. And definitely not both at once."

A chorus of laughter rose. Riley chimed in with a humorous comment as Will relaxed back in his chair and sipped his drink, enjoying the banter flying around the room. He'd been far too antisocial since the breakup and he was glad he'd taken Riley up on his invitation.

* * * *

A few hours later, Will reluctantly excused himself. He'd had a wonderful time and had enjoyed the witty conversation. It had left him feeling lighter and more relaxed than he had in a while. "I'm going to head home. I have an early game of racquetball planned with Charles tomorrow. I had a great night," Will said. "Thanks for inviting me, Riley. Carter."

"I'm glad you came," Carter said with a nod. He offered Will a sincere smile that crinkled the corners of his hazel eyes and Will grudgingly admitted he could see Carter's appeal. His jealousy had blinded him too much to appreciate Carter's broad-shouldered, long-legged build and handsome face before.

Will said goodnight to everyone and Jesse stood to shake his hand. "Please come back any time. I'll add your name to the list, so even if Kyle and I aren't here, you'll be let in. We do have a seat limit of forty and try to keep private events on the smaller side, but feel free to bring a friend or two. Especially if they're hot and single." He winked. "And maybe save that for when I'm here."

"Jesse!" Carter sounded exasperated and Will couldn't hide his smile.

"I'll keep that in mind," he said.

"We're trying to turn this into a regular thing," Kyle said. "Riley and I had the idea of meeting here the third Thursday of every month. Nothing formal, and if you can't make it, no problem, but it would be great if you could join us."

"I'll try to make it," Will said. "And thanks for a great evening. You make a mean sidecar."

"Any time," Kyle responded.

Will turned to leave. "I'll walk you up," Riley said. He fell into step behind Will.

"Tell Charles I said hi," Riley said as they walked up the stairs.

"I will."

"How are he and Gabe doing?"

"Good. They're both pretty busy right now. Charles is teaching classes this summer and Gabe is looking into opening another restaurant." Charles was an ex of Will's, and one of his closest friends and a colleague at NYU. Charles had married Gabe the summer before, and Gabe owned a high-end Vietnamese restaurant in Tribeca, not far from Will's home.

"You're welcome to bring them to Under anytime," Riley said. "If you think they'd be okay with that."

Will pushed open the door leading into Lock & Key. "I'm sure Gabe will be. Charles is still holding a bit of a grudge," he said. Will and Riley's breakup had rocked Riley's friendship with Gabe and Charles.

Riley sighed. "I deserve it."

"No, I should talk to him. You and I have mended some fences. There's no reason he needs to continue to shut you out." Will walked through the exit of the bar and turned to Riley when they stepped onto the sidewalk out front. "Thanks for inviting me tonight."

"I'm glad you came. I know it was asking a lot but—"

Will cut off Riley's statement. "I meant it when I said I wanted us to be friends. You're happy with Carter and *I'm* happy for you. Honestly, it's been great hanging out with you guys and your friends."

"I'm relieved to hear it," Riley said with a smile. He leaned in, then hesitated and Will closed the distance to hug him.

"Have a good night, Riley."

"Night, Will."

Riley disappeared back through the door of Lock & Key and Will sighed. Hugging Riley left him with a bittersweet feeling, but he was glad he'd come to check out the speakeasy. And he'd meant it when he said he'd try to come back on Thursday evenings in the future. He'd needed some time to lick his wounds and recover, but his self-imposed isolation only made his loneliness worse.

He glanced up and down the street. There wasn't a cab in sight so he pulled out his phone and brought up the Lyft app. He leaned against the wall of the brick building while he waited and a few minutes later a car slid to a stop in front of him.

Will made small-talk with the driver as the car traveled from Morningside Heights back to Tribeca. When they got caught in a traffic snarl near Central Park West because of a protest, Will took out his phone to kill the time. He was scrolling through articles on a news app when his phone vibrated in his hand.

Mom flashed across the screen and he hesitated before he accepted the call.

"Hey, Mom," he answered.

"Will." Agnes Martin's voice sounded strained, with none of the usual groomed sophistication it typically held.

He straightened. "Is something wrong?"

"Will, your father..." Her breath hitched. "I have some news. Your father has been ill lately."

Serves the old bastard right, Will thought grimly. "Ill?" he said aloud.

"Tired, losing weight, stomach pain. At first, we blamed his stress. He's been working so hard lately—"

Yeah, probably passing more anti-LGBT legislation, Will thought.

"But when we noticed some yellowing of his eyes, we got concerned. We were hopeful it was a gallbladder issue, but after some testing, we were referred to an oncologist."

His breath caught. *Oncologist? Shit.* "He has cancer?"

"Yes. He has something called a—a non-functioning neuroendocrine tumor. Pancreatic cancer. It's quite large and the doctors are concerned it's spread to some nearby lymph nodes. It's stage III and the—the prognosis isn't good."

Will took a moment to let the words sink in, but didn't feel much of anything about the news. A wave of guilt washed over him. "I'm sorry, Mom," he said gently. She loved his father and while Will had many, many issues with William Martin Sr. as a father and an elected official, he had always treated Will's mother well. There had never been a hint of infidelity and after Agnes had suffered a serious car accident years ago, Bill hadn't left her side until she'd recovered. "I know how hard this must be for you."

His mother sniffled. "I can't lose him. I know you and your father have your...differences but—"

"We don't have *differences*," he retorted. Any goodwill he'd felt dissipated. "He detests me. He thinks I am less deserving of the same basic human rights he affords everyone else. That's more than an ideological difference, Mom, that's a complete lack of respect for me as a human being."

"Come to Garden City," she blurted out and the words rang in his ear for several seconds before he could process them.

"What? You must be *kidding*," he said. "You can't think I'd come to Long Island to sit by his deathbed and hold his hand." He winced. His cruel words served only to remind Agnes her husband was probably dying. "I'm sorry, Mom, but I can't do it. I can't pretend like everything is fine between us. We haven't spoken in over ten years and it's not only because *I'm* pissed at him. He's the one who cut me out of his life, remember?"

"He wants you here," she said softly. Agnes had used the same tone during Will's years growing when she tried to get him to do something he didn't want to do.

Will sat back in his seat. "Really?"

"I asked him if you could come home and he said yes."

Well, that was more plausible than Will's father specifically asking for him to come home. He sighed. "I-I don't know. I suppose I could come for a long weekend or something. School's out and I could work on my edits while I'm there."

Agnes went silent for a moment. "I hoped you'd stay longer. Your father is undergoing surgery next week, but it'll be exhausting for all of us. If the surgery doesn't work, we may only have a few months left with him." Her voice broke.

"You want me to spend the entire summer in Long Island?" he asked, incredulous.

"Please, Will. If you won't come for your father, come home for Olivia and me. Your sister and I need you. We can't do this alone."

Will glanced out of the window, surprised the bright lights of the city were blurred by tears. He wasn't sure who they were for.

"I'll think about it, Mom."

PUBLISHING

Sign up for our newsletter and find out about all our romance book releases, eBook sales and promotions, sneak peeks and FREE romance books!

About the Author

K. Evan Coles is a mother and tech pirate by day and a writer by night. She is a dreamer who, with a little hard work and a lot of good coffee, coaxes words out of her head and onto paper.

K. lives in the northeast United States, where she complains bitterly about the winters, but truly loves the region and its diverse, tenacious and deceptively compassionate people. You'll usually find K. nerding out over books, movies and television with friends and family. She's especially proud to be raising her son as part of a new generation of unabashed geeks.

K. loves to hear from readers. You can find her contact information, website details and author profile page at https://www.pride-publishing.com